"This splendid debut novel is so charming, so whimsical, that its incisiveness sneaks up on you, slowly, gradually, until at last you look up from the last page, dazed, marvelling at how exactly Yeoh pulled it off. *Impractical Uses of Cake* is a wise and wondrous book."

KIRSTIN CHEN

author of *Bury What We Cannot Take*

"A fascinating novel, written with economy, sophistication and wry humour. The porous nature of the boundary between 'normal' and 'abnormal' is explored with sensitivity, along with a neat balance between the mundanely ordinary and the seemingly nonconformist. Yeoh Jo-Ann exhibits emotional depth in telling her story with tact and nuance."

PROF RAJEEV PATKE

Epigram Books Fiction Prize 2018 Judge and Director of the Division of Humanities, Yale-NUS College

"Yeoh Jo-Ann exposes the cracks in Singapore's gleaming façade with wit and compassion. An impressive debut."

JEREMY TIANG

Singapore Literature Prize-winning author of *State of Emergency*

Epigram Books UK
First published by Epigram Books Singapore in 2019
This Edition published in Great Britain in April 2020

Author photo by Joanne Goh. Used with permission.
Cover design by Lim Qin Yi.

A CIP catalogue record for this book is available from the British Library.

ISBN 978-1-912098-94-1

Printed and bound in Great Britain by Clays Ltd, Elcograf S.p.A.

Epigram Books UK
53 Baker Street
London, W1U 7EU

10 9 8 7 6 5 4 3 2 1
www.epigrambooks.uk

IMPRACTICAL
Uses of Cake

YEOH JO-ANN

EPIGRAM BOOKS
SINGAPORE • LONDON

For my parents, for putting up with all the noise

A man and a woman are in a supermarket. They do not speak, except to announce items on their shared shopping list.

"Eggs, check."

"Cereal." The box lands with a thud in the trolley.

"Pears."

There are fifteen items on their list.

The woman is dead. She died today. The man knows this but isn't sure how he feels about it. Why should things be different now? But they must be.

They finish their shopping and he drives them home. It's his home, really, but he has grown used to sharing it with her. Sharing his books, his bathroom, his kitchen, his television (which she doesn't ever watch, but he would be fine if she did), his six-seater dining table and three-seater sofa. One of the pillows on his bed smells of her, combined with his shampoo. He hopes she won't leave, now that she's dead. Her death has put a ring of anxiety somewhere between his chest and belly.

They go to bed and he holds her, wondering what he wants from all of this. It cannot be reasonable to want anything, and he is a reasonable man.

She lets him hold her, wondering what he wants from all of this. It cannot be reasonable to want anything, and he is a reasonable man.

I

THE DAWN SKY is full of pinkish clouds, but Sukhin goes out anyway. None of the other early-morning runners are about, not even the nutter from the condo down the road. He feels a little smug. *Hah. Afraid of a little water.* The smugness makes the next couple of kilometres much more bearable than usual, and a little while later he is halfway through—finally. As the air around him thickens with the smell of a thunderstorm brewing, he strains to run a little faster, willing himself to take longer, quicker steps.

Sukhin hates running. It bores him. It makes him feel stupid, all this ridiculous gasping and heaving, this inelegant, unimaginative pavement-pounding that he practises every morning to get from his flat to…his flat. Zero displacement—how ridiculous. But he is sticking to it. It's cheap, it's convenient, and he needs the exercise.

"Unfit people just aren't productive," he heard Ken tell the new coordinator a few months ago. "They tire easily—there's just no stamina. It's not even a question of being willing or unwilling to work." They were in the staff pantry and Ken was looking right at him—clearly, he meant that Sukhin was unproductive, tired easily and had no stamina, and, just as clearly, he wanted him to know this.

There was a time when Sukhin would have said something cutting, when he would have refused to exercise on some prideful principle, not wanting to prove Ken had any sort of point. But denial took more energy now than it did when he was younger, and he found himself looking closely at his growing paunch in the mirror, checking his energy levels throughout the day, comparing his stride to Ken's and Tat Meng's and Dennis', and, after exactly a week, coming to the decision that exercise would have to be dealt with.

This morning, as the rain courses down in streams, drenching him all the way to his insoles, he wonders if he should have joined a gym instead.

The trouble with gyms, though: the people who go to them.

Years ago, Sukhin went to a gym. The people maddened him. Men in front of wall-to-wall mirrors, trying to isolate obscure back muscles. Women in perky ponytails, checking themselves out in the same mirror, gushing about how much their thighs hurt after class. And bright Lycra, everywhere he looked. Why would anyone dress in bright Lycra to engage in repetitive actions with other bright-Lycra-clad people, usually while being falsely cheered on by a gym-appointed bright-Lycra-clad chieftain, whose employment depends solely on people being unable to motivate themselves without being shouted at while dressed in bright Lycra?

This was all lost on Dennis, who had dragged him there, who only rolled his eyes, saying: "Sweetie, relax. You sound crazy. Worse—you sound angry. With Lycra." And off he bounded to spin class, whatever that was. Sukhin went home.

So no. No gyms. No bright Lycra.

Sodden, Sukhin reaches his apartment building. He can hardly see—his glasses are misted up, the rain is in his eyes—and it takes him five tries to punch in the correct code at the gate. He feels like shouting but doesn't. Instead, he takes comfort in stomping across the lobby and jabbing repeatedly at the Up button, even after the lift doors open.

"Zero displacement," he growls, once the doors close and the motor starts to whir. "Zero displacement." There's a metaphor in this somewhere, he feels—he just hasn't pieced it together.

ᴧᴧ

"See? #04-03 talks to himself." The night guard gestures at the CCTV monitor marked Lift A. The morning guard has just clocked in.

"Mr Dhillon? Teacher lah." The morning man is older and used to be on duty in the CBD, where he saw all sorts of crazy types and stored them as anecdotes for friends and family. "Lawyers, teachers, all the same. All talk a lot, all crazy. Have I told you about the one who took off all his clothes and threw them into traffic?"

The digital wall clock in the security booth beeps twice. It is six o'clock.

ᴧᴧ

It takes Sukhin exactly thirty-seven minutes to shower, dress and cycle to the junior college where he works. He is exceedingly proud of this. Every two months, he uses the stopwatch app on his phone to make sure he's keeping the proper time.

Two minutes to chain his bicycle to the gardening shed and walk to the canteen. His morning teh si gao kosong is always ready—he keeps a tab with Mrs Chan, and she makes his tea just before he arrives at 6.45. Four minutes from the canteen to his office, one minute to start his computer, ten long, beautiful minutes for his cup of tea. Then he gathers his books and notes and heads down to the courtyard for morning assembly. He takes the back stairs to avoid meeting any of his colleagues. Sukhin likes to keep his mornings his own for as long as possible.

Today, he finds Dennis waiting for him at the bottom of the stairs. Sukhin grimaces.

"God, you're hot when you're angry."

He wishes he had a clever retort, but he's never ready for Dennis. "Just tell me what you want."

"Cover for me—I've got 2SO2B for first period, but I need to run out and do something very quickly." Seeing Sukhin frown, he repeats, "Very quickly."

"I might have a class for first period, Dennis."

"You don't. Thursdays you have the first two periods free."

"Ah. How convenient." Sukhin realises—as usual, too late—that Dennis hasn't even factored in his option to refuse. While he fishes for something snide to say, Dennis dashes off, waving, mouthing: *Love you.*

Also as usual, Sukhin feels equal parts affronted and impressed by Dennis' thickskinnery—a word that, in Sukhin's head, exists just for Dennis. Sukhin would never, ever run off and leave someone else in charge of his class. But of course he will cover for Dennis—it's easier than getting him out of trouble afterwards.

The walk to the Science block feels a little odd—he never has cause to be there, and the last time he moved through this part of the school was back when he was still a student here himself, lost on his way to a talk at LT6, the small, damp-smelling lecture room that was killed a few years ago and resurrected as the art studio. After ten minutes of increasingly frantic searching, he finally finds 2SO2B.

Expecting—some of them even having prepared for—their Thursday morning Further Maths tutorial with Mr Yeong, the students are baffled at Sukhin's entry. He rather enjoys this. He hands a stack of photocopied poems to the nearest student and tells her to pass it around.

"Mr Yeong has gone to see a doctor," he tells the kids, fighting the urge to roll his eyes. "Today, we're going to do what's called practical criticism—something neither practical nor really critical, but rather fun to do if you like to show off."

He starts by reading out an old favourite by Philip Larkin, his face straight and serious, his voice dry and pedantic. It's the poem he uses for the first lesson in poetry with every new class he takes on, but he still enjoys the rush of dropping that first line, that rueful "They fuck you up..." cutting through the classroom, cutting out all the chatter. And just like his did when he was seventeen, as Mr Brooke's booming *fuck you up* sliced through the tepid afternoon air, their eyes light up with something like glee and they lean a little closer towards him. Ah, the power of the four-letter word in the Singaporean classroom. For the rest of the lesson, Sukhin coaxes as many awkward responses as he can from the class, marvelling at their sheer pep and how it makes up for the lack of instinct and sensitivity. He dishes out the usual prac crit prompts: "Why 'fucked up', guys? Why not just 'ruined'? Or 'miseducated'? Read the last stanza out loud—what does that sound like?"

It ends up being his favourite lesson of the day—fresh blood is always sweeter, he tells the new teachers. They always laugh—but these days he's a little suspicious of the laughter, now that Mr Narayan has retired and Sukhin has taken over as head of the English department.

"Call me Ramesh," the illustrious Mr Narayan said to Sukhin on his first day, nearly eight years ago.

Sukhin tried. But he couldn't do it; he couldn't casually say something like "Ramesh and I are thinking of making Beckett part of the required reading this year" without feeling like an asshole or an iconoclast. So Sukhin went on calling Mr Narayan Mr Narayan, just as he had done when he had been fresh blood in the man's classroom. He knew the other teachers always laughed at *that*.

~

"Mr Dhillon is so handsome…those eyebrows!"

"He's okay lah—nice face, but everything's a bit too…pointy. Do you think he and Mr Yeong are dating?"

"Oh my god, really?"

"I'm *asking* you. Jesus."

~

In the canteen, it is the usual lunchtime frenzy. Waving away impatient orders for coffee and sandwiches from a group of students—"Wait lah! Or you come back later!"—Mrs Chan is looking out anxiously for her favourite, her Mr Dhillon. It is 1.15—he should be here already. His lovingly prepared sandwiches are all wrapped up, and his extra-large cup of teh si gao kosong is ready. She checks the clock again—another two minutes and she'll make him a new cuppa. No extra charge—there's no way she'd let him suffer lukewarm tea.

Ah, he's here. She fusses over him as much as she dares, telling him that he must "drink more water, sleep more, cannot work so hard", pressing him to accept a free banana.

Hers is an irrational devotion—she knows that Mr Dhillon has never done anything to warrant any of it, but she can't help wanting to make this grim, tired man a little less grim and tired.

Today, she forces him to take a banana *and* a curry puff—poor thing looks more tired than usual, and is he getting thinner? Must be working late. Probably not sleeping well. She sighs as he walks off, laden with carbs and tea. *Aiyoh, Mr Dhillon, must quickly get married.*

Marriage, if it had entered the mind of the irate Mr Dhillon, would have very quickly made its exit. It is the hottest time of the day and Sukhin is at his grumpiest, his sense of charity dulled and tongue sharpened. Making his way through the loud, tireless horde, he tries very hard not to frown.

Or shout. It will be the noise, surely, that will one day make it impossible for him to continue. A class of kids—fine. But the cacophony of a whole sea of them, with their easy, unfettered chatter and their stupid boundless *energy*—it makes him want to kick things. The tea sloshes around inside its tight-lidded paper cup, a little storm in his hand to match the one in his head. He eats a sandwich but doesn't really taste it.

There is hardly anyone in the staff room—most of the other teachers are eating their lunch together in the adjoining pantry. When he first arrived, Sukhin had felt obliged to join them. And so he endured the small talk, the whingeing and the occasional unwanted confidences, and then one day, just as he'd unwrapped his sandwich, someone said, "Hey Sukhin, it's been a year! Happy anniversary!" The horror—he'd spent a whole year essentially paying court to these people, most of whom he didn't have anything in common with, all of who he suspected thought him unreasonably quiet and strange even when he was trying his best to be pleasant and good and sociable. The next day, he ate his lunch at his desk while reading *Dune* and felt content for the first time since he'd joined the school. He never ventured near the pantry at lunchtime again.

And now, in the tiny, windowless office that used to be Mr Narayan's and is now Sukhin's, he eats his second sandwich.

The door opens and Ken walks in. No knock, no hello, just: "Saw you with 2SO2B when they were supposed to be having F Maths. What was that about? Where was Dennis?" Ken is speaking in his interrogator voice—pitched low, slightly gruff—the same one he uses to grill the boys on misplaced balls and bats, the one he always uses when he wants to convey that what he's talking about is a Big Deal.

"Hey. I'm busy, actually." Sukhin's computer screen is off; he's reading Stephen King's *Christine*. He hopes he sounds rude.

"Hmm." Ken doesn't budge from the doorway. "So you took his class, right? Don't think that's allowed."

Sukhin goes back to reading. "Okay. Thanks."

"I won't tell anyone."

"Yup. Okay."

"You owe me. You and Dennis."

Sukhin refuses to look up from his book. He starts counting backwards from twenty in his head. At the count of twelve, he hears the door shut.

Ken is head of PE—in Sukhin's mind, head of nothing. He joined the staff just two years ago, and from the very start they detested each other. Sukhin can't remember how it began, possibly something to do with a misquotation—but it ended with Ken saying he would never allow his children (he has two) to take "a nonsense subject like English Lit" and Sukhin saying he couldn't imagine anyone taking serious academic advice from a PE teacher. And from then on, regular volleys of barbs and darts flung both ways.

Sukhin believes he could cheerfully watch Ken drown. Ken isn't just Other People—Ken is Vermin. Ken must be removed or destroyed... when Sukhin has the energy.

Ken's name isn't even Ken. It's Kheng Joo.

Ken had Lasik surgery done last year.

Sukhin squirrels away scraps like these whenever he finds them. One day there will be a war, and he will win it with one (or all?) of these seemingly insignificant details.

Ken is allergic to penicillin. And macadamias.

ᨓ

"Who's the cake for?"

"The diligent, dapper Mr Dhillon." Dennis is arranging candles in concentric circles on a cream-engulfed monstrosity.

"Did you make it?"

"No lah—Advocakes and Solicitarts. Their yuzu coconut cream is the best."

A gasp, exactly as Dennis intended. "But they only accept orders three months in advance!"

Dennis smirks. "My sister knows the owner—they used to work at the same firm. So I managed to order this three weeks ago."

"They deliver?"

"I wish. A bakery like that doesn't have to bother with delivery. I picked it up first thing this morning—it's been sitting in the pantry fridge all day. I've had to watch it like a *hawk*."

"This morning? Didn't you have class?"

Dennis laughs. "Made Sukhin take it."

The candle arrangement goes on and on.

"Wow, that's a lot of candles."

"The man is older than he looks. Ageing very gracefully, in spite of all the frowning." He steps back to survey his handiwork, then resumes the task. "Almost done—go gather people. We're ambushing him in his office."

Sukhin is sleeping. This isn't intentional—his last class of the day is done and if he hadn't rested his head on his desk for a moment just before packing up, he would already be cycling home. He is dreaming—he is walking in a field of giant saguaro cacti, all identical, all with thorny arms raised skywards.

"Happy birthday, Sukhin!" says the nearest cactus.

What the fuck.

"Sukhin! Sukhin!"

He springs upward and awake. There are about twenty faces looking down at him. Feeling violated, he glares back at them. Dennis sets the biggest cake he has ever shared a space with on his desk. Sukhin is horrified—this is for *him*, he realises. The cactus was right. It really is his birthday. God, so many candles.

"Happy birthday! Did you think we'd forget?" And then, seeing Sukhin's odd expression, Dennis realises that it is he who has forgot. *Nuts. His own birthday.*

A pause. Everyone eyes Sukhin. Sukhin eyes the cake. Dennis congratulates himself again on the choice of yuzu coconut cream.

And then a tuneless warble, rather heroically led by Dennis: "Happy birthday, dear Sukhin, haaaaaaaappy..." Sukhin feels like crying, or throwing up. *I'm thirty-five and this is my life.* And then, the next instant: *Oh god, I'm thirty-five and I'm about to have a mid-life crisis. How cliché. How sad.* All he wants to do now is get as far away as possible from these smiling faces, this stupid song, this ridiculous cake. When the singing finally stops, Sukhin forces himself to smile, thank everyone, then cut up the monster into little bits so that everyone can stuff their faces while seeming not to eat very much. He even pretends to eat a slice. Anything to have them think he's pleased, anything to have them get the fuck out of his office as soon as possible.

Sometime during the night, the woman awakens. She finds herself on her side, facing the wall. Behind her, he's breathing softly in the way she has learnt to recognise as a sign he is sleeping deeply. Carefully, she turns over. He is turned towards her, but his face is half-buried in his pillow, under which both his hands are tucked. His knees are raised towards his chest, making it all look like an elaborate yoga pose.

The woman slips her hand under the man's pillow and onto one of his hands. How warm this feels, nestling between his skin and the weight of the pillow. He stirs slightly.

In the morning, he will remember this weight on his hand, the sudden cold of hers.

In the morning, if he asks, she will deny everything.

II

THE FORTUNE COOKIE reads, "Be sincere with all you meet. For the charming social networking."

Sukhin pops the cookie fragments into his mouth. What awful advice—even if he were the kind of man who'd take ungrammatical advice from a cookie. Be sincere? With all you meet? How…unsound. Charming people lie—how else are they charming? And people expect to be lied to, and they'll lie to themselves, believing they believe in honesty and all that crap about just being yourself. What if being yourself meant not liking other people being themselves? Sukhin could think of a whole lot of people who could be improved by being other people. If only everyone had a reset button—though that would mean having to wear some sort of security vest all the time so that people couldn't just reach out and reset you because you said something mean about their hair or something.

Had he been mean about Vera's hair?

His thoughts wander back to the afternoon. He was getting a glass of water in the staff pantry. Dennis was there talking about something—what was it? Some new gym routine he was trying out. Something like that. Vera, the new geography teacher, the transfer from

Methodist Girls' School, bounded into the pantry and said hello. As she approached, Sukhin noticed how tall she was—nearly as tall as Dennis, who was only a little taller than Sukhin. Which made her, very possibly, his own height.

"You've done something to your hair." Trust Dennis to notice this.

"Yes! I decided to go shorter. What do you think?" She patted her hair and grinned.

"Very nice, very nice. Makes your neck look longer." Where did Dennis get all this from?

She turned to Sukhin. "And what do you think?"

He stared hard at her hair, searching for something to say about it. It wasn't very interesting, just hair. At last, he noticed something worth pointing out. "Is it meant to be lopsided?"

"Lopsided?"

"It's longer on the left side. Just a bit—about a centimetre here." He gestured at her left ear.

She tugged at the section. "Really? I don't think so."

"It is. Dennis, look. Isn't this bit longer than this bit?" He added: "Should be easily fixed. I'm sure you could do it yourself."

"It's not lopsided!" She turned a little red.

He wasn't going to argue—he hadn't planned on having a conversation with her about her hair; she had forced it on him. He was happy to let her win this. "Hmmm. Okay. Maybe your left ear's higher than your right ear? That would explain it." He was rather pleased with the reasoning. It was perfectly logical, and most people didn't have symmetrical heads anyway.

Her eyes widened. "Now my ears are lopsided?"

"No, they're not lopsided—lopsided describes unevenness on a single object," Sukhin explained—rather patiently, he thought. How did people get these things confused? "So your hair is lopsided. A mouth could be lopsided—no, not yours. Ears are two separate objects. So your ears—I'd just say they aren't level. Yes, I think that would be *best*."

"That would be best?" She glared at him.

"The best way to describe them." He tried to reassure her: "But yours look level, actually. So it's your hair that's lopsided—and that's much easier to fix."

At that point, she turned and walked away.

Dennis cackled. "You must find her attractive. Usually it takes more than a week for you to offend anyone new."

No, he hadn't been mean about her hair. He only pointed out that it was lopsided—not her fault, and not even a permanent state. If his haircut were lopsided, he would like someone to tell him. He would want to know. Why wouldn't anyone? That woman was clearly far too attached to what she thought her hair should be. Delusions of symmetry. What a nut.

Sukhin makes himself a cup of tea, wondering if he does find Vera attractive.

The second fortune cookie reads, "Breathe deep and often."

What rot. Who wrote these things? Manufactured Chinese exoticism for the simple American—and now the simple Singaporean. Dennis had seen them at a shop in Chinatown and bought Sukhin two giant packs of fifty. One hundred ridiculous cookies. ("Look, sweetie, you can read *and* eat! Your two favourite things in a convenient little cookie. You love me.")

Vera isn't his type. Far too tall. And far too unappreciative of symmetry.

~

At the old house, Sukhin arrives to find his mother in the kitchen stirring sugar into a pot of coffee. It is blacker than ink, completely opaque—

if you can see the spoon, she's told him since he was a child, then it's not strong enough.

"Kopi?"

"It's okay, Mum. I'll make some tea."

It's been years since I gave up coffee, he wanted to say. Mum, I don't drink coffee any more. He satisfies himself instead by creating a louder clatter than necessary as he fills the kettle and puts it on the stove, then reaches into a cupboard for the tea.

Usually, they sit in silence, needlessly stirring their drinks over and over again. But today she appears determined to have a conversation. She tells him about her morning, about the bargain she managed to pull off at the fishmonger's, about the phone conversation with her sister. He says nothing, only half-listening, refusing to press her for more information. She stops and looks at him expectantly. He stares down into his mug.

"How was your day?"

Sukhin sighs. "It was okay. Exams in three weeks. The teachers are going nuts; the kids are going nuts. Of course, quite a few are pretending not to care."

"Teachers or students?"

"Both."

Sukhin watches as his mother removes all her rings and bracelets, puts them in a pile on the table, then puts them all on again. He has never asked her why she does this. He doesn't ask now.

They sit in the kitchen because the living room is never used. It must have once been meant for lounging around, perhaps even entertaining guests—there's a sofa somewhere, an armchair, a coffee table even.

But then the boxes took over. The largest squat in the corners and line the sides of the room, sentinels against marauders. Inside these boxes:

more boxes, arranged neatly, to maximise space, and gently, so no box presses uncomfortably against another—no box, little or large, will stand for being squished. Other boxes in boxes have sidled up to these giants over the years; some perch rather audaciously on their smooth cardboard tops. In the centre of the room, the cool crowd lolls about on the former coffee table. These delinquents—hexagonal, pyramidal, heart-shaped, star-shaped, panda-shaped (just one, but one is enough)—won't fit into other boxes and resist all attempts to put them into orderly piles, but they are the best loved.

After tea, Sukhin goes into the living room and squeezes himself into the narrow space between a pile of boxes and the delinquents' pedestal. With a hand-held vacuum cleaner, he carefully removes the dust from every odd-shaped box. The panda is the hardest to do—so many awkward flaps—but Sukhin hasn't done this for years for nothing. He's a pro, nudging every flap open with the vacuum cleaner's blade-like nozzle, then swiping left to right in quick, even strokes. He works meditatively; he forgets where he is, who he is, even what he's doing.

Some of the boxes have been around since Sukhin was a child—the box that the rice cooker came in, the one that held the family's first microwave oven and the Cadbury tin, once full of chocolate eggs, that Aunty Siew Peng gave them for Christmas when he was a boy and still liked sweets. One of the cardboard sentinels once protected the (at the time) state-of-the-art front-load washing machine that remained the apple of his mother's eye for years because it meant she didn't have to hand-wash all the clothes she'd had to protect from their previous washer, a pale violent monster whose sole purpose was to push Hooke's law to its outer limits. Elsewhere in the cuboidal sea: boxes that once were home to various electronics, crockery, lamps, toys and many other objects long dead and discarded.

Once he's finished with the delinquents, he moves on to one of the weekend's designated stacks, one that nearly reaches the ceiling. As always, Sukhin is efficient. He splits the stack into two, carrying the top section off and into the narrow pathway through the living room that the boxes have decided to allow the family. Then he sets to work on each demi-pile, cleaning, checking for damp and damage, until every box is cleared—and then they all go back into the stack to wait for their next round of TLC. Sukhin moves on to the next designated stack.

Not every box makes it here, to what could be called the Dhillon Family Retirement Home for Boxes—there is a stringent selection process.

To qualify, a box must fulfill at least one of the following requirements:

1. It is large enough to be useful should the family decide to move. "Large enough" is a completely arbitrary measurement, decided entirely by Sukhin's father, Dr Jaswant Dhillon. (The family has not moved houses in the last thirty years, but if they decide to, they would be very well equipped where boxes are concerned.)
2. It is a box that once contained:
    a. What Sukhin's mother, Doris Dhillon, considers a "milestone" electronic.
    b. A set of something or other—Doris believes that things that come in a set must always be transported in the box they came in, because it was designed for that very purpose.
    c. A good memory—a vague, often exploited, category of box.
    d. A "first" anything.
3. It is a Really Nice Box. For a box to be kept under this category, the entire family must be in alignment that it is indeed a Really

> Nice Box. (The panda was a point of contention in its day—Sukhin and his mother were keen on it, but his father thought it was too kitsch. Eventually, he was won over—with veto rights over the next Really Nice Box.)

Over the years, with very little success, the family has tried to edit their collection, trim it down, get rid of excess. Most attempts are spurred by the threat of some impending visit by relatives, but the last one was brought on by an attack of home-envy Doris experienced while looking through the pages of *Home and Decor* in the waiting room at the dentist's. Suddenly, she found herself dreaming of Scandinavian-chic interiors, all soft, poetic edges and stark walls. The family spent an unhappy weekend arguing over which boxes to keep, which to give to the karung guni man. In the end—exhausted, angry—they gave up and put all the boxes back in their old spots. Doris has not breathed on an interiors magazine since.

The old turntable, a relic from Doris' single-girl days as an undergrad in 1970s London, plays an even older Beatles record. Sukhin doesn't realise this, but under the calming influence of the family boxes, he is singing along to "Lovely Rita", a song he despises.

"Are you staying for dinner?"

Sukhin turns off the vacuum cleaner. "No, I've got to go to Chinatown. Need to buy decorations for the staff party."

It isn't the answer she wants, but she knows better than to try to ask again. "That's nice."

"No, Mum, it isn't. It's a pain." Sukhin moves, crab-like, out from among the boxes. He doesn't notice his mother's poorly concealed disappointment. "And it's stupid. No one enjoys the CNY party. Everyone just pretends—it's just a big show for the Tay. She likes to think we're all a big happy family."

"But it's not *unhappy*, right?" Doris wonders for the nth time why her clever, prickly son decided to be a teacher. Probably to irritate his father.

As if on cue, her husband's car pulls up outside. The automatic gate whirrs into action, and a few seconds later, the car is purring on the other side of the living room wall. A sudden quiet as the engine is shut off, and then Dr Jaswant Dhillon bursts into the house, talking rapidly, already in mid-paragraph as he removes his shoes and socks.

"...rubbish 'Punjabi' food—not even close, darling, we must never go. I tell you, that Ranjit couldn't tell proper Punjabi food from random curry house stuff. Spent too much time abroad—not even in England, where some of the Indian food is the real thing, but in Scotland. But of course he had to go to Edinburgh lah, couldn't get into Cambridge."

Sukhin's father is a big man, taller than Sukhin, towering over his petite wife. His voice is even bigger—rich and strident, with all the drama of the old-time storytellers. In another age, he would have been one of them, the men who went from village to village telling stories of Hang Tuah, Hang Jebat, Badang and the rest of the old Malay heroes.

Now he holds up a small plain cardboard box like it's a jewel. "Anyway, the rose barfi was decent enough—not too sweet, so I got you some. Don't eat all of it at once, yah? And keep it away from me!" A loud laugh as he presses the box into her hands. "You know what happened when Meera Auntie's daughter—Rina? Rani? Rathi? Something starting with R, what is it?—got married and she made us take home all that jelebi." Another loud, happy laugh, accompanied by a dramatic gesture, a cross between it-was-this-big and the standard both-arms-waving. "Two days and it was gone! Gone! For weeks I couldn't look patients in the eye when I told them to please, for your own good, cut down on the sugar."

"Hey, Pa."

"Sukhin!" His son's presence is unexpected and Jaswant needs time to warm up. He stalls by offering nuggets of affirmation: "Ah, you're looking well. Doing a good job at school, I'm sure. Hard to be a teacher these days, children so different from what they used to be."

The same combination of personalised nothing each time. Sukhin has often wondered if all doctors needed to master this technique, if this is, at root, the foundation of a good bedside manner. *God, my father is a fortune cookie.*

Sukhin only half-listens as his father talks on, saying something about seeing an article somewhere about English Literature being taught in schools "with outdated books, from centuries ago, that have nothing to do with our way of life now".

Five years ago, even two, that would have been enough to send Sukhin into a rage. He might have jumped on his father, even knowing that he had only brought up the article as a matter of interest and not as provocation. He might have raised his voice; he might have roused himself into a sneering, growling thing.

But now Sukhin only manages a tired shrug. He picks up the bag he left on the shoe rack earlier. "I'll see you guys soon. If I don't head to Chinatown now, all the shops will be closed." He pauses. "Should I buy any cookies or whatever for Ah Mah?"

"Your grandmother doesn't need any more encouragement—your Aunty Lillian is already killing her with cake."

"Jas!" his mother shouts.

"It's true lah, darling, your sister really needs to stop all the baking and baking. Can't she get another hobby? It's a miracle Bobby doesn't have diabetes..."

Doris hisses. "How can you say things like that? So suay. Every year you eat so many of Lillian's pineapple tarts, so don't pretend..."

Sukhin slips out the door and out the gate, which he opens by flicking a switch next to the front door. The automatic gate used to annoy him because it deprived him of a step in his routine—the flick of the switch didn't have the finality of the heavy, clanging latch of the old gate. But these days, the soft whirring, followed by the click, of the new gate has come to suit him, now that his exits have, over the years, lost their drama. The boy Sukhin was a slammer of doors and gates, a shouter of rude things calculated to shock. The man Sukhin doesn't like noise.

As Sukhin gets into his car and drives off, his parents notice that he has left.

"Why does he do that?" says Doris, irritated. Absently, she has opened the box of rose barfi and is nibbling on a large piece. "He never says bye properly."

Dr Jaswant reaches for one too. "He makes me worry, you know." He adds quickly, knowing his wife's protective instinct will launch her into an argument with him faster than he can pacify her with sweets: "Yes, yes, he's a good boy, good job, seems to be fine. But something's missing."

"Ah, don't start—if you're going to try the matchmaking again, he'll stop speaking to us. Remember what happened the last time."

He does, and eats another piece of barfi to stifle a sigh. How do barfi-less parents cope?

The day they met, the first time, they were enduring a chemistry lecture in the coldest lecture theatre in school. They were both late, and this meant having to sit all the way up front. She had the seat next to the aisle. He was two seats away, having left an empty place between them—exactly as unknown-persons protocol demanded.

He fell asleep. She didn't. When the lecture ended, she grabbed him firmly by the shoulder and shook him. He jumped, ran out and didn't look in her direction for the rest of the year.

For years after, she would recall the horror on his face and laugh.

For years after, he would drink copious amounts of coffee at lunchtime.

III

BUYING THE CAR was a mistake. He doesn't drive to work, so he feels he must drive on weekends. Which means he must endure parking on weekends, a special circle of Hell designed for the local driver, that privileged class of Singaporean willing to part with more money than it takes to put a child through a lifetime of school for the pleasure of not putting up with public transport and its promise of other people.

But three years ago when Johan told him he was relocating the family to Brunei and offered him the car at fifty per cent off the market value, Sukhin had jumped at the chance and bought it. Which was so unlike him, he who never made any big (or small) purchases without careful research. He'd felt weak and stupid for weeks afterwards, but put it down to the fact that he'd been rereading *King Solomon's Mines* at the time and was therefore in a bit of a state, wondering if he'd ever feel compelled to follow a map into unknown deserts and jungles and mountain ranges. *Victorian adventure novels—always a bloody mistake.*

For the third time, he drives through Mosque Street, then Trengganu Street, eyes peeled for a parking spot. No luck—everyone and his brother are in Chinatown. And probably for the same reason that he is: to buy hyper-kitsch Chinese New Year décor and ridiculously expensive snacks that no shopkeeper would be able to shift from his shelves if it weren't for the mixture of sentimentality and desperation that drives people to fritter away hard-earned cash on things they don't even want—everyone decorates to please everyone else, and stocks up on cookies, fried seaweed, peanut brittle and cashews to feed other people.

In the end, he finds a spot far from the chaos of Chinatown and has to walk fifteen minutes to reach the main street. By the time he gets there, all Sukhin wants to do is turn around, walk back to his car and drive home.

"Towkay!"

Sukhin sets his teeth. He hates being called "towkay"—sure, it's meant to be deferential, but it also means that anyone using it on him thinks he can be buttered up by being called boss. He waves the man off.

"Towkay! You looking for what?"

Sukhin looks at his feet and walks to the end of the street without stopping to look at anything. Feeling ridiculous, he turns and goes down the next street. Here, it's even more crowded. Appalling. Even though it's past five, the heat is thick enough to grill steaks on the pavement. The people make it worse, crowding around the shelves, squeezing past each other. Someone brushes against him. Sukhin stares at his forearm, at the streak of sweat the stranger has left on him, wanting to scream. He can already feel the beginnings of a Very Bad Headache.

The tall man is hardly making sense, but she nods anyway.

Ai Ling knows his type. Desperate, completely pliable. Everything fast fast fast, never mind the price. Her favourite kind of customer—much, much better than the little old ladies with plenty of time to kill, the ones who want to inspect every last item and bargain down everything to its cost price.

"What about pineapples? Do I need a gold pineapple? Is that still a thing?" He is babbling, looking down at a handwritten list. It is wrinkled and damp; the ink is already smudged.

"Ong lai," she pronounces with a sweeping gesture towards the store ceiling, from which hang hundreds of pineapples of different sizes. Cardboard, plastic film, crepe paper, sequinned, glossy, covered in glitter—all he has to do is choose. "Which one you want?"

Her customer stands very still for a minute, blinking at the ceiling. Ai Ling realises she shouldn't have bothered asking—you had to be very careful with his sort. They got scared easily—one wrong move and they'd give up, run off.

Smiling widely, she goes to a shelf and takes four large flat packs, each holding a folded-up pineapple. "Nice one. Okay?"

He nods, looking grateful. She picks out more things for him and piles them into his arms—strands and strands of plastic firecrackers, cardboard cutouts of the god of prosperity, two dozen carp made out of bright red felt, a three-metre golden banner proclaiming the arrival of the new year. Ai Ling wonders how far she can push him, then decides to take a risk—she lifts a large furry yellow lion from the middle of a display table and plants it right on top of the pile. He looks at it for a moment, confused, but says nothing.

"Okay! Can already!" Her work is done—any more and the man will crumple. She leads him to the cashier counter, where he pays for everything without protest, then leaves the store with three bulging plastic bags, bumping into everyone in his way.

If every customer were like this one, Ai Ling wouldn't mind her job so much. She might ask for a bit more overtime pay today—Mrs Lee will be so pleased when she hears that the lion from two years ago has finally sold.

~

A light drizzle keeps Sukhin company as he trudges back to the car, cumbersome plastic bags swinging in every direction, and, inside them, plastic and cardboard in random motion—*not Brownian, that's only for particles in suspension, or is it? Better ask Tat Meng.* He glares at the sky. *Of course.* He stops and checks each bag he's carrying to make sure it's tied up tightly enough to withstand the rain—there is no way he's coming back here, so these stupid, garish things *cannot* be ruined. And he's forgot all about the snacks—well, too bad.

The rain gets heavier. Sukhin's first instinct is to launch himself and his plastic charges forward in as much of a sprint as he can muster, but very soon this proves to be a poor decision—one of the bags breaks, and a heap of plastic firecrackers spills onto the pavement.

All he wants to do is throw himself onto the ground and howl, but that would just be wasting time. Grabbing the firecracker strands, he winds them around his neck, then picks up the two remaining bags and dashes into the nearest shelter. This is a multi-storey public car park, and as Sukhin waits out the rain, walking aimlessly around the first level, he finds himself mulling over how effectively soulless it is designed to be—no one would ever linger here longer than necessary. Like its fellows all over the country, it is floor-to-ceiling concrete, a hollow cuboid with punctures for air circulation that could never count as windows. No one growing up in Singapore could be faulted for not having the capacity for poetry, Sukhin thinks, feeling a sudden indignation on behalf of all the students he's ever heard say, "I just don't get it"—*the Romans took concrete and made the Pantheon; in Singapore, we just keep making more and more of these things.*

There is a lull in the rain and he decides to make a run for it.

He dashes out of the building and into the nearest alley, a long and darkish gap between the backs of two buildings he doesn't quite recognise, but at least there's shelter—the roof of one of the buildings extends across most of the gap, and only a sliver of light and rain passes through. He isn't sure where this alley leads, but tells himself he will figure it out once he gets to the end. The bags bounce along, mocking him, depriving every step of its potential speed.

Near the middle of the alley, a pyramidal stack of boxes is piled high against the more sheltered wall, taking up most of the walkway. As he tries to edge past it, one bag irreverently, violently throws itself against the cardboard structure, which trembles for a moment and then comes crashing down. And then Sukhin is surrounded by boxes—boxes in his path, boxes behind him, and a large box that only narrowly missed his head and lies next to him. *Of course*. Now would be the time to howl, but then he hears a muffled sound from beneath the pile, close to the wall. *OF COURSE*.

Another sound. What remains of the structure shudders a little, and then a figure emerges from among the boxes.

"I'm so sorry," he hears himself say. "I'm so sorry." He drops his bags in a sudden wave of mortification—he's just brought someone's makeshift home down with his CNY crap. All the rage at the rain and the bags and the soulless car park vanishes. "Let me help you put all of this back." He starts picking up the boxes nearest to him.

The figure takes a step towards him. Sukhin is a little afraid now, but he is more ashamed than afraid. "Sorry, sorry. Please, let me help." He starts stacking the boxes on one side of the alley, instinctively grouping them by size, already thinking of how he will rearrange them into a cardboard igloo.

A rustle among the boxes, as the figure approaches.

He looks up. Backlit, it is thin and insubstantial, all long limbs in loose clothes. Another step towards him—and as he bends down to pick up more boxes, he can feel it moving even closer. He is now equal parts remorse and fear, quickly tipping towards the latter.

"Sukhin?"

All fear now. He throws a box at the figure and runs, runs, runs.

It is past eleven and still raining as Sukhin makes his way down the alley again. He tells himself he's here to retrieve the bags of decorations, but he's really here because he's embarrassed that he allowed himself to become so worked up earlier that he ran away like a cockroach thinking this random stranger was calling his name, instead of being logical, i.e. staying put and speaking nicely to the guy, who was probably just asking for money or something. So he's back—and he needs to prove to himself that he's not a mean, stupid coward.

The house of cardboard has been rebuilt against the wall. From inside comes the sound of a radio playing softly—not music, just voices, could be the news. Outside, a large box sits apart, also propped against the wall. A firecracker strand peeks out of it. Sukhin leaps towards it, then springs back.

SUKHIN—upper case, black marker, on the side of the box. What the fuck is going on? His heart pounds like a wild thing, but his head is empty—nothing in his life has prepared him for this.

A sort of shuffle, from behind him.

It's like a bad movie. He turns around and it's the figure from before. It's difficult to see by the street light left over from bouncing off other buildings, but the guy appears relaxed and unarmed.

The guy takes a step closer.

It isn't a guy.

"It's me."

It's her. It's her. It's her.

They are younger and she is alive. They've just seen a movie, the plot of which neither will recall in the years that follow, and they're walking aimlessly through the city. It is past eleven, and later they will both be in trouble for this.

He wants to tell her he loves her. Instead he says, "When I was a kid, I wanted to be a palaeontologist because I thought I'd actually get to meet dinosaurs." He has never told anyone this, so for him this is the same as a declaration of love.

She doesn't laugh. He takes her hand for the very first time and holds it tight.

She tells him she wants to be a rock, thrown into the sea, flying straight to the bottom.

IV

"YOU CAN'T HIDE in here forever—just get in there, smile at the Tay and get it over with." Dennis slinks into Sukhin's office and drapes himself over a chair, head grazing the floor and legs over its back.

"You sound like one of your stupid fortune cookies."

"So you've been eating them!" Dennis picks a scrap of paper off the floor and reads it: "Sea of change, not the stagnant puddle."

"One of my favourites." Sukhin allows himself to smile, but refuses to look up from his marking.

"Really? But you're such a puddle kind of man."

"Shapeless, wet and ruins shoes? I can live with that."

Dennis swings himself upright. "Come on then, puddle—let's go. You know you can't miss the party."

Sukhin does know. The school board, prominent parents and select alumni are invited to the Tay's annual suck-up fest, and every head of department—sadly, this includes Sukhin—is expected to entertain them, talk pointedly of the year's glorious plans, and hopefully elicit a donation. It's also the principal's chance to indulge her fantasies of herself as goddess-guide-queen-mother, swanning around the room doling out scraps of praise, crumbs of encouragement and sugary promises that won't be remembered the week after. ("You're doing such a wonderful job in the Physics department—I don't know how Tat Meng ever managed without you!" "Ganesh, we must arrange for an overseas training course for you in June—maybe somewhere in New Zealand, where they're doing some really interesting marine biology research?" "We're so lucky to have you—so rare to see someone with such a natural gift for teaching!") Still too cheap to hire professionals, though—the food is mostly whipped up by Mrs Chan in her tiny stall in the school canteen, and Sukhin cringes as he recalls his décor-buying trip to Chinatown two weeks ago. What a horror that was, even if it did lead him to *her*—not that he'd decided that *that* was a good thing.

Seeing Jinn again—that was a level of drama he hasn't allowed in his life for years. And seeing her like that—it shook him to find her so changed. It wasn't just that she looked different. What unsettled him more—far more than the short, jagged hair and the sparseness of her face and frame—was her new quietness. Every word, every movement seemed pared down and restrained. This wasn't the girl who once told him, at the top of her voice and in the middle of a very crowded train, to go fuck himself because she never would.

Well, this *could use a little restraint.* It is far too loud in the teachers' lounge, even from the outside. Some sort of pseudo-jazz blares overhead, refusing to be relegated to background music, forcing everyone to raise their voices to be heard over it. As he enters the room, Sukhin is assaulted by the sound of about fifty simultaneously shouted conversations and a soprano saxophone dragging on "How Deep Is Your Love"—someone's idea of culture, probably Ken's. The party shows alarmingly little sign of winding down and the Tay is nowhere in sight, which lays waste his plan to pay court and leave in the next half-hour. As Dennis is swallowed up by a group of young trainee teachers who want to know why he's late, Sukhin heads straight for the buffet table and piles his plate high. *Those who can't leave, eat.*

"Wah, you very late yah."

"Not late enough."

Tat Meng grins and shrugs—nothing ever bothers Tat Meng; Sukhin's brand of morose doesn't even register. "Never mind lah, once a year only. Eh, try the butter cake. My wife made it."

He takes Sukhin by the elbow and leads him to the dessert section. Sukhin doesn't feel like eating cake, but he cuts himself a sliver of Tat Meng's wife's almond-encrusted handiwork and takes a large, dutiful bite. "Very nice."

This gets rid of Tat Meng, who sails off to find more people to force-feed. And the cake does turn out to be very nice—when a few colleagues try to strike up conversation, Sukhin leads them to the cake and tells them they must try it, then slips away. He slinks into a corner and stuffs his face with fried noodles.

What does she eat? He can't recall seeing any food in her house of boxes. All he can remember: a mat, a sleeping bag, a trolley suitcase and some newspaper. Not that he imagines she'd leave food strewn all over the place. Maybe she goes to soup kitchens—are there soup kitchens in Singapore? Are there places that give out free food? He should have asked her, instead of mumbling over and over again, "Let me take you somewhere," to which she only replied, once, "I'm okay here." And he shouldn't have left her there, but he did. He didn't know what else to do, after staying with her for about two hours and failing to summon enough courage to ask her why she lived how she did—tackling the elephant in the room has never been Sukhin's strong suit. Where is the dummy's guide for asking the woman you once loved why she's living under a pile of boxes in an alley?

"Only you could look good eating mee goreng, sweetie."

Sukhin pretends not to hear Dennis, who edges closer and passes him a paper cup full of something orange. He takes a sip and stares. "There's vodka in this."

"Vera snuck in a bottle. You know, she of the lopsided head."

"Lopsided *hair*."

"Whatever—the one you pissed off." Dennis makes a vague gesture at the ceiling. "Great job with the decorations."

The golden "Happy New Year" banner hangs across a set of cupboards. Two firecracker strands dangle from the ceiling in each of the seven corners of the odd-shaped room. Six cardboard cutouts of the chubby, grinning god of prosperity line up in a precise row on the wall right above the buffet. Above them, thirty large red carp swim in a straight line, making their way along the walls to the opposite side of the room, towards the air conditioner.

"Inspiring. It's like the war of the clones." Dennis looks across the room to the coffee machine. "And *that* is magic."

Perched on the coffee machine, looking a lot bigger than Sukhin remembers it being at the store, is the yellow lion in all its furry, embroidered majesty, long-lashed glass eyes smugly surveying the chaos. It fixes its amused grin on him. *Wow, Sukhin,* this *is your party?*

It sounds exactly like her, the Jinn he remembers. She would have found this party hilarious—the ass-kissing, the bad music, the clones, the crone. Even the new Jinn smiled when he took the decorations from the box she'd put them in and told her what they were for. But she said nothing, and because he didn't want to talk about the party when there were clearly bigger things to talk about, he said nothing. He stood for a few minutes cradling his bags of decorations, feeling ridiculous, and then he left, telling her he'd be back.

He hasn't been back. *I'm an asshole.*

"I see her—let's go, let's go." Dennis grabs his arm and pushes him forward. Half the room away, the Tay is simpering at a stranger, probably one of the new members of the school board.

Sukhin takes a deep breath. *Showtime.*

Chinese New Year used to mean madcap days of running amok with his Ipoh cousins in the old house on Rose Lane, chasing each other up and down the stairs and round and round the garden in a never-ending game of catch they called celok duduk, while his parents and his aunts and uncles crowded around the dining table drinking cold beer and ice cream soda, playing blackjack and gin rummy.

These days, only his Uncle Desmond and his wife make the drive down from Ipoh. Aunty Mary insists she's far too old to travel. His cousins are all married, and he hasn't seen them in years. Sukhin and Philippa, Aunty Lillian's daughter, are the only two left—and he doesn't like Philippa, who's a year older and always considered herself too cool to join the cousins in their games. The old house is still the same, but now all he does is sit in a corner and read while everyone else drinks and plays cards and talks about food, who's dead or dying, and whether property prices will go up this year.

"Frankie says I should wait—but should I? Bought the condo five years ago, then prices straight away went down. And now they're finally up, but should I wait a bit more? Am I being greedy?" Sukhin's Aunty Lillian sighs as she deals another round of cards.

"*I'm* going to be greedy—these pineapple tarts are as good as ever. Better!"

"Jaswant! Enough! You've had at least fifteen."

"Fine—what about a slice of your sugee cake, darling?"

"Pong!"

"Desmond, we're not playing mahjong."

"I'm just joking lah—I'm not senile, Lillian. Relax."

And on, and on, and on.

Sukhin gives up trying to read and wanders over to the coffee table, where the snacks are set out. Glass jars take up every inch of the table's highly polished surface, each filled with a different kind of cookie, tart or cake made by either his mother or his Aunty Lillian. He helps himself to a few peanut cookies, checking first that his mother isn't looking—she would consider it betrayal that he's choosing Aunty Lillian's cookies over hers.

"Someone turn up the air-con, please! I'm melting."

Sukhin grimaces. Turn up the air-con, indeed. He'd like to raise the temperature a couple of degrees and watch Philippa fly into a fit of rage—stupid brat. He pacifies himself with a very large slice of his mother's sugee cake.

He cracks open a window and quickly shuts it again. Outside, it is hellish. Blazing sun, and not the faintest whisper of wind. Nothing moves in his grandmother's garden—it's like looking at a photograph.

It must be hotter in Chinatown. All that concrete, no trees, barely any shade anywhere. It must be suffocating in that alley at this time of the day. And where does she get water? He imagines there must be a toilet nearby, but how nearby is nearby? He can't recall the last time he saw a drinking fountain anywhere in the city. For the first time in his life, this strikes him as ungenerous.

~

In the kitchen, a conversation.

"Can you go talk to Sukhin? Poor fellow."

Philippa glares at her mother. "What? Poor fellow? He's just super weird lah, Mum." She peeks through the doorway at her cousin, who is muttering to himself as he stares out the window. "See? He's talking to himself."

"Aiyah. Some people never recover from a broken heart, you know."

"Oh my god—seriously, Mum, that was so long ago. And he's always been weird."

"Pah, sayang. Kesian dia. He's been through a lot. Don't be mean."

Doris overhears all of this, unseen, as she pours herself another gin and tonic on the other side of the wall. Is that what it is—a broken heart? Across the room, her son is at the window, sullen, mumbling to himself. Then he catches her eye, points to the slice of cake he's eating, and rolls his eyes and opens his mouth in a mime of ecstacy. She smiles and shakes her head. *Nonsense. That Lillian watches far too many Korean drama serials.*

~

This year, as ever, his mother has spared nothing in her preparations—the reunion dinner the night before was excellent; the cookies and cakes were planned a month ago and executed last week, filling the house with the smell of caramelising sugar, brown butter, pandan, coconut and pineapple. She's never said it, but Sukhin is sure that her determination to make every single dish, dessert and pastry that her mother (his ancient Ah Mah, who's crushing everyone at poker now) deems right and proper for Chinese New Year has much to do with her marriage to a Punjabi man. Well, if his mother having a point to prove meant homemade sugee cake every year, the marginal social benefit of that mixed marriage was quite evident—many family rifts have been repaired (or prevented) by that very cake. And the cake itself—a point proven. Sukhin takes another bite. Definitely QED.

He sees his mother watching him—probably wondering if her cake is up to the usual standard. Sukhin does his best impression of his father's sugee-cake-appreciation face for her benefit. Only because it's Chinese New Year.

Maybe he should bring Jinn some cake. He would if he knew she'd like it—but what if she thought cake frivolous now? It strikes him that there is something incongruous about eating sugee cake and living under a pile of boxes. But why? Sukhin feels a stab of shame. He's turned into one of those awful people who hold it against hawkers who drive BMWs, as if luxury cars must stay forever out of reach for them in order to have meaning for the rest of us.

He will bring her cake—and she can decide if she wants it or not.

Every morning, when he wakes up, so does she. But she pretends to be asleep, and she lies still as he carefully climbs out of bed, dresses and goes out for his morning run. Then she rolls over to his side of the bed and lies where his body has been, stretching out in the warmth that he has left behind.

When he returns from his run, he will find her in the kitchen, showered and dressed, drinking tea. She will hand him a mug, strong and sugarless, the way she drinks it.

In the bedroom, the bed is already made. Everything is folded, tucked in, smoothed out, perfectly lined up. No evidence that anyone has slept in it.

V

"THE MOROSITY OF the poem is made more apparent by the style of the poet, which is sad and lonely."

Fuck me. Sukhin throws his pen against the wall. Morosity? Morosity! Does no one own a dictionary any more? Probably not. The thought renders him, yes, morose. The style of the poet is...lonely? Did this boy—this Kevin Seah, according to the spidery scrawl at the top of the page—actually think it acceptable to describe a poet's style as lonely, or did he mean the poet himself was lonely, which was just as ludicrous? And what, what exactly was Kevin even trying to say? It's like he put together a bunch of words that could perhaps describe a poem and just hoped for the best. Sukhin puts his forehead down on his desk and takes a deep breath. *Kill me kill me kill me.*

The gods ignore him. After a minute or so, he sits up straight and decides it's time to call it a day. The pen lies defeated at the other end of his office. *The morosity of the pen is made more apparent by the sigh of the teacher, which is sad and lonely.*

~

Sukhin doesn't know that he's been the focus of the department store security team for approximately fifteen minutes.

It's been years since he's spent this long at a department store. Once every two years, always in March—specially timed to exclude any sort of local festival and avoid the Singapore-wide mid-year sale—he allocates a small part of an afternoon to replenishing his wardrobe. A list is drawn up weeks beforehand, detailing what needs replacing: shirts, T-shirts, trousers, shorts, underwear, socks, shoes, in exact sizes and quantities. That way, he can round everything up, pay and make his exit (hopefully) within an hour.

Today, though, is different. Sukhin has decided that, along with sugee cake, he will bring Jinn practical things—socks, underwear, a windbreaker, some clothes, a towel, a thermos. The socks, the windbreaker, the towel, the thermos—easily done. The clothes—he's picked out a couple of T-shirts and track pants, very versatile. The underwear is the hard part. He's been in the women's underwear section for about forty-five minutes, scrutinising the merchandise and reading labels while checking online reviews of each brand on his phone. The salespeople, all women, having offered to help and been refused, watched him peer at various bras for a while and then called security.

The security team watches Sukhin on the surveillance camera as he methodically picks up one of every kind of bra, fingers the fabric, reads the label, then puts it back. He doesn't know that they're wondering if they should approach him; they don't know that he's looking for a bra that's one hundred per cent cotton.

In the end, no altercation is necessary. He settles for three ridiculously expensive organic cotton bras and two box sets of what the label mystifyingly claims to be "midi" panties and, more mystifyingly, all of it is supposed to be made of combed cotton. He has no idea if any of these will fit—but he is determined to buy underwear because everyone needs underwear. There is nothing more practical than underwear. Even organic combed cotton underwear. Groomed underwear! Sukhin imagines scores of tiny cat-like creatures running combs through tangled masses of cotton. He raises a hand to his head—when did he last comb his hair?

~

She offers him tea from a thermos. *She's got a thermos.* He eyes the paper bag he passed her earlier, the one she's put aside without looking inside of.

They are eating cake. Sukhin is relieved to find that this, at least, hasn't changed about her—she eats one buttery slice after another with obvious relish, licking her fingers, a half-smile on her face that he's sure has nothing to do with what he's telling her about his job. He goes on for a bit, meandering through the mundane but determined to stay on safe territory. He tells her that he's doing *Hamlet* for the fourth year in a row, and *Wuthering Heights* for the second. He tells her about cycling to work. He tells her that the common tests are in March, that he's already dreading having to read and mark about seventy essays, half of which will be incoherent—if he's lucky. Throughout, she says nothing.

And then: "Is it weird?"

"Is what weird?"

"Being back at school."

Sukhin hasn't thought about this in years. "No, not any more—but at the beginning, I felt like the man from that Japanese folk tale. The one about the fisherman and the turtle and the underwater kingdom. Do you know it?"

She shakes her head, reaching for the last slice of cake.

"A fisherman rescues a turtle—I think it gets trapped in his net by accident—and it takes him deep, deep down into the water to meet the king and queen of the sea. Everyone's really pleased that he's saved the turtle—can't remember why—so they put on a performance at the palace in his honour, and he gets to dance with the princess. She convinces him to spend three days with them, and he does—better than fishing anyway, he must have thought."

He has her full attention now—all the cake is gone.

He wishes he hadn't started telling this story. He cannot tell it well enough—his words land thin and tepid; he knows he's robbing the story of its mystique its power its beauty, and he feels stupid. But he can't stop midway—that would need even more explaining.

"The three days pass, he says goodbye to everyone and the turtle takes him back to shore, but now he can't find his house in his village and there's no sign of his family. It gets worse—he learns from some guy that a hundred years have passed, not three days, while he was gallivanting underwater. Everyone he used to know is dead, and he's all alone in a strange place that isn't a strange place. So he goes back to the shore and sits on the beach and waits."

He stops, remembering how much the ending had disturbed him as a child.

She is looking at him expectantly. He realises his telling of it is so bad that she doesn't know that the story has ended. Apologetically, he forces himself to continue: "And that's how it ends. Rather mean of the turtle, I always thought. No? Some guy rescues you and you decide to take his life away—or maybe the turtle didn't know. Do we know what time is like for turtles? Maybe theirs is a completely different concept of time. Turtles live a long time—I saw a turtle at the butterfly farm in Penang and the sign said it was three hundred years old." *Oh god, I'm babbling.* Sukhin clamps his mouth shut.

He pours himself more tea. The tea comes from the Sacred Tooth temple down the road, Jinn tells him—the monks give her as much tea as she wants. The cup is a tiny plastic thing that holds less than a third of a mug's worth. She's drinking from a small bowl—he doesn't ask why; he suspects she's given him her only cup.

"And now you don't feel like a fisherman out of an old Japanese tale?"

"Not every day."

Even the fisherman, cheated of a hundred years, would have had to pull himself together and just get on with it. Sukhin, cheated of nothing—he knows he is his own turtle; he *asked* to be assigned to his old school—has long reconciled himself to spending most of his days in a strange place that isn't a strange place. Knowing all the blocks and corridors, but getting the classrooms wrong so often because his instinctive navigation of the school remains stuck in time, even after nearly ten years there as a teacher. Checking the largest flower pot in the foyer every time he passes it because Jinn and Melissa were always hiding his things there. Quickening his step every time he passes the gym, which even with its new equipment and air conditioning and bright white floors still reminds him of the rugby boys who once tied him and Renyi to the banana trees at the back gate.

"I've never been back," she says.

This surprises him. *But you always seemed happy there.* At the tip of his tongue, but he decides not to say anything. No point, and Sukhin never likes not having a point. They sit in silence for a while, and then he asks if she would like more cake when he comes again.

ᨓ

"This year, like last year, we're focusing on *Hamlet* and *To the Lighthouse* with the first years, and *Wuthering Heights* and *The Doll House* with the second years. For the poetry option, we have Marvell, Pope and the usual sonnets."

No one is listening. No one is even pretending to listen. Not Natalie, his deputy head of department, who is busy drawing tiny intersecting circles in her notebook. Not even Dennis, who is attending the meeting as acting head of the Mathematics department while Alice is away on maternity leave.

There are no windows in this room, and no pictures.

Sukhin presses on in the monotone he has adapted specifically for these monthly inter-department update meetings. "This year, like last year, I'm leading *Hamlet* and *Wuthering Heights*, while Natalie will be in charge of *To the Lighthouse* and *The Doll's House*. Lynnette, Ian and Hanis will all take two texts each. Natalie and I will divide the poetry."

Natalie looks up briefly from her drawing and smiles.

The only door to the meeting room is all the way at the other end of the room from Sukhin. There is no way of leaving without anyone noticing.

Mr Leong, the vice-principal, looks at his watch and then at Sukhin. Notebook open, pen in hand—but Sukhin can see he hasn't actually made any notes. "Any change to the syllabus?"

"No."

"Any change to the coursework?"

"No."

"Applying for any teaching aids or tools?"

"No."

"Applying for any Ministry grants?"

"No."

"Field trip?"

"No."

"Okay. Next—Maths."

Sukhin suppresses a sigh and reaches out for a curry puff from a box in the middle of the table. It's delicious—flaky, crisp pastry around a centre of curried potato yumminess. The curry puffs, specially ordered from a shop in Holland Village, are his sole source of comfort during these ridiculous sessions. How much longer will this one last? It is nearly four—and he is desperate for a drink.

Dennis is bored and boring. He speaks to the bit of table in front of him. He doesn't use a single adjective in his brief rundown of the Mathematics department's plans for the year. He uses the word "Mathematics" in every sentence. He summarises at the end: "We plan for this plan to be the plan for the year."

Sukhin eats another curry puff.

~

Finally, a drink. A cold pint at a bar just a five-minute dash from school. And dash they did, leather soles clip-clopping against the pavement. The bar is still empty—the only good thing about being a teacher is being able to start drinking before five.

"I thought I would die in there. Is it always so bad?"

"Always."

"How was I?"

"Perfectly awful. Planning for the plan? Wow."

"I almost called him sweetie at the start, you know."

"Pah."

"Don't get jealous—I'm just being honest."

"Pah."

"Sweetie, please. You need to work harder on your vocabulary. You're an English teacher."

~

"I'll be back in half an hour."

"Take your time—I brought a book."

Sukhin and Jinn have settled into a routine—he is stunned by how easily and quickly it happens, but he doesn't let this stop him from running with it. He goes to see her every other day now. He cycles home after school, makes tea and puts it into the thermos he bought her (he doesn't like the tea from the temple), then drives to Chinatown. They talk for a bit—mostly it is him talking about his day—and then he waits in her house of boxes while she goes off to take a shower at a yoga studio nearby, where the door to the fire escape opens from the outside.

"Not very smart," he says when she tells him. "So anyone can get in?"

"People don't think anyone would sneak into a yoga studio. Not in Singapore." A smirk. "Nobody ever notices me."

"Well, you're not the archetypal bum."

She doesn't look the part. Or does she? Sukhin doesn't know any more—she's the only homeless person he's ever known. Nothing about her—not her uniform of track pants and T-shirts, not her thin, bare face, not the vague, uneven haircut—makes any sort of statement about her homelessness. No one passing her on the street would think, that woman definitely lives in an alley under a pile of boxes. Someone like Dennis might say something snide about the hair or the track pants, but that was the end of it. *Oh sweetie, make an effort—sportswear doesn't have to be ugly.*

He has to try very hard not to look around while she's away. He wants to know, so badly, what has led to...all of this, and maybe the answer is somewhere in the trolley suitcase, or in the small stack of books next to it, or under the mat. She doesn't have a phone—or he would have been tempted to check that as well. This disturbs Sukhin—he never thought of himself as the snooping sort; before this he's never felt any sort of compulsion to look at, let alone inspect, anyone else's stuff. But now he's desperate with curiosity and surely, surely, there's a reasonable explanation in here—somewhere—for vagabond Jinn.

A week ago, he finally summoned enough courage to ask:

"How long has it been?" No preamble—it was like lifting the filter-trap between his brain and his tongue and just letting whatever was there tumble out.

Jinn didn't pretend not to understand—thankfully. He wouldn't have been able to repeat the question—or worse, rephrase it. *The vagrant life—how long have you enjoyed it?* Or: *When was the last time you experienced the security of permanent shelter?*

"Five years, eleven months, nineteen days." She didn't have to think about it. And offered no elaboration.

He didn't know what he'd been expecting, but he wasn't prepared for this. Almost six years. He couldn't say a word, but he quickly anchored this new piece of information with his own markers. While he fished for a week in Sabah last year; when he was made Head of Department the year before; three years ago, while his parents were scurrying around behind his back trying to marry him off; when he broke his ankle four years ago falling from a stepladder while changing the lightbulb in the bathroom—she was living like this. What was he doing five years, eleven months and nineteen days ago? Probably marking essays. Raging at essays. Reading. Drinking tea. While she—sized up alleyways. Gathered boxes. Folded up her life and chucked it into a suitcase to make it easier to carry around.

"What are you reading?"

She's back and he looks up from the book he isn't reading. Her newly washed hair is fluffy, practically standing on end, and reeks of the strong lemony smell of the yoga studio's choice of cheap shampoo. She's changed into a different T-shirt. He hasn't asked her how she manages her laundry, but he suspects she washes her things while showering and hangs them to dry in the car park nearby—it's what he'd do.

She takes the book, looks at the cover and hands it back. There's a grin on her face. "Greene? *The Heart of the Matter*? You poseur."

He laughs, and it's mostly relief. Every time he meets her, all he wants is one more sign that she is who she is, that she isn't deranged, that she knows what she's doing, even if he doesn't, that he's not somehow turning into an accomplice of some heinous plot to end the world through a zombie apocalypse that for some twisted reason begins with the clone of his ex-girlfriend.

She packs her things into the trolley suitcase—Russian-doll style, cup into bowl into hood of windbreaker, thermos into hollow of rolled-up mat—and they go for a walk. This, too, is part of their new routine: a man, a woman and a large suitcase, zigzagging through alleyways, slipping out onto the main street, making their way past shops and people and street vendors. Waiting for the lights to change. Crossing the road. They find the small, nondescript path in the middle of a row of shophouses that leads to Duxton Plain Park and down it they go: the man, the woman, the large suitcase.

Whoever called this area a park was either wildly ambitious or delusional—Sukhin wonders why anyone even felt the need to name it. It isn't much more than a paved path under the cover of trees on both sides—but maybe it exceeded the quota of trees for a pathway, or failed to obey a government-designated tree-to-pavement ratio, and had to be called a park or be destroyed? But park or not, here, parallel to the chaos of the main roads, it is suddenly and surprisingly quiet. Jinn has a favourite bench—this is where she reads when she's by herself, and where they both read when Sukhin is with her.

He wants to know what else he can bring her—books, food, tools? More combed cotton underwear?

She looks up from her own book, frowning. "The Koh-i-noor."

He brings her peaches.

~

Three weeks later, Kevin Seah sits down in a frigid lecture theatre for his very first English Literature common test and refrains from using the word "morosity" in his essay on *Hamlet.*

Sukhin reads the essay the next day, in Jinn's cardboard hut. He shows it to her. "Morosity boy."

She reads the first couple of paragraphs out loud. "Very earnest. Rather like my old Lit essays, don't you think?"

Kevin gets a B—the highest grade he will ever receive from Mr Dhillon, who makes up his mind never to mark scripts around the woman and her boxes again. Clearly, they combine to weaken his intellect.

The woman sips her tea at the balcony, wondering if death will somehow change her. For a long time, it was all she looked forward to.

So far, nothing. She wakes up feeling the same; she goes to sleep feeling the same. There is nothing light or giddy about being dead. She's a little surprised. She expected a lift of sorts, some change in emotional weight or substance. An unbearable lightness of being? She smiles. Well, perhaps. She liked that novel.

She stands up and looks out into the neighbourhood. It is the same. Lazy, silent and still in the late afternoon except for the wind in the trees. A little later, the piano lessons will begin and the quiet will be punctuated by the practice drills of reluctant children repeatedly gnawing off little chunks of classical pieces. Still later, buses will draw up, bringing home the tired, listless horde, all aching for home. Some are brisk, others steady and sedate.

The woman sits at the balcony for hours, watching. The people all go past; no one sees her watching.

The world seems completely unmoved by her death.

VI

IT REALLY WASN'T Seethal's fault. She was okay—she didn't talk too much, she wasn't stupid, and she actually seemed to think that being a teacher was a fine thing.

They met at his cousin Gurmit's sangeet. She was the awkward woman hanging around the dessert table, stacking jelebi on a plate in various formations and trying not to make conversation with anyone. He was the awkward man hanging around the tea dispenser, drinking much-too-sweet tea and trying not to make conversation with anyone. The dessert table was next to the tea dispenser, and at some point, a nosy aunt (hers) introduced them. They talked about tea, then jelebi, and across the room, one and a half sets of Punjabi parents looked at each other and smiled. It would have made a nice anecdote if he had married her (met at a wedding, bonded over tea and jelebi, literally a sweet story)—but that would have been the only reason, and Sukhin was well past the age of doing things for the sake of an anecdote.

By the end of the evening, Sukhin's parents knew how old Seethal was (twenty-seven—perfect), what she did for a living (something to do with insurance pricing—sounded okay), whether she had a boyfriend (no—very good), what her parents did for their living (dentist—good; stay-at-home mum—very good), and whether she had been engaged before (no—very good). And Seethal's parents knew all of that about Sukhin, with bonus points going to them for finding out that he had just been made Deputy Head of Department, that he had bought his own place, and that he'd worn braces as a teenager. Numbers were exchanged—not Sukhin's or Seethal's, but their mothers'—through another nosy aunt (Sukhin's—the bride's mother, another plus for the anecdote).

By the time they got home, Sukhin's parents were discussing when the wedding might be (August would be nice—not too warm or rainy—but not National Day weekend), who they would invite (not Uncle Milan, who got drunk at Gurmit's sangeet), and whether the children would be tall (Seethal couldn't be more than 1.6 metres).

By the time Sukhin got home, he was unbearably bloated, wondering why he drank all that sugary tea. He went to bed annoyed with himself, and woke up with only the barest recollection of the evening.

"Call her." The number was written on a memo sheet from his father's clinic. This was a week after Gurmit's wedding dinner, during which he'd muttered hello to Seethal on his way to the gents', once. One damn hello.

Sukhin wasn't half-Punjabi for nothing—he knew the significance of a woman's number thrust at a son along with those two ominous words. He folded up the sheet and put it into his pocket, knowing that if he didn't, he would spend the next couple of hours enduring his mother sighing about never having grandchildren.

A week went by. He didn't call; he didn't intend to.

"She might call you, Sukhin," said his father. "I think it's okay, yes? Modern times now—who says boys must call girls? I told her mother you're always busy; she says she'll give your number to Seethal, and then you two can do the WhatsApp. Easy!" He had evidently taken over as the household negotiator of this dark business.

The three of them were having dinner at his parents' house. They looked sly and pleased with themselves. Sukhin wanted to change his name and never speak to them again. *Do the WhatsApp, indeed.*

Three days later, Seethal texted.

Hi Sukhin, how r u? This is Seethal.

A woman who couldn't type "are" and "you" in full—how could he possibly marry that? Inconceivable. But he replied—no point being rude; she had probably been goaded into this by her parents and he could certainly empathise. Weeks went by. Her texts grew longer and friendlier; his didn't.

"It's okay to meet her," his mother said one day, apropos of nothing—she had been talking about whether it was worth getting a bread-making machine. "Go ahead and take her out to dinner."

He did—partly to shut everyone up, partly because he wondered if he should make a greater effort to just get on with it. He and Jinn were finished. It had been years. He should at least see what—well, who—was out there. It wasn't as though he was holding out for her return—he knew her well enough to know there would be no return. For all he knew, she was probably married to some smug lawyer or banker, or even worse, a rich hipster.

She didn't know what she wanted, she'd told him, but it wasn't *this*. They were at a cinema, mulling over the movie selection. He didn't particularly feel like seeing anything and he'd been quieter than usual all evening—it had been a long week, and he had an essay due. It was his first term at the National Institute of Education and he hated it. The coursework was dull, the other trainee teachers were vapid, the twice-daily two-hour commute was exhausting—who knew that sitting in a moving train could be so debilitating?

He'd heard various versions of her refusal of an unnamed "this" over the last few months. *There must be more than this. This is all so ridiculous. I deserve better than this.* Sukhin hadn't thought much of it. Her love-hate relationship with her job was making her moody, he'd decided. She seemed to constantly vacillate between derision and outright envy, and that had to be tiring.

Jinn had spent the previous year and a bit working at an events company owned by one of her mother's friends, a company that existed solely to plan parties for very bored, very rich people. For a child's fifth birthday, she supervised the filling of two swimming pools with gummy bears. For a bunch of eighteen-year-olds, she organised a burlesque cabaret on a private jet. Recently, for an anniversary party, she arranged for thirty crates of the vintage from the year the couple got married to be flown in from the vineyard in Burgundy where they first met.

He pretended not to understand. "We don't have to see a movie."

She blew up. It wasn't the rant-rage-repeat of her usual outbursts—he was accustomed to her tendency to fly into dramatic fits of temper, but this time she had just gone quiet. Her eyes flashed, her lips moved, a muscle in her cheek twitched, but she didn't make a sound. He couldn't find anything to say, nothing that could cut the tension without sounding like a platitude, and their silence amplified the chatter of the crowd around them, turning the debate over some cheesy thriller, the giggling over Ryan Gosling, all the general indecision and inanity of the cineplex lobby, all the peopleness of people, into a sea of grating, vibrating tension.

"I don't want to do this any more." Softly, just above a whisper.

He refused to ask her what she meant, but he could tell he had become part of *this*.

She walked away. He didn't walk after her. When he called the next day, she cancelled the call. He didn't call back.

Three weeks later, a box arrived at the house. Neatly taped up, SUKHIN on one side in black marker. He didn't open it. When he moved out and into his own place five years later, he left the box behind in his parents' house, under the coffee table, where the Really Nice Boxes sat.

Dinner with Seethal wasn't terrible. She was polite; he was polite. He listened with interest about reinsurance; she said that teachers were underappreciated and that it was a shame. But it wasn't good. She didn't like poetry; he didn't like pottery. She read self-help books; he wasn't friends with anyone who did. She didn't understand why he wouldn't consider vegetarianism; he balked when she ordered an organic soy latte instead of cake for dessert.

"I don't like cake," she said when he offered her a bit of lemon sponge.

"You don't like cake?" Sukhin didn't like how incredulous he sounded. While he wasn't at all out to impress her, he didn't want to come off sounding—of all things!—like some sort of weirdo who judged people on their dessert preferences. Even if he was. And what exactly was wrong with cake? This unspoken question hung in the air for a few minutes—for Sukhin. He finished the slice of lemon sponge, frowning, his thoughts jumping from cake as dessert to cake as a kind of connective tissue between people. *His* people, anyway—obviously, there were people out there who didn't see the point of cake, who didn't see and therefore could never enter the community of cake, and who would never be his people.

Seethal, to whom his shift in attitude and attention was immediately noticeable, tried to explain. "I'm not really a dessert sort of person," she offered, forgetting all about tea and jelebi and the half-baked jokes she'd made.

Sukhin hadn't. He pounced on this jarring logical gap. "But all those jelebis at Gurmit's wedding…"

"For my mother. I can't stand those things." She made a face. So did he.

He didn't text her again, making a mental note to ask women about cake before considering anything even remotely resembling a date.

His parents wheedled and whined, after his father got repeated calls from her mother inviting the family over for tea. Tea! One of the many euphemisms for pre-engagement talks. Sukhin refused to engage.

That was when things really got out of hand. His aunt and uncle invited Seethal's family to their annual barbecue, and Sukhin was ordered to grill skewers of peppers, halloumi and mushrooms as her mother looked on. "So careful you are, Sukhin—no wonder you're a teacher!" He found himself dragged to random weddings, and then: "Isn't that Seethal?" His father would wave, and he would be marched over to her and left to have a non-conversation, in which they would take turns making random, stand-alone observations that didn't interest each other. She didn't seem to mind, which made the situation all the more dire—every encounter with her, he knew, went towards racking up enough points (or hours, or whatever this system was counting) before their parents decided it was proper to insist on an engagement. Seethal seemed to have placidly accepted this, which made her one of the enemy.

Sukhin did the most logical thing he could think of—he behaved like a complete asshole. It was an exit strategy.

Whenever he saw Seethal at a wedding or a party, he would make an about-turn and stride off, trying to knock over at least one chair along the way. When his aunt asked if things with Seethal were going well ("Such a nice girl, and looks a bit like Madhuri Dixit, doesn't she? You know, that Hindi film star, hmmm maybe you're too young to know who she is"), he gave her a long, cold stare and abruptly walked out the door, to his parent's horror and embarrassment.

His father ran after him. "Sukhin! Don't be rude to Aunty Malkit!"

He pretended not to hear—quite a feat; the neighbours two doors down had probably heard Dr Jaswant's bellow. Sukhin got into his car, slammed the door as loudly as he dared, then drove off.

Aunty Lillian and Uncle Bobby were treated to the grand finale. Aunty Lillian had brought over pineapple cake, made with a recipe she'd pried out of a retired pastry chef. Sukhin's mother, not to be outdone, had spent three hours making kaya and scones. They sat at the dining table in Doris' kitchen and gossiped, and were still at it when Sukhin dropped by. He made himself a large mug of tea and was about to join them at the table when Aunty Lillian inadvertently set the scene in motion.

"Exciting times, Sukhin," she began, buttering a scone. "I've just ordered some silk from Shanghai to make my dress—I'm not going to wait until the last minute! Your father says he's expecting the engagement party to be in a couple of months, and a good cheongsam takes about thirty days to make, you know, fittings and all!"

He looked grimly from one parent to the other. His mother was all tight lips and shifty eyes; his father kept eating cake, refusing to look up from his plate.

"What kind of weird fantasy are you people living?" Sukhin snarled. "What the fuck is wrong with you? This is not your life!" He glared at his father. "If you want a wedding so badly, you marry her!"

He threw up his arms—Sukhin is very much his father's son when he's angry—forgetting about the mug he was still holding. Trailing an arc of scalding hot tea, it went sailing into the middle of the dining table, smashing itself into angry little shards of porcelain that promptly jumped onto the cake and scones, into the pot of kaya, into every cup of coffee on the table.

He laughed at their horrified faces and didn't stop laughing until he was out the door and driving away.

~

One evening, as he walks Jinn back to her alley, he tells her about Seethal.

"Stupid man. You might have been happy, you know."

"No."

They walk in silence for a bit.

"She was so different—from you." He regrets it the moment he says it.

"Nonsense. She lost you at organic soy latte."

~

The doorbell rings, just as he's about to do the laundry.

"Heyyyyyy."

Dennis, through the door. He rings the bell again. Sukhin wonders if he should pretend he isn't home.

"Open up, sweetie—I checked; your car's here. You're home."

Through the peephole, Dennis is mostly head and shoulders, leaning towards the door. He's also mostly bright orange, dressed to go join the neon army at a gym somewhere. He jabs the bell switch again. On the other side of the door, Sukhin rolls his eyes. No. Not opening the door.

Dennis switches tactics—four sharp raps against the wooden door, followed by the doorbell, then four knocks, then the doorbell again.

"Sweetie, I'll scream."

God, Dennis. Sukhin unlatches the door, pulls it open. "What do you want?"

"Where are your manners? Have you got any coffee?"

"I don't drink coffee."

"Whatever—water then. You have to offer me something."

By now, Dennis is in the kitchen, opening cabinets at random and peering into them. He opens the fridge and squints at its contents. "Milk. Aren't you lactose intolerant?"

"No."

Dennis is well acquainted with the apartment—two years ago, Sukhin reluctantly suffered him in the role of self-invited houseguest for three weeks while Dennis had his own place repainted (it started out as two weeks, then got extended because the fumes were "simply too much, sweets"). Dennis had been unable to stop himself from invading Sukhin's privacy—he reorganised the cupboards, replaced the worn-out rugs, threw out Sukhin's old clothes, ordered furniture.

That had caused a major scene at work.

Sukhin was in the staff room looking through the lesson plans of two trainee teachers, trying his best not to sound condescending or bored, while the rest of the English department tried not to snicker. Who hadn't been the object of Sukhin's poorly concealed disdain? "Such a know-it-all. He must have been insufferable as a student," said one of the younger teachers, who had been told to "go home and read *Fifty Shades of Grey*" after he had failed to recognise a racy bit of Marvell.

Dennis bounded up with an interiors catalogue. "Sweet cheeks, great news—they have the sofa in peacock, and they can deliver tomorrow."

"What sofa?"

"This one," Dennis pronounced, flipping the catalogue open to a dog-eared page. It was incredible, Sukhin thought, in the truest sense of the word—in what looked to be a flowering forest glen, a shaft of sunlight falling across one arm, a sofa languished, cool, casual, a dryad of polished wood and blue-green upholstery with an expensive sheen.

A squirrel and some other woodland animal stared down at it from an overhanging branch.

"I don't need a sofa."

Dennis sighed impatiently. "You have two chairs and some sort of large cushion thing. You need a sofa."

Sukhin stood up. He had to unclench his teeth to say: "I don't want a sofa."

"Well, I'm buying it for you—it's coming tomorrow. Don't be difficult, Sukhin." Dennis shut the catalogue primly, then turned to walk away. Sukhin stared after him. The insouciance. The utter thickskinnery.

"Dennis, I don't want a sofa." Perhaps a little too loudly—though everyone in the English department and most of the History teachers were staring openly by this time anyway.

Dennis had the gall to look surprised, as if the sofa were some sort of shared life goal and Sukhin was laying waste to years of careful planning. Sukhin bubbled over. He reached out, grabbed Dennis by the shoulder and whipped him around. He took a step closer, and the incongruous thought hit him that Dennis was the taller man as well as the better built, and in ancient Greece would have been considered the better man—"kalos kagathos": good looking and therefore a good person.

It was possibly this thought that sent him over the edge. Kalos kagathos—what the actual fuck.

"I don't want a bloody sofa!" The Physics department, on the other side of the wall, would later report hearing this loud and clear. "Even Susan heard it," said Tat Meng, who was on the phone with his wife at the time.

Still holding on to his shoulder, Sukhin gave Dennis a shove—light, but enough to send him a step backwards. Dennis glared, then stomped off. But a moment later he was back. He seized Sukhin's copy of *Hamlet*—

a yellowing relic from Sukhin's own junior college days, with SUKHIN in black marker across the cover—and flung it theatrically across the room, but even he was unprepared for the binding to come undone in mid-flight and the ensuing explosion of pages over the English team.

Breaths were held, eyes widened, faces turned up towards the paper storm.

Sukhin felt a page land on his head and reached up to catch it. He read—out loud, without meaning to: "I am but mad north-north-west. When the wind is southerly, I know a hawk from a handsaw."

He passed a hand over his face. Dennis' mouth was cast in an O, his chest heaving, a hand raised protectively to his throat. "Sorry, sorry, I'm so sorry."

Sukhin stared past Dennis, at the pages littering the floor. He wanted to grab Dennis and break him, but he couldn't move. The period bell rang. A few of the other teachers gathered their notes and books and slowly shuffled out the door, careful to avoid the scattered pages. Sukhin left the scene quietly, cycled to East Coast Park and spent the rest of the afternoon walking along the coast. When he finally got home, Dennis had made clam pasta, and they ate in the kind of heavy, brooding silence that reaches perfect pitch when one party is clearly and irrefutably wrong, while the other is clearly and irrefutably wronged.

The sofa arrived the next day. It was there when Sukhin got home—queening over the living room, vivid, peacock-hued and as glorious as the brochure promised. On it was his copy of *Hamlet*, put together again and rebound, SUKHIN and all. Dennis was in the kitchen, noisily rummaging through the fridge. "I'm throwing together a salad, sweets—we're going to have us a little picnic on that gorgeous sofa. Where are your wine glasses?"

The same sofa—the only object in Sukhin's apartment that isn't grey or greyish—is now under scrutiny by its patron, his nose only a couple of centimetres or so from the fabric. A frown, a "hmm". Dennis goes into the bedroom and inspects both pillows, then lifts the duvet. "Have you changed your sheets recently?"

"Last week—not that it's any of your business."

Sukhin watches as Dennis slides open the wardrobe and rifles through his shirts. "What the hell are you looking for?" He is surprised to find himself more mystified than annoyed. Is this what it means to grow mellow with age?

Dennis moves on to the underwear drawer. "Who is she?"

Sukhin is aghast. "What?"

Dennis straightens up and crosses his arms. "You've been missing astronomy club meetings, and you've left before four every day for the last three months. Every day."

"Work-life balance, Dennis. It's a thing." He walks off. Dennis shuts the drawer and follows him into the living room.

"And you've lost weight."

"I've been running."

"Aha. You've been running. And you gave out thirteen A's in the common test. In October, you gave six." Dennis looks smug. "It must be love."

"I'm exercising so I won't be a useless lump when I'm eighty. And maybe the kids have improved." Sukhin pauses. How does Dennis know how many A's his students got for their Literature papers? "Are you stalking me? I don't even know what to call it—how do you know about the A's?"

"It's called a database, sweets—you put all your scores on a spreadsheet, yes? Well, where do you think that ends up? For a smart man, you can be very stupid sometimes."

Sukhin sinks into the sofa and sighs. What do other people do with sticky, aggressively nosy friends? Some people must like having them—there are those who seek attention, and those who seek to give it. Tinder be damned—why isn't there an app pairing up these people? It would save him (and presumably there were others like him) so much time and energy. Maybe if all the desperately private people in the world banded together and funded the app...

"I see you're not denying that there's a woman somewhere. Just not *here*."

"I just can't imagine why you'd think that. And what are you looking for? Lipstick stains?" Sukhin slowly rearranges the pile of books next to the sofa, hoping he will appear bored.

Dennis begins pacing—he walks to the kitchen, then back to the living room, then back to the kitchen. "I can't understand why you're lying to me," he whines. Sukhin continues to stack books, splitting them into two equal piles, then into four equal piles. *Remain calm—he'll tire himself out.*

"Aha!"

Sukhin's head snaps up. *God, no. No, no, no, no.*

In the kitchen, Dennis is kneeling beside the washing machine, holding up a pale blue bra. Its pale green sister has followed it partway out and now sits idly across the edge of the door. If Dennis were curious enough to check, he would find "100% organic combed cotton" printed in tiny, tiny script on the sides of both brassieres.

"My dear Mr Dhillon, please take your time. I've got all day."

They used to fly kites after school at the great big field beside the bay. She loved it because it was so green—grass, grass and more grass as far as her peripheral vision stretched. He loved it for the kites. He made many of them, mostly because he enjoyed making them and sometimes because he wanted to please her with something witty or silly that she could release into the wind. Her favourite was a pineapple, the earliest and ugliest of his kites. He never understood why.

After they parted, when there was no one to make her kites, she would go to the great big field to watch other people fly their kites.

She never saw him there again.

VII

SHE IS NOWHERE to be found. Her suitcase is missing, and the cardboard structure is empty. Sukhin has come to think of this large, unwieldy thing, held up and together by the mysterious combined forces of luck and physics, as Jinn's house. A house can pretty much be anything, he muses, as long as someone is willing to live in it. Or under it—he recalls how, as a child, he turned his mother's dining table into his house for a few weeks, insisting on eating all his meals under it, surrounded by his toys and books. His father alternated between threats and pleas, but in the end Sukhin was forced out from under the table by a cockroach that had sauntered over to look for crumbs (it couldn't have set out to chase him out from under the table).

It's just a toilet break. Everyone has to pee.

As he waits for Jinn to return, he inspects the boxes. Some are beginning to look a little wilted—time to put in some new ones. He wonders if he should insist on moving her to some sort of shelter, or to his place, anywhere that doesn't involve living outdoors in a DIY fire hazard. He's been wanting to talk to her about her living arrangements, but hasn't found the courage nor a good enough excuse—the old Jinn would resent it, and he doesn't want to give the new Jinn any excuse to walk away.

Where the hell is she?

He waits another fifteen minutes and then tries not to panic, but panics anyway. Where can she have gone? Well, pretty much anywhere. He decides he will find a way to put a tracking device on her. Or pay people to set up watch round the clock. Or get her a phone.

There's a post-it stuck on one of the boxes on the inside of her house.

"S—53 Kerbau Road, 4pm. J."

He's relieved. But it is 3.47.

Without stopping to think, he rushes to his car and drives like a madman from Chinatown to Little India, feeling like he's starring in a spoof of a Singapore Tourism Board ad.

If you ignore all considerations for safety and spare no thought for pedestrians, it is possible to see the one-hundred-and-eighty-six-year-old Jamae Mosque—note the combination of South Indian and neoclassical architectural styles—and the more recently constructed Buddha Tooth Relic Temple—see how the Tang style of this building departs from the dominant South Chinese typology of Singapore's Buddhist temples—in just under three minutes. Over the next ten minutes, push your vehicle farther: race down Eu Tong Sen Street, then Hill Street—the flash of white on your left is the Armenian Church, consecrated in 1836, making it the oldest church in Singapore—and cut across Orchard Road, then Selegie Road. Dash across the intersection and onto Serangoon Road. Now see Tekka Centre whizz past, then the Sri Veeramakaliamman Temple—people say that the goddess Kali, for whom the temple was built, made sure that it survived the Japanese air raids in World War II. Sharp left onto Race Course Lane, then Race Course Road, home to the famous Banana Leaf Apolo, where meals are still served on, yes, banana leaves. Swerve onto Kerbau Road, park, then admire the multicoloured façade of the former residence of old-time candy tycoon Tan Teng Niah—you might as well; you are five minutes late and what is a few more minutes to catch your breath, now that you've arrived alive?

She is where she has asked him to be and doesn't look surprised to see him. She doesn't look particularly pleased either, which disappoints him.

"This way."

He follows her through an alley and they emerge facing Tekka Centre. The wet market is closing for the day, and the vendors are busy packing away equipment and goods, cleaning their stalls. Some of them are pushing wheelbarrows of vegetables and fruit towards a large rubbish bin by the side of the road. The bin, about the size of a large van, is already teeming with unwanted produce, so the vendors have begun to pile the rest into boxes next to it. Some simply empty their wheelbarrows onto the street. A small, nondescript group of people rifles through the discard piles next to the bin.

"They're saving vegetables so that they can be redistributed instead of just rotting here," Jinn tells Sukhin, and she's helping with the collection today. She takes two sacks from a pile on the street and hands him one. "Pick out whatever you think is still edible. Like this." She shows him a dirty-looking cabbage. "If you remove the outer leaves, this is perfect." She puts it into her sack. "And hardly anything can kill a carrot."

He picks up a carrot and examines it. It's a rather ugly specimen—twisted and gnarled, not something he'd choose at a supermarket—but otherwise undamaged. He puts it carefully into his sack, along with two other ugly carrots and an evil-looking potato. Some of the stack he's sifting through is damaged beyond redemption, but a lot of it is just puny or ugly, thrown out because a kinked cucumber or a carrot with a forked tail just isn't sexy.

Jinn and the others are quicker than he is. They work for over two hours, making sure they don't miss anything. A few vendors begin to hand over their discards directly, bypassing the bin. Passers-by stare openly.

Some are rude. ("Wah! Like that can eat meh?" "You all got no other work ah?") Others stop to ask what they're doing, and one of them—a tall, lanky man who appears perfectly at home sifting through refuse piles—explains that they're trying to reduce waste. His tone is measured, polite and unapologetic. He shows off some of the bounty, opening a sack for the benefit of the curious onlookers. The others work in silence. Watching Jinn, Sukhin can see that she is an old hand at this—she's developed an instinct for which vegetables to check, which to ignore, which parts to check for damage, how much damage is acceptable—and he realises that this must be how she gets some of her food. *Well, one mystery solved. Progress.* But the thought of her picking through rubbish for food makes him feels angry and uncomfortable—and guilty. Sukhin manages to convert all this rather quickly and efficiently into missionary zeal, falling onto the next pile with a dogged determination to rescue as much fruit and veg as possible from ignominious, stinking death. "Ulysses" by Tennyson bubbles up in his mind:

Death closes all: but something ere the end,

Some work of noble note, may yet be done…

In the afternoon heat, on the steaming asphalt pavement, he subjects countless carrots and potatoes and brinjals and pineapples and persimmons to careful, pedantic scrutiny. It's very much like marking student assignments, Sukhin realises—scrutinising specimen after specimen, desperately trying to keep an open mind, desperately wanting to see promise, all while fighting rising waves of nausea.

"Is that your Lit teacher?"

"No, Mum. And it's *tutor*—I'm in JC." Her daughter is texting a classmate and doesn't bother to look up.

"I'm telling you, Prema, it's him—look!"

Prema looks—and stops regretting that she let her mother talk her into going shopping for Punjabi suits after school. It really is Mr Dhillon, squatting beside a rubbish bin at Tekka Market, rummaging through a pile of veggies someone has thrown away. Mr Dhillon, a dumpster diver!

"Is he actually going to eat that stuff?" She makes a face. "And he didn't even bother to change. Wow—dumpster-diving in this heat, in shirt and trousers." Prema, torn between admiration and disgust, takes a picture.

"Stop that!" Her mother swats at her phone.

"Damn." The photo is a out of focus; it looks like Mr Dhillon, but it's hard to be certain. "Dammit."

"None of that language, please, Prema. Come, let's go. Don't let the poor man see you." She shakes her head. *Goodness, are teachers so badly paid?* Back in her day, teachers were pillars of the community. No teacher would have ever picked through rubbish for food; no community would have allowed it. She sighed. *Does his mother know?*

ʍ

They are in a stranger's kitchen and Jinn is giving orders. Cool and calm, with a quiet authority that invites everyone to assume she's grown up running a kitchen, though Sukhin knows her family had a helper and she was never even allowed to boil water. In low and measured tones, she tells a man who's just arrived to chop up carrots and another to dice peppers. Sukhin, tasked by Jinn with cleaning and slicing up lotus root, is just one of her seven kitchen minions. The woman next to him is busy removing the outer layers of about thirty onions.

The man who spoke to the passers-by at the market bursts into the kitchen, bearing a large basket. "X, the supermarket workers just dropped this off." He beams at Jinn, offering up the basket for her inspection.

She removes a stalk of leek from it. It's beginning to yellow, but otherwise there doesn't seem to be much wrong with it. There are more weary-looking leeks in the basket, all in various stages of depression. Jinn sets them reverently on the kitchen counter. She is smiling like she does when she's about to eat cake—a tiny, private smile of anticipation. "Wonderful, Kim Seng. When you return the basket, tell Yasin we're very grateful."

She extends a long thin arm towards the man chopping peppers. He turns. "Gopal, when you're done, can you slice the leeks? Thin, not too fine."

Gopal nods vigorously. "Okay, X, no problem."

Jinn comes over to check on Sukhin's progress. "Are they calling you X?" he asks, careful to speak in an undertone. "Or is it Ex? E-X."

She raises an eyebrow. "As in the prefix? Or the former lover? You can call me Ex if you like."

"Fine. So it's X. The letter. Not very original."

"No one's trying to be original, Sukhin."

Chastised, he returns to his task while she finishes her round of the kitchen, talking to the other volunteers, making minor adjustments. No empress in silk and indigo ever had more willing, adoring subjects—Sukhin notices how they all defer to her, how they're immediately alert when she's looking their way, how they lap up her faint praise. Incredible. The girl who once hid his books all over school in a spiteful fit of rage is now the serene godmother of this covert soup kitchen operation.

Well, *seemingly* covert soup kitchen operation. To be fair (and to protect himself from unnecessary knowledge), Sukhin hasn't asked any questions. All he knows so far is that they brought the vegetables they salvaged from Tekka Market to this shophouse on Rowell Road, right next to what appears to be a brothel—or some other enterprise involving women and hourly rates. They entered from the back alley into a large, surprisingly well-equipped kitchen and have been joined by others also bearing rescued fruit, vegetables and canned food from supermarkets and sundry shops in the neighbourhood. Jinn hasn't introduced him to anyone, but she greets them all by name.

"X. All done."

Finally, the vegetables are all chopped, waiting for her. The kitchen goes quiet as she takes final stock of the ingredients. She counts the onions, checks the leeks, peers at the tomatoes, considers the canned goods. She picks up a piece of blue ginger that has had its dry bits lopped off. "Let's do something cool with this—we don't usually get lengkuas."

She looks like she's trying to remember something. No one rushes her.

A smile. She nods at everyone. "Okay—I know what we'll make. Lina, can you pound these?" She hands a woman all the pieces of salvaged blue ginger. "With these." She gives her some salvaged turmeric root and garlic.

She turns to Kim Seng. "Let's grill these leeks. First, you'll need to blanch them. Do you know how?"

One by one, the dishes are decided, the tasks portioned out. Sukhin has no idea where or when she's learnt to cook, or whether this is all some great pretence and no one has called her bluff. No time for conjecture—he has to help Gopal make garlic rice.

~

As Kim Seng grills the leeks over the bare-bones grill that a retired satay hawker donated to the cause, he watches X teach Lina and Weixiong how to make vegetarian soto, with canned mushrooms, potatoes, carrots and celery instead of chicken. He feels at once proud and awed. So graceful, so soft-spoken, but she makes it clear she's in charge. A real woman, just like his late mother. *And I found her; it was me!*

He is fond of telling the story; he tells it to every new volunteer and never misses a chance to repeat it to the rest of the team. How he found her looking through the dustbin of that bakery on Keong Saik Road for leftover bread, how he knew there wasn't any—he'd already looked. How he offered her some of the fruit he had taken from Tekka earlier, how he told her about the group of food salvagers he had started, how she had shown up two days later at Tekka, on time, to help the group with their hunt. How she'd had the idea to cook the food nearby, so that even the larger items and the more badly damaged or too-ripe produce could be saved. Which meant more food could be shared with more people—there was often more than the salvagers could consume themselves.

It had all come together after that.

Gopal's brother offered up the shophouse on Rowell Road—perfect; just ten minutes' walk from the market. He had taken over what used to be a café, and was using the three floors of shophouse space to grow dainty organic vegetables that he sold for outlandish sums to fine-dining establishments that wanted to be able to say they were supporting local growers (but didn't want to stoop to incorporating actual local vegetables into their dishes). Gopal's very smart brother Raj supplies them with the elegant solution of edible flowers and micro-greens grown in carefully controlled micro-climates under artificial UV light, right in the heart of Singapore. (Kim Seng understands that these micro-greens are in fact very small turnips, leeks, pea shoots and carrots, and Raj has explained that "rich people are extreme; they like their cars as big as possible, their vegetables as small as possible.") But the more important point was that Raj wanted to support his little brother's efforts at social work, so Free Kitchen was born. "Let the rich people pay for it," he said, offering to waive all the costs of electricity and water. Raj is the group's other hero, next to X.

X, who from day one has run the kitchen, teaching every volunteer how to prepare and cook the food that they rescue and how to store it and reheat it the next day, adding new ingredients if there are any.

X, who makes sure everything they cook is delicious and dignified, not just ingredients slapped together over a stove. It was also X who insisted on using proper cutlery and plates. "No plastic shit," she snarled, losing her composure that one time.

X, who is now beside him, telling him the leeks smell amazing. They do—who knew that just olive oil, garlic, salt and pepper could make something magical out of leeks?

X, who is herself magical. Whose name no one knows, but maybe that's part of the magic?

"Who's that?"

"The new fella? Came with X. He was with us at Tekka too."

Lina still isn't sure what to make of X, even after a year. X looks like she could be Lina's daughter's age, which makes Lina a little more sensitive than she should be—but she isn't aware of this. Yes, X is a good cook. Yes, she's very organised. Yes, she's creative. But why does she do all this? She's clearly had an education—her voice has that telltale "good school" ring to it; her English is excellent—so what is she doing here, when she could be out there working, or getting a job? And doesn't anyone else think that it's strange she won't tell them her name? And why do all these grown men behave like children around her, so eager to please? So stupid. The woman isn't even pretty—look at her hair! It's like someone threw a hedge clipper at her.

What kind of mother would let her daughter run around like this, looking like this?

It makes Lina angry but she doesn't let it show, and she never speaks against X. Why waste energy? She adds tomatoes and carrots to the soup and, while watching the pot, looks out of the corner of her eye at the stranger, now busy cutting up a watermelon. *Aiyoh, so bad with a knife.* She winces as he slips and nearly cuts himself. Honestly, some men in the kitchen are just accidents waiting to happen.

He puts down the knife and rolls up his sleeves, getting watermelon juice on his cuffs.

She shakes her head. Back to the pot. She gives it a stir—it does smell good, this soto.

A clatter to her left—the man has managed to drop the knife. As he bends over to pick it up, Lina notices his shoes—black leather, polished—and his trousers—pleated, carefully ironed. His hair is short, neat but not styled. Maybe some sort of salesman? Well, definitely not a cook.

~

More people arrive. At first, Sukhin assumes they've come to eat, but soon he realises that they're also here to help, and most of them have brought foldable chairs and tables. Some leave these behind, heading off after saying hello to the group in the kitchen; others stay to help set up. He puts the container he has filled with watermelon slices into the fridge and goes out into the alley to watch them.

Very quickly, in a practised rhythm, the tables and chairs—all varying in size, colour, style—are laid out next to each other in a row that stretches over half the alleyway. Sukhin counts fifteen tables, about sixty chairs. Tea lights and candles are placed on the tables and lit, casting a warm glow over everything, and suddenly it's possible to ignore the mismatched cutlery, the mismatched tables, the mismatched everything. The kitchen team begins to bring out the food, and Sukhin rushes to help. Some of the later arrivals have brought food that they've prepared themselves—among the hodge-podge of offerings, Sukhin spies kueh, a dish of lasagna, some sort of cake.

Doris Day's "Perhaps Perhaps Perhaps" starts to play on portable-speakers.

This must be their version of the dinner gong. People begin to arrive, walking in from both sides of the alley, to take their places at the table. Most of them are older, shabbily dressed, tired-looking. They come alone, but some of them greet each other. Some are construction workers, probably from Bangladesh and China. Others are harder to pigeonhole—middle-aged, not quite dishevelled, listless rather than tired. After everyone is served, a few of the salvager-cooks sit among them to share the meal, while the others eat in the kitchen. No one speaks, but it is a relaxed, companionable silence. The music—now Nat King Cole's "Mona Lisa"—romanticises it all somewhat, but nobody seems to mind.

Sukhin and Jinn eat in the kitchen, standing side by side. She looks tired. He wants to ask her so many questions, but holds off. He'll be fine in the dark for one more day.

"Thanks, Sukhin. You know, you don't have to."

He takes the bag from her. "It's fine. I told you, I don't mind."

She sighs. "Fine. But I can do this myself."

Sukhin fights the urge to roll his eyes and succeeds. "Yes, of course. But let me, okay?"

The anti-princess goes into her cardboard castle. The man who is not her prince walks away, feeling like he's been entrusted with the crown jewels of a kingdom instead of a crummy bag of dirty clothes.

Is this love? He hopes not. But he's become thankful for the gentle setting on his washing machine—and he's bought fabric softener.

The woman stands outside a shop she doesn't recognise any more. She can't see inside—a display window now takes up the entire shopfront. It is all glass shelves with rows and rows of cakes and pastries, with a panel of gleaming wood behind them. The door is smoky glass, impossible to see through, with a polite sign asking customers to ring the bell for service.

The cakes—they are so much grander than she remembers. So beautiful too, but she cannot imagine eating any of these.

The woman stands outside the shop for a very long time, then she leaves and never returns.

VIII

HE'S GOING TO do it.

He's poured himself a gin and tonic, even though it's barely two in the afternoon. Outside, it's sunny and cloudless, and everyone is indoors, escaping the heat. His clothes are drying on the balcony—whites today. Inside, the air conditioning is on, he's put on a Radiohead album and through the wall comes the faint sound of the neighbour's vacuum cleaner. It's like any other Sunday, except it isn't—it's The Day He Googles Her.

He's thought about doing this before, of course. Too many times. Each time, he's managed to either put it off (this comes quite easily) or reason it into something vaguely sinister (not so easy; Sukhin isn't really the moralising kind, least of all with himself). He knows the truth, of course—he's petrified of what he might find out. But it's been six months since she dropped back into his life, six months of wondering whywhatwhowhenwherehow, six months of waiting for her to tell him. So far, all he's found out, beyond what he learnt in the first month or so, is that she sleeps in the multi-storey car park if the rain is too heavy, joins the food-salvager folks (he still doesn't know what they call themselves) at least twice a week and is now reading a copy of *Paradise Lost* that she found in a recycling heap.

Not a crumb on what her life was like before, nothing whatsoever about what combination of circumstances could have brought her to this.

His first thought had been that she was a fugitive. Had she killed someone? Embezzled millions? Had she been part of some sort of complex terrorist plot? Dramatic, ludicrous, but perfectly possible.

Then it struck him that she might be running from some sort of domestic horror—an abusive husband? Unlikely—he'd have an easier time believing she'd been part of a terrorist plot. So mass murder for a higher cause, yes; victim of abuse, no. But wasn't that part of the problem, though, that you could never tell who could or would be a victim? Or who could or would be an abusive psycho, for that matter. He remembered his Aunty Malkit telling his parents about an old friend of hers from dentistry college ("Such a good girl she was, always studying, no discos, volunteered at the orphanage on weekends") whose husband had filed a suit against her after fifteen years of marriage for physical and mental abuse. "She beat him with a garden hose, can you imagine?" Aunty Malkit sounded deeply horrified, but something in her voice, an undertone of an undertone, seemed to ring closer to schadenfreude than sympathy. It made Sukhin wonder if hers was a horror of the beating or the garden hose.

Was it a question of money? He'd heard about people losing their jobs and their homes and not being able to pick themselves up again. At first, he thought this had to be what happened—not quite as dramatic as embezzlement or terrorism, but it would explain her reticence. Always too proud to ask for help, and he couldn't imagine her asking anyone for money or a place to live. But Jinn, clever minx, always resourceful, good with people—she would find something, or something or someone would find her. No, *this*, all of *this*, whatever *this* is, is her not wanting to find anything. Jinn 2.0 is deliberately unplugged.

The few tentative, carefully considered questions Sukhin has dared to ask haven't yielded anything useful.

"Is anyone trying to find you?"

"I hope not. But maybe."

"Are you hoping they'll find you?"

"I'm hoping there's more of that banana cake."

"Why don't you come live with me?"

"Why, are your boxes nicer?"

"Would you like something to do?"

"I have lots to do. Is there something you'd like me to do?"

"No. Nothing in particular."

"Okay. You let me know if there is."

He types Jinn's full name into the search bar and waits. Google hurls more than twelve thousand results at him. Twelve thousand! What the fuck. And just from the first page, it's clear that at least three other women out there have the same name.

"Jinn Hwa." She stuck out her hand—rather formally, he thought. He shook it, mumbling his name. This was at some school production or other, probably the annual drama fest. Sukhin can't remember who introduced them or why anyone even bothered, but he remembers sitting beside her for the entire performance, feeling baffled every time she laughed at something because he didn't find anything on stage funny. But without wanting to, he paid more attention to her laugh than to anything else in that crowded hall, and he could still hear it in his head the next day—the loud, unchecked, ungirly cackle that he would spend the last year of junior college listening for in the corridors as he went from one class to another.

Sukhin shakes his head at the memory, caught between ridiculing his seventeen-year-old self and wanting to do it all over again. Read *Hamlet* in the library hoping she would suddenly appear; dawdle between any two points, hoping to bump into her in transit; scan the foyer, the canteen, the field, the basketball court every time he passed them, hoping to see her. And then, if by some chance he did bump into her, scurry away without saying a word.

God, to be seventeen again. With no baggage other than the books he'd read and some ragging from the rugby boys. No crushing anxiety—wait, was that true? It is far too easy at thirty-five to dismiss the struggles of being seventeen, but what really qualifies thirty-five to look down at seventeen? Not much, in Sukhin's case—thirty-five-year-old Sukhin isn't even taller.

He makes himself another G&T, weaker than the first. Twelve thousand results, three or more Jinns—he's going to need a bit more of his brain than he assumed.

What does he really know now, that he didn't at seventeen? His thoughts run back to this, over and over. Eighteen years since junior college—has he learnt anything useful? Well, maybe. The teenage Sukhin would never have dreamt of being a teacher and kudos to him for self-awareness—he would have been terrible at it. It's taken years for him to admit this to himself. It's taken him years to understand what works for him in a classroom, how to set and control the rhythm of a lesson, how to cope with the disinterested kids and the smart-asses, how not to talk to his shoes. He cringes at the memory, arriving unbidden but sharp, of his first lesson as a trainee teacher.

"So is it an urn or a woman?" the student who had been staring out of the window since the start of the lesson suddenly piped up.

Before Sukhin could answer, a girl in the first row snapped, "Urn, dumbass. Haven't you heard of personification?"

"Why is he talking to the urn?"

Sukhin pounced on this. "Yes, good question, Alex—why? Why doesn't the poet just address his reader?"

Alex hesitated, but only for a second. "Urns don't talk back?" he ventured.

The girl burst into derisive laughter. Sukhin felt an urgent need to slap—Edwina? Erina? Erica? He cannot remember her name now, but he can still see her smug round face after all this time. He took a deep breath, thankful that none of the senior teachers was observing the lesson.

"That's a good point, actually, Alex," Sukhin tried to smile encouragingly but failed. "So what difference does it make that the urn doesn't talk back? Let's look at..."

"Are you taking his side because he's a guy?"

"What?"

She didn't back down, not this girl. "Are you taking his side because he's a guy?"

Sukhin was so baffled that he made the mistake of defending himself. "I'm not taking sides. If we consider—"

"That urns don't talk back? That's what he said. Are we seriously going to discuss this?"

Sukhin glared. "Yes. Yes, we are, because..."

"Because you say so and you're a man?"

He should have studied engineering. Or economics. Palaeontology—oh, for palaeontology.

He leapt towards the teacher's desk, where his lesson notes were. There was nothing in them that would help him handle this situation, but he desperately wanted something to hold. Anything that would prevent him from covering his face with his hands and walking backwards out of the room.

"This is nothing to do with anyone being a man," he said. Firmly and kindly, he hoped.

"The poet is a man, right?" Someone else. Daft question, but thank god.

"Yes. Keats was a man." Easy enough. And just ten more minutes until the end of the tutorial.

"Are we only doing male poets?" Edwina-Erina-Erica again, eyes narrowed.

"No!" Sukhin was horrified to hear how shrill he sounded. "In fact, for our next lesson, we'll be—"

He takes a step forward, clutching his lesson notes. Edwina-Erina-Erica looked ready to bite. Fate intervenes: a sudden, intense pain shoots up his leg.

"Mr Dhillon! Mr Dhillon, are you okay?" Not Edwina-Erina-Erica or Alex.

No, no he wasn't. He was in a heap on the floor, his ankle twisted spectacularly. The unbridled, unfortunate, collective force of a shoelace come undone and a small depression in the concrete classroom floor. Sukhin felt a wave of dizziness. He tried to stand but couldn't. *If I faint now, I will never live it down.*

He fainted.

But he lived it down, though it still horrifies him that he's now head of the English department. Sukhin can't decide if he's got away with a crime or is the victim of one. How has he managed to not only keep a job he never thought he was good at, but somehow end up alpha wolf? All he's done, all along, is aim to survive—forget outwitting or outlasting or whatever. But what kind of logical, prudent higher power decides that a man who hates the thought of speaking to people—of which teenagers are the most terrifying, unfiltered specimens—should spend most of his waking hours doing exactly this, with the express duty of transferring knowledge and the unexpressed but expected duty of inspiring even the most cabbagey of students? What kind of perverted cosmos arranges for him to be good at this—or at least thought to be good at it—while combining the elements that make this man ensure that he will fear every moment, be in conflict with every moment, be ever equidistant from paralysis and nirvana?

Okay. Another drink. Now for twelve thousand results and four Jinns.

None of the Jinns on the first page appear to be his. One isn't even a person—it's a stationery store somewhere in Johor. Just to be certain, Sukhin checks out the website. Hopelessly amateurish, site menu laid out like a calculator, not the slightest sign anywhere of anyone called Jinn. Good—one down. Sukhin modifies the search to exclude the name of the bookstore. Close to ten thousand results. Good—two thousand-ish down.

The Jinn that now appears on top of the pile is a prolific—Twitterer? Is that the term? Tweeter?—whose handle is @jinnjinnlovesjinnjinn. *Fucking hell, what are you, thirteen? Why do you think anyone cares what you think about anything?*

He reads her last tweet, from about five minutes ago:

"So hungry can die but McDonald's not delivering because raining. Huh?? U all no umbrella ah. So lousy service. Boo!"

And exactly fourteen minutes before that, a rather cryptic missive to someone in particular flung into the world at large:

"Always like that. Never ask what I want, just do whatever then say why I always so angry. Just take me for granted."

He scans the rest of the page before he can stop himself.

"Dare to say me fat then cannot breath in the dress she stole from me. Can die."

"Try to sabo my diet, say can eat avocado. 300 calories! Now must go walk one hour. F U, bitch."

It's a wonder that her handle is grammatical.

She has 7,582 followers. And 32,473 tweets, lapped up by so many feeble minds. Two weeks ago, Sukhin discovered that, eight months into the academic year, more than half of his second-year students hadn't finished reading any of the texts required for their A-Level exams.

This generation—no, the world—is doomed.

And so is his laundry—did she say it was raining? He looks outside. Yes, it is. Hang this changeling weather.

Another modification to the search. Goodbye, @jinnjinnlovesjinnjinn, and this time, Sukhin scans only for images—that should filter out all the Twitter rubbish. And then he sees it, halfway down the results page, buried among photos of smiling women in corporate suits, a surprising number of floor plans and technical drawings of pipes and windows, sketches and illustrations for some sort of anime production—a photograph of Jinn. He doesn't recognise her immediately; his first thought is only that the woman looks familiar. But it's her, staring unsmiling into the middle distance, her expression taking baby steps towards serenity. The background is fuzzy, but it looks like an outdoor shot—sunlight has softened the usual shadows under her eyes and cheekbones, given her pallor the barest semblance of a glow.

There's another photograph a little further down the page—this is clearly the one that the first photograph has been cropped from. Four women; a bride and three bridesmaids. Jinn stands on the far left, next to the bride, the only one not smiling. The bride holds one of Jinn's hands close to her chest instead of the bouquet, which has ended up with one of the other bridesmaids. She is leaning slightly towards Jinn, who doesn't reciprocate but appears indulgent and at ease. Sukhin realises that the bride is Jinn's elder sister, whose name he can't remember now. Xing Hwa?

Ling Hwa? He clicks on the photo and is taken to some sort of photo-sharing platform, where he's asked to sign in or create an account. No.

Back to the first photo then. The link takes him to a local news site and an ad automatically pops up: "Don't miss out. Get the latest news and updates for just $0.99 a day!" *Fuck off.* He remembers why he stopped bothering with the news, besides the substandard writing.

But clearly he should have bothered—how did he even miss this? The article is six years old, brief and completely devoid of emotion. Jinn has been missing for days. The police have searched her apartment—no indication of robbery; passport and documents found in a drawer; wallet missing.

"Teo was reported missing by her sister, Teo Ping Hwa, on Wednesday evening. By this time, Teo had not been seen by friends or family for a week.

"It is not known exactly when she went missing. When questioned by the police, none of the other residents of her building reported seeing or hearing anything suspicious at any time during the week.

"Witnesses or anyone with information pertaining to her possible whereabouts are urged to come forward."

At the top of the page is that photo of her, cropped to remove her sister and the two other bridesmaids. It is the same photograph, but for Sukhin her expression has changed—it has lost all its quietude; what remains is a calculating patience, like that of his grandmother's cat as he sits among flowers watching a bird that has not yet seen him.

~

"You left a note."

They are in the park and Sukhin has been pretending to read for the last hour.

She closes *Paradise Lost* without marking her page and gives him a long look. He has to force himself to look her directly in the eyes, keenly aware that he has not felt this anxious since he was a teenager. It's like a clamp closing over his throat and chest and brain—he finds it hard to speak or breathe or think. Damn this woman. He is suddenly angry. What on earth is she doing, what point is she trying to make and why is he here? Does she even know what she's doing? Does he? Well, he can answer that—no, no, he doesn't.

"I did." Evenly.

"What did it say?"

She says nothing but doesn't look away. In the end, he does. What right does he have to demand an answer? Who is he to her, she to him? Two people sharing a bench in a park. Two people who once shared a school, a handful of friends, an economics textbook, a blanket, a few hundred kisses—maybe. Two people who talked together of children and careers and dreams and other things when they didn't know enough not to talk about these things. Two people on a bench in a park that really isn't.

"Forget it. It's okay. You don't have to tell me." Sukhin picks up his book again and wonders what he's doing. Why does he keep coming back here, to her? Is it inertia? But surely inertia would mean not coming back, since the act of coming back is what takes him off the path more easily travelled. Unless *she* is the path more easily travelled. God. So much ridiculousness. Sukhin wants to slap himself.

Her hand on his shoulder. "Sukhin. Let's walk."

They walk. It is nearly six, but because Singapore standard time is a big fat lie to make sure the country gains an hour's trading time with Japan and Hong Kong, it is still bright and the sun won't set for another hour. They walk. Slow and silent, through the long, linear park, past the backs of shops facing the din of the main road, past the alleyway overlooking the kitchens of the fashionable joints on Keong Saik Road.

Two teenage girls wander out the back door of a café into the park and stare, disorientated. A group of kitchen staff from a nearby restaurant hovers near a rubbish bin, smoking.

One of them recognises Jinn. "Eh. Boyfriend ah?"

"No. Slave."

Laughter. She waves as they walk past. Sukhin avoids meeting anyone's eyes.

They walk. Through the underpass, under Neil Road, out of Chinatown and into Tanjong Pagar. Along the back of another row of shophouses. The paved path is much wider now, and children from a nearby condo tear up and down it, screaming. At the end of the path is a small playground with the unimaginative plastic usuals—a low slide, a few animals on springs, a see-saw. There are more children here.

"Stop, stop. We have to turn around or stop." Sukhin squeezes his eyes shut, but of course he can still hear the little monsters.

"Okay. Let's stop."

They stand still for many minutes. The sun sets. As if this is her cue, she begins to tell him about the note and why she wrote it and where she left it and who she wrote it for. She recites the note from memory. The telling is calm but the pace is erratic—sentences tumble out in bursts, then nothing, then another burst, like a verbal version of Morse code. The note is short and horrible. Sukhin's heart pounds and pounds and he stops listening to her.

They face the back of a vintage store. It is dark and dingy and old, and a balcony hangs overhead, crowded with random furniture, a jukebox, some sort of large stuffed animal.

"...had to be a certainty of free will and a possibility of death..."

A giant handwritten sign hangs across the balcony rails. Red letters, neat and perfectly legible even in the falling darkness:

We buy junk and sell antiques
Some fools buy, some fools sell

The sky turns a deep liquid blue as it uses up the very last of the evening light. The street lamps have not come on. The children have all disappeared.

"I didn't want to be part of any of it any more. I couldn't bear it." A pause. "I don't want to talk any more."

He takes her hand and gives it a squeeze. Not a loverly gesture, more of an admonishment. Silly woman. When has he ever made her talk when she didn't want to?

~

"So. You want to tell me about her?"

"No, Dennis. Still no."

"Combed cotton. Organic. She must be fussy."

"Shut up, Dennis."

"So hot when you're angry. Does she tell you you're hot?"

The woman is in the bathroom, looking into the mirror. Her hair is so much longer now. She says this to him, her voice full of surprise. She hears the surprise in her voice and laughs.

The man is in the bedroom. He can see her from where he is as he sits up in bed, reading, waiting for her. He doesn't laugh. He wants to know if she wants him to take her to a hairdresser, or to whoever crops it short.

She cuts it herself, she tells him. It felt right, before, to cut it before the curls crept in. It kept her from recognising herself immediately in the mirror. It kept her from seeing their eyes their faces their hair.

He watches her tug at her hair and look at it, turning her head this way and that. He remembers how long it used to be, when they were younger. She had read Gone With the Wind *and she wanted her hair like Scarlett O'Hara's, so long it could go around Rhett Butler's neck.*

You're mad, he told her then.

Now he wishes she will let her hair grow long again, and he will wind it around his neck.

IX

IT IS THE best of times, it is the worst of times. All around: wisdom, foolishness, belief, incredulity, light, darkness, hope, despair.

Exam season.

Sukhin cannot go anywhere in school without being accosted by students in various degrees of panic. His office is no longer safe—it is the first place they look. Dennis has taken it over—no Further Maths student ever wanders into the Humanities section, so he's safe as long as he avoids all the main corridors. This leaves Sukhin with Dennis' desk in the Mathematics department, which works out rather well—most of Sukhin's students will not darken that section of the staff room, for fear that their Maths tutor will corner them and demand six months of unsurrendered homework. What Sukhin doesn't know is that a small, resourceful group of students does know where he is, but is biding its time—they are planning a proper ambush, to be launched in a couple of days once they have all properly finished their mugging.

He dashes out of the staff room, taking care to use the least popular exit, and down the back stairs. It is three o'clock. Too late for lunch, too early for tea. Perfect.

Mrs Chan is ready with his cup of tea—he called her from the phone on Dennis' desk five minutes ago. Sukhin wants to take his tea and scoot off, but as usual she needs him to indulge her in a little small talk. If Mrs Chan didn't make such a good cup of tea and if she wasn't so obliging, Sukhin would not allow her these trespasses—he never speaks to the man running the junior college bookshop, who once sold him a dud pen and refused him a refund.

"You getting thinner, Mr Dhillon." She stares at his shoulders, his stomach. He half expects her to make him turn around.

He assures her that he's not getting any thinner and takes a step away to actively discourage conversation.

"All the children, very stress. You? Teacher also very stress?"

Indeed. "The children are stressful, Mrs Chan." *The children are so bloody needy.*

"Last time, you young, you also stressful."

Touché. Sukhin is amused in spite of himself. He bows, startling his tea mistress. "Back to work. See you in the morning."

Mrs Chan manages a parting shot before he can move out of range: "Don't stress. And cannot just drink tea ah, must drink water, okay?"

The tea break, even the banal chat with Mrs Chan, is a welcome distraction. Sukhin is having a particularly lousy day. He has to reset an entire exam because one of the trainee teachers thinks she might have hinted too much at what the *Wuthering Heights* excerpt would be in next week's nineteenth-century paper.

"They were so worried, and I just wanted to make them feel like they could do it. I'm so, so sorry. I'm such an idiot!" She found him at Dennis' desk this morning and cried for a whole half-hour while Sukhin watched the clock and wondered just how supportive he had to be, given the magnitude of inconvenience she was causing.

"Lynnette, it's fine." *No, it isn't. But I have to get to work. Work that you've created.*

"I'm such an idiot!" *Yes.*

"Please calm down. Everyone makes mistakes." *Yours is just stupider and more of a time-suck than most.*

And this morning, he took thirty-eight and a half minutes to get to work after his run. It's the first time he's timed himself in a very long time. The last time was two weeks before his birthday and he'd clocked in thirty-seven minutes, which has been his timing for the last three years, ever since he'd started cycling to work. And now he's unable to break thirty-eight, even after trying for a week. This morning, he was sorely tempted to skip shaving to see if that would make up for things—but that would have just been pathetic. And he knows he isn't taking longer to dress or shower—the clock in his bathroom makes sure of that. So it's just the cycling bit that's taking a minute longer—a minute and a half—damn.

Is this what happens at thirty-five? What's next? Or worse, what has already happened or died or given way that he hasn't discovered yet?

Sukhin sets down the paper cup of tea, grimacing. Renchun, Dennis' neighbour, sees him and raises his eyebrows.

"You okay?"

"Have to reset the paper for next week. God."

Renchun's eyes widen. "Aiyoh. What happened?"

Sukhin tells him, trying not to be mean about it. But he doesn't bother hiding his irritation. Why should he? At thirty-five, in the face of rapid physical deterioration, surely he is allowed to be cross with dumbassery as long as he refrains from calling it dumbassery? And that dumbass Lynnette is costing him an afternoon's extra work, which means he will be late—he still has to get that coffee pound cake from his mother before he goes to see Jinn.

ꟿ

"Wow, Lynnette, you've really done it."

"What?"

"Sukhin is telling everyone in the Maths department how you fucked up the Lit paper."

"But he told me it was fine!"

"Well, it's not. Diyana said Sukhin said he will never let trainee teachers breathe onto exam questions again."

"I really really didn't mean to do it. Should I talk to him?"

"Are you kidding? It's Sukhin. I think you should just pretend not to exist for the rest of the week."

~

"Stop that. We're not supposed to eat in the library."

Jinn has the foil-wrapped coffee cake on her lap and is sneaking a slice out of the tear she's made in the packet. "Sure."

He frowns. "You'll make everything sticky."

"I won't touch you."

It's raining and they have decided to venture farther away from Chinatown for proper cover, into the depths of the National Library instead of their usual rainy-day coffee shop on Keong Saik Road. Sukhin is poring over his much-marked-up copy of *Wuthering Heights*, trying to find a passage to replace the one he'd previously chosen for the exam. *Stupid Lynnette.*

Why did it even have to be a stodgy essay question? Why bother? Maybe ten of his first-year students will be able to consider, structure and write a clear essay on any text in any of the exams they're about to take; the rest will muck about until the middle of next year trying to find their footing and then miraculously pass their A-Levels—it's the same story for every batch of students he's ever had. If only he could set a quiz instead, like the ones his Russian literature professor at university used to deal out at random.

What is the colour of Heathcliff's eyes?

What season is it when the narrator first encounters Heathcliff and family?

What is the name of the dog that has just had puppies in the first chapter?

Next to him, Jinn eats another slice of cake, engrossed in an issue of *Singapore Tatler*. On the cover is a couple on a sofa, in what looks like an obscenely expensive apartment. They are dressed in black, flying goggles around their necks, rugged and stark against the soft beige tones and flowing fabrics of the rest of the shot. Against his will, Sukhin's mind drifts. What kind of scene is being played out here?

Hey, darling, shall we get kitted out in modernist pseudo-aviation gear and watch television?

Great idea—let me plug in the wind machine first and change the curtains. It's time we saw leather juxtaposed with bleached linen around here.

"Cake?" Only half of it is left.

"No. All yours."

Later, when she gets up and takes a walk to stretch her legs, Sukhin picks up the magazine. The headline on the cover reads: "Power Trip: Carey and Ching to Conquer the World". He would never have thought Jinn to be the type to read society magazines. Is this a sign that she's having doubts about the vagrant life, that she wants to return to more prosperous times? Her family is markedly well off, he recalls—large, tasteful house in an old-money neighbourhood, quiet, expensive furniture, both girls indulged with esoteric hobbies and language lessons. It must be brutal for her, living on the streets after decades of a life in which cold showers could be considered physical assault, and surely this is all well past the point of novelty. He knows he is being unkind—he knows that she isn't driven by anything as daft as novelty or the need to experience the other side, that hers isn't an indulgent journey of self-discovery (*Don't Eat, Pray, Love?*)—but there's a big logical gap somewhere. Or, more likely, there's a whole chunk of missing data.

"*... I can't talk to anyone because I will only say terrible things. I must go. I'm not coming back—count on that. Forgive me for what I do.*"

Her recital of the note springs on him at random moments on most days, but never in full. Sometimes he only hears the beginning; sometimes, like now, the end. But his thoughts are always the same: why walk away from everything and everyone, when you can just ignore it all? And that becomes the cue for him to wonder when this will all end—at some point, she'll realise she didn't have to walk away and then she'll go back to whatever's left of her life and do her own laundry and get her own cake.

On page seventy-two is a double-page spread dominated by a photograph of a woman in a bright red dress perched on a table, surrounded by cakes and pastries of different shapes, sizes, colours and textures. The header reads "Queen of Tarts"; her smile is big, bright and beatific. Her face is familiar—why? Sukhin reads the kicker.

"'Never look before you leap,' says our entrepreneur of the year. It's certainly worked for her—in just two years, lawyer-turned-baker Teo Ping Hwa has turned an old family cake shop into boutique pâtisserie Advocakes and Solicitarts, where reservations must be made months in advance, even if you're visiting royalty. Sue Selvarajah grills her on the subjects of risk, family and the perfect pandan chiffon."

So this is what Jinn's sister looks like perfectly coiffed and dressed by someone else—like someone else. Even the birthmark on her left cheek has been airbrushed off.

He skims the article—a whole slew of gormless details about clothes, a couple of mentions of her past life as a lawyer, more talk of clothes, a brief history on her decision to convert her grandmother's bakery in Tiong Bahru into a pâtisserie, an anecdote about the Bruneian princess not being able to get a sea salt caramel coconut cream cake, something about the family. Aha.

"Teo politely declines to talk about her sister's disappearance five years ago, but shares that the family has done its very best to move on. 'It's brought us closer, in unexpected ways,' she says. 'And my husband has been my rock through it all.'"

Followed by some nonsense about work-life balance, some random titbit about pandan juice extraction, then a trite, formulaic ending.

Sukhin checks the cover—the issue is from a year ago, so most of this must still be accurate. So much drivel, though. Distilled, the article could have been shrunk to a single paragraph. *One day, one of my students is going to write something like this and I'll see it and feel responsible.* This sends his thoughts back to the exams, back to Brontë—the children will just have to suck it up and write an essay, for their own protection.

Half an hour later, having decided on the passage he will use for the exam, Sukhin shuts his book, stretches and wonders where she's gone. He knows Jinn's propensity to wander off—it's how they ended up becoming friends, after all.

The girl with the cackle from the concert was in the drama room, talking to Rashid, the leading man. Sukhin was helping with the sets, working on a contraption that would release paper rain from the stage ceiling. He put down his tools quietly and wondered if he should leave. He didn't know why he thought he should leave—in fact, he knew it was irrational, but at the same time, it felt like the sensible thing to do.

Too late. Rashid was already bringing her over; obviously he wanted to show her the sets. A crude mixture of anxiety and indecision kept Sukhin rooted to where he was. To his amazement, she recognised him.

"Hey, it's you."

"Yes. I think I sat next to you at that concert last year."

"No, no. It was that chem lecture—you fell asleep and I woke you up." She laughed. "I think I frightened you!"

Oh. That was her, was it? Sukhin felt horrified all over again. "Are you helping with the production?"

"I don't know. Maybe. I just got here. I'm really supposed to be in bio lab but I got bored."

It became their contraption, the rain machine.

Outside the library, it is raining for real. Torrential. Tropical. The kind of rain the colonial planters on Cameron Highlands must have written home about. *In Malaya, dearest, the rain is different. Umbrellas are no match for the monsoon, and we have been stuck indoors for three days. Everything is wet.* There must be something like this somewhere in a Somerset Maugham story.

Jinn is sitting on the steps at the edge of the library's central atrium, an expanse of sheltered outdoor space extending from the main entrance to some sort of stage area. She's watching the rain. Sukhin sits down next to her. Her face is rain-splattered and her hair is wet, but her eyes have a lively gleam.

"Ready to go?" He wants to suggest dinner somewhere, but she's never said yes so far, so he keeps quiet.

She nods. "Let's."

A rain like this makes everything harder in Singapore. Traffic slows down to a crawl, no, a struggle to crawl. Pedestrians move in slow motion, avoiding puddles, wrestling with umbrellas and slippery sidewalks. Visibility ends at two metres. Tempers are short. Queues are long. The world is grim and wet and dim and cold.

The car park near Chinatown is almost full and it takes him more than twenty minutes to find a space. Silent and glowering, he takes her suitcase out of the boot. She holds his large black umbrella over them both as they walk to her alley, the suitcase skidding occasionally on the slick pavement.

"Fuck."

She says nothing. Her face is calm as she hangs on to the umbrella with both hands, holding it down against the tugging, insistent wind.

The cardboard house is a sodden mess. The rain gutter along the roof overhang is partly collapsed, the overflow drowning part of the house. Most of what's still standing is now a wet amorphous blob, the rest roughed up and scattered by wind.

They stand very still; they don't approach the wreckage and neither knows what to say. Sukhin's head is full of stupid platitudes; he bites them back. Jinn looks occupied; she is watching a cockroach crawl up the wall behind the lump of boxes.

"You're coming home with me."

Sukhin is surprised by how firm he sounds, and even more by how quickly she relents.

~

Family conference. Sukhin is doing his best to be nice.

"Is this a school project?"

He wishes he hadn't bothered to ask their permission. "No, Mum, not a school project. But my friend needs some boxes—she's moving house." *Sort of true.*

"And what if *we* need to move house?" Dr Jaswant still thinks of their box collection as the moving-house hoard.

Sukhin allows himself one eye roll. "We've lived here since I was four, Pa. Are you really thinking of moving?"

"No—but the point is to be prepared. In case."

Doris senses that their son is about to lose patience and leave. She shoots her husband a sharp look. "How many boxes does your friend need?"

"Quite a few—these should be enough."

Sukhin has set aside about thirty boxes of various sizes—he has an idea for her new house that requires some amount of flexibility.

"Oh! So many! I thought you were cleaning these!"

"I was, Mum—I can't bring her dusty boxes."

Doris wonders who this woman is. She can't remember the last time Sukhin mentioned a friend, let alone a woman friend. Does he have a girlfriend? Or is he at least interested in someone? The prospect is thrilling. She must do her best to help this along.

"Of course, of course—and go ahead, take the boxes for your friend."

"Maybe not the vacuum-cleaner box, that one is such a nice size for—" But Dr Jaswant is silenced by another, more menacing glare from his wife.

"Take the vacuum-cleaner box, Sukhin."

"Maybe Punggol."

Jinn stands at the kitchen window, looking out. There's nothing much to see—the back of Sukhin's apartment overlooks the gardening shed and the bicycle lots.

Sukhin has just returned from work and, even after three days, is unsettled to find her at home. He leaves his bag next to the sofa and goes into the kitchen. "Punggol? We can go take a look around after dinner."

He would have asked her to remain, but she's been talking about where she should live next since she arrived and he doesn't know how to approach the subject of her living with him. Not that he's thought it through—but he's willing to. Willing, but unable to take the plunge and say, "Forget Punggol, Jinn. Just stay here."

Instead, after looking up how to drive to Punggol from his apartment, Sukhin loses himself in peeling potatoes for dinner. He will make her a nice casserole. Cauliflower, potatoes and plenty of cheese and paprika.

The highlight of the week was the very real chance that the stupidest of all the conversations they would ever have was over and done with.

She wanted to sleep on the sofa. Absolutely not. It would ruin the sofa, he told her. And then she wanted to lay her mat down in the living room and sleep there. Out of the question, he told her. He didn't want her sleeping among the stacks of books he keeps on the floor or anywhere near the unfinished 3D puzzle of the Guggenheim—it has taken him two months to reach a point where it is starting to look like a building.

"Are you saying I should sleep with you?"

"No!" Damn this woman. He should have just let her sleep on the sofa. "Yes. It's just easier. There's enough space. And it's a bed." He doesn't know what else to say. "I can take you to a hotel, if you like."

"That's going to be a lot of money."

"It doesn't have to be fancy. And of course I'll pay."

"I don't want you to pay for a hotel."

Round and round they went. By the time Jinn agreed that sleeping with him was the most logical thing to do, he was too tired to find her choice of words even the slightest bit amusing. Overcome with relief that the conversation had finally ended, he even let her take the right side of the bed, which is his side, and now he can't say anything about swapping without sounding strange and petty.

He has forgot what it's like to share a bed. It's a nightmare. He goes to sleep hoping he won't flail about and kick her, and then wakes up wondering if he did. He wakes up cold in the dead of the night, the covers snatched away, and he has to pry them away from her gently, so gently that he wants to scream. He goes to sleep hoping *she* won't flail about and kick *him*. She does. It's like sleeping with a goat—he remembers thinking this years ago. *Still the same cloven-footed terror in the bedroom, my girl.*

"Why are you smiling to yourself?"

"I like casserole."

"You're making that cauliflower thing? Oh, yes."

This morning, he woke up to find her close, her nose only centimetres from his, her head nestled in the recess between their pillows. How strange, how surreal, that she was here, in this bed, in his bed, in this home he had made for himself so that he could be alone. How strange, that he wanted her here. He thought of the years in between them then and them now, all submerged by this moment, and it made him gasp for air.

He puts the casserole in the oven and sets the timer. Forty-five minutes and dinner will be ready.

There used to be one set of drawers in the man's bedroom. Now, there are two.

The second set is for the woman's things. It surprises her that she has enough to fill two out of the four drawers.

The man is not surprised. It is he who has filled them, slowly, slyly. It is he who has, over time, carefully selected and planted every item so that nothing stands out, so that everything feels and looks like everything else even though no two items are identical.

The man is very pleased with himself.

X

THE STUDENTS HAVE become relentless in their pursuit of enlightenment—they will take anything the teachers throw their way: random titbits on any subject, advice on sleep, nutrition and the best kind of pen to use, repeated entreaties not to spot questions and to "answer the question that is asked, not the question you would have liked to be asked", all of which they eagerly lap up and then invariably ignore.

Hilda and Rohan, who have waited outside the staff room for twenty minutes in order to intercept Sukhin on his way to the canteen for his afternoon cup of tea, feverishly scribble into their notebooks: "Don't forget about Polonius. Or Horatio."

Sukhin smiles grimly. He has said this about a hundred times in class, and now, now, two days before the bloody paper, they are writing this down.

"Which acts should we focus on, Mr Dhillon?" Hilda's voice is a small, harassed whisper. A whisperlet. She braces herself for a put-down but cannot prevent herself from hoping that Mr Dhillon will soften, pity her, say something that will give them some inkling of what the exam question will be. Rohan has insisted that it must be her who asks the question ("Mr Dhillon looks like the kind of guy who can't deal with crying girls").

He sighs. *This is going to take a while.* "They're all important. You have to think about the play as a whole—what each act reveals about every character, what patterns appear when you lay all the acts down next to each other. It's Shakespeare; everything is cleverly linked because he can. For example, take Act III, Scene 3—"

He allows Hilda and Rohan to walk with him to get his tea and they sit with him in the canteen while he drinks it. More students join them, then still more, and Sukhin finds himself giving an impromptu seminar on divinity and morality in *Hamlet*.

In another corner of the canteen, next to a girl who looks close to tears, Dennis is looking through her frantic workings of a problem he set as homework two months ago.

Their eyes meet and Dennis makes a face. Sukhin bares his teeth.

Exam season. Driving teachers mad twice a year since institutionalised education became a thing.

But now it's also the perfect excuse to keep Jinn around, to put off the move to Punggol.

"I'm going to help you move," he told her yesterday, trying to sound as casual and pleasant as possible, "but give me a couple of weeks. The students are going mad, I'm going mad—and then I'll need to mark the scripts. Two weeks, okay? Meanwhile, help yourself to my books. Go nuts."

Jinn doesn't protest—he suspects she rather likes being back under a solid roof. And the books must sweeten the deal: the entire wall on one side of the flat, floor to ceiling, and as much of the bedroom wall space as possible have been conquered by bookshelves; his study is a massive bookshelf in three and a half walls (he left the window as is, but was very much tempted to close it off). The corridor separating the kitchen from the study is one big bookshelf (Sukhin likes to think of it as a bookshelf turned into a corridor), broken up only by the need for the door to the study. Even the balcony has a bookshelf; the kitchen has two—why waste space? His mother isn't a fan of his take on interior design; she's asked him too many times where he plans on putting up all the family photographs, and "what about the portraits of the children when they graduate?" Photographs? Portraits of *the children*? Sukhin's books, which occupy every bit of space in every bookshelf, which have begun to creep over the furniture and are plotting a takeover of the sofa, are the only friends he has chosen for himself. It is a never-ending source of comfort to him that every book he has ever had the pleasure to claim, every single one, lives here with him.

Now that Jinn is also here, Sukhin is often overwhelmed. Overwhelmed with what, he doesn't quite know.

But he likes having her around. Even if she mixes up the jam lids and he found the marmalade lid on the apricot preserve jar this morning.

~

She's been watching him.

While he prepares dinner. While he sorts out the laundry. While he cleans his records and wipes down the bookshelves. While he vacuums and mops and disinfects the kitchen floor with lemon juice. While he reads. While he pretends to work and is thinking about a book he wants to go back to reading. While he puts on his shoes before he leaves for work. While he takes off his shoes and puts them back on the rack when he returns.

She watches him openly, not bothering to hide her curiosity. He tries not to look at her—if there's anything more disquieting than knowing she's watching him, it's watching her watch him.

She's doing it again, right now.

It's Sunday night and he's ironing his clothes for the week ahead. Sukhin really likes ironing—he likes watching all the wrinkles disappear, lining up the seams, making sure all the pleats perfectly align.

Jinn has been at the kitchen table with one of his books since they cleared the dinner dishes. She's just made a cup of tea and is sipping it while watching him iron, the book overturned on the table to mark her page. Under her scrutiny, he feels like he should say something, tell a joke, share ironing tips. He also feels like telling her to use a bloody bookmark.

"You're very neat."

"I like to be."

"You're neater than I remember."

She goes back to the book. He goes back to his black pleated trousers, wondering exactly what she remembers.

∿

"Mum, do I need fresh crab?" Sukhin is at the deli section of the supermarket, examining the rows of tinned seafood, phone to his ear. "Or is the canned kind okay?"

"Hello?" Doris is a little breathless—the phone rang while she was upstairs. Sukhin and her husband have told her many times, take it with you, it's a *mobile* phone, but out of habit she still leaves it on the kitchen counter, next to the cookbooks, where the old telephone used to sit. She thinks she heard something about crab, but it's Sukhin, so she can't be sure.

Sukhin grits his teeth. "The crab. Does it need to be fresh?"

Doris shakes her head. How does he manage to teach anything? Always saying things without a head or a tail. "What crab? What are you making?"

"Bakwan kepiting, Mum. Why do you think I asked for the recipe on Sunday?"

Ah yes, and he wrote everything down in his notebook and made her repeat everything while their dinner got cold.

"Fresh crab, fresh crab. Always fresh crab."

"Okay—so I can't use canned crab at all for this? Ever?" Sukhin picks up a can of Alaskan crab meat and reads the ingredient list: Alaskan crab meat. Seems straightforward.

They are in her territory now. Time to put him in his place. "Sukhin. Canned is canned; fresh is fresh. If you wait ten years, does this change?"

"Right. Yes, Mum."

"And did you think your grandmother's recipe would have canned crab? Do you know where your grandmother's from?"

"Penang."

She corrects him. "*Telok Bahang* in Penang. Your great-grandfather was a *fisherman*. Your grandmother is a *fisherman's* daughter."

"Yes, Mum. Okay." Sukhin wishes he could have just texted his mother—but neither of his parents reads a text message the day it is sent.

"Do you think your grandmother's recipe for bakwan kepiting would use canned crab?"

"No. No, Mum." He should have gone straight to the wet market.

"The next time your Ah Mah cooks her bakwan kepiting, I'm going to tell her you thought *maybe* she uses canned crab. *Maybe* you'll get half a bowl." Doris pauses. "Why are you cooking bakwan kepiting?"

Sukhin isn't prepared for this. "I'm making it for a friend" is the shortest and least informative honest reply he can muster.

"Is this the friend you're helping to move house?"

"Yes. That's right."

Doris smiles. There's definitely something going on. "Well, it's a difficult dish. Let me know if you need help. Just call, yah?" If her son means to cook his way to a woman's heart, he is going to need her help.

"Yes, Mum. Thanks."

He hangs up. Doris spends the rest of the afternoon thinking about how she will entertain her future grandchildren—is there a box of Sukhin's old toys around somewhere?

~

Jinn has decided on Punggol—prematurely, in Sukhin's opinion. They've only been there twice to look around, but for some reason she has become fixated with the idea of living along the river.

"But we haven't looked anywhere else," he said. "And it's mostly open. Where are we going to build the house?" The boxes he picked out for her are still at his parents' place, set aside from the rest of the family stash, sighed at by his father every time he passes them.

"I don't think I'll need a house."

He thinks of all the hours he's spent online researching cardboard furniture, all the sketches he's made for her new and much-improved cardboard igloo. It was going to be grand—modular, strong, modifiable, collapsible.

"But where will you sleep?"

"In the open," she tells him. *So much for a solid roof keeping her here.* In the pretty park the National Parks Board so meticulously maintains. "It leads all the way to the sea," she says, "did you know?" Yes, he does, though he can't understand why this is any reason for living along the Punggol River. Then again, he lives near the sea and it makes him happy—no, that's too strong a word, but it's a good feeling—knowing there is that stretch of water only fifteen minutes away.

"What about showering and all that?"

"Toilets everywhere—didn't you notice? I'll manage."

And when it rains, her plan is to sleep under one of the many pavilions in the park, typically used by people taking walks along the river as a rest stop or momentary respite from the elements. Kim Seng, leader of the veggie pirates, has offered her an old bicycle. She will trade her suitcase for a backpack—one of the Free Kitchen volunteers is keen to swap; he has a massive one lying in his storeroom that hasn't seen daylight since his uni days.

Everything is planned and logical, but Sukhin looks at her and thinks, *she's mad*. It's a welcome thought—over the week and a half that she's been around, he has alternately confused and terrified himself by imagining life with her, not just for a couple of weeks, but for the rest of his life. He's quite sure he isn't in love with her—and he's a teacher of English literature; of course he can recognise the signs of a man in love. He feels none of the heady rush, the constant desire to be with her, that gripped him when they were young—in fact, much of his ruminations involve plans to reclaim some of his personal space—perhaps he will give her the study so he can have his living room back, or can he turn the balcony into some sort of reading hole for her? And now, listening to Jinn's plans for Punggol and pronouncing her mad, he is relieved. His internal logic is clearly intact. It must therefore be logic that compels him to return, over and over, to the thought of having her live with him indefinitely. Of course it's logical—it will cost her nothing, it will cost him very little more in terms of household expenses, it will mean he won't have to travel to check on her, it is far easier to cook for two, it will even increase the utility of his books and that ridiculous sofa.

"What do you think?"

"Makes perfect sense. I'll drive you there next weekend—the bicycle should fit into the boot."

~

It doesn't. After many, many attempts to fit the bicycle into the boot, in as many different positions as a bicycle may be imagined to occupy in that fixed, finite space, Sukhin decides to put Jinn and her backpack in a taxi and cycle to Punggol Park himself.

"See you in a couple of hours."

Congratulating himself on this very sensible decision that will clearly contribute to his goal of keeping somewhat fit in order not to become decrepit before he's seventy (which seems a decent age to start creaking—the origin of decrepit being the Latin "crepare", i.e. to creak), he sets off. The conditions are perfect for a morning ride—slightly overcast, just a bit of a breeze—and it's too early for the picnicking crowd to have descended upon East Coast Park and its paltry strip of beach. He's decided to take the longer route through the parks and along the eastern coastline instead of cutting through housing estates—after days and days of marking poorly written, terrifyingly inane exam scripts ("The energy level of this paragraph reverberates like an engine, forcing the reader to climb with it"), cycling, just being outdoors, will be a treat.

It's a better machine than he expected from something that looks so old—Kim Seng has obviously taken good care of it. It's a heavy single-speed, but everything works and nothing rattles, and he reaches the beach in under ten minutes, just slightly over the timing he clocks with his own bike. The weekend horde isn't out in full force yet, but there are enough of them—and enough of them who ignore the signs warning pedestrians to stay off the cycling paths—to turn the ride into something of an obstacle course. Except, of course, that Sukhin would rather decimate these obstacles than avoid them. To make it harder for him to resist the urge to run people over, Kim Seng's bike doesn't come with a bell—making it necessary for Sukhin to shout for people to get out of his way. But he finds a way to derive some enjoyment from this.

"Run, dumbass, run out of my way!" To a speed-walking woman in a blinding pink tracksuit.

"Get onto the grass, you cow!" To a pudgy man walking his very small dog.

Normally, Sukhin detests shouting, but this feels okay. In control, rather than out of it.

"Fuck off, dimwit! Read the sign!" To a jogger cutting across the cycling path.

"Go away, you fuckwit! That's not cycling!" To a rollerblading teenage boy.

The looks of frozen horror on their faces before they scramble off the cycling path to flee a verbally abusive madman on a bicycle—Sukhin hasn't had this much fun in a very long time. Maybe he should pursue this as a serious hobby. With a helmet camera.

A while later, there's no longer any need for shouting—he's finally past all the parts of the park that keep it crowded: the hipster bit with its mandatory Starbucks, the fast-food belt with its enormous kid-magnet playground (the designer must trace his lineage to the Pied Piper), past the seafood restaurants, past the massive hawker centre, where he stops for a cold sugarcane drink. The sun is higher now and the sky has cleared up, but it isn't sweltering—yet. *This is actually really nice.* Sukhin looks out at the sea, at the vessels in the distance and the soft swelling waves and the wide expanse of water water water, and he can feel his mind unscramble and lighten. He straightens his shoulders and lifts his head a little higher.

We carry too much weight to move, or think, gracefully.

He doesn't know where this thought comes from—a book, a poem, something someone said?—or where it's trying to lead him. But it must explain Jinn's new grace, her unhurried movements and her decisiveness, all uncomplicated by any consideration of current obligations or future regret. He recalls her reaction weeks ago to the destruction of her cardboard home—no angst, no fist-waving, just a calm, collected acceptance of what was. He thought of the scene for days, stricken by the loss of what he'd come to think of as the locus of her, while she turned her attention to settling into his flat for the time being and started planning for Punggol.

If her grace and clarity come from weightlessness, what of him—what weight does he carry? Or is he carrying too much weight to recognise it for what it is?

Is this what people call a paradigm shift, or the beginnings of one? Sukhin makes a mental note to return to this. *Maybe it's time to think a little further ahead, instead of just getting through the days, the hours. Seek enlightenment or purpose or whatever.* He snickers. It's a little funny—the thought of enlightenment coming to a man who just called a stranger a fuckwit for rollerblading on the wrong path. To be fair, though, it's precisely the people who will call other people fuckwits for rollerblading on the wrong path who are in desperate need of enlightenment. If he were a divinity with a fixed quota of people to enlighten, he'd go straight for the twisted, angry ones—higher returns on investment and greater marginal social benefit.

Like Jinn of old—totally twisted, often angry. Disproportionately pleased and displeased, swinging in and out of anger and joy and resentment and excitement. When a boy in one of her classes at university said something snarky about girls from her old school, she raged for a week, then poured sugar into his motorcycle's fuel tank.

"It'll still run for a while, but slowly and surely—caramel."

The time when the bus broke down on her way to take an exam—she walked along Nicoll Highway screaming her lungs out, throwing her meticulously handwritten notes onto the road. She was quickly hauled up by traffic police for littering and causing a disturbance.

"Control yourself," he told her outside the dean's office, where she'd been taken by the TP officer. "When something upsets you, you've got to shrug it off. Move past it. You can't keep flinging yourself at everything." *I can't spend my life watching you do it.*

Now she doesn't even have to shrug things off—they simply don't attach. *Lucky Jinn.* This jumps out from the back of his mind so suddenly that it nearly causes him to lose his balance. Steadying himself, he begins pedalling furiously, but he cannot distract himself from the magnitude of this, this recognition of his strongest feeling when it comes to her—envy.

~

It's nearly eleven and he's finally reached Punggol Park. The nearly-forty-kilometre ride has been surprisingly punishing—especially the lifeless, straight, sun-blasted stretch right after East Coast Park that went on and on for nearly an hour. If it weren't for the promise of chendol at Changi Village soon after, he might have given up then. But buoyed by chendol, here he is—at last.

Ten minutes later, he spots Jinn under one of the pavillions. She looks happy to see him.

"Thanks for bringing the bicycle." She gestures at the wooden boardwalk, the water lilies. "It's nicer in the daytime."

He props up the bicycle and sits down next to her. "Quite a ride. You might try it. Not with the backpack, though." It is indeed massive, exactly as promised—two small children could fit into it easily. Three, dismembered.

She unpacks the sandwiches he made this morning while he tells her about the chendol at Changi Village. "Delightful. I had two and wanted a third, but I wouldn't have made it here."

"Chendol coma." She hands him a sandwich.

"Exactly."

"You may need to appease the chendol gods—I think they wanted you to have that third chendol."

"You didn't tell me there were chendol gods."

"I don't tell you to put one foot in front of the other, but you walk just fine."

He should have put off the move for another couple of weeks. It's still the rainy season—would the evening storms be worse out here? "You're going to be okay? You can always come back."

"You worry too much, Sukhin. I rather like it here, so let's see."

Like most parks in Singapore, Punggol Park is a bit of a princess—prim, proper and manicured. All the circulation is planned—cycling paths, boardwalks, lookout points—to cover enough permutations of movement that no one feels tempted to wander off the paths. And if someone did? It would be a bit awkward—guardrails to climb, hedges to jump, water features to wade through—but hardly impossible if being stared at by the people on the designated pathways isn't an issue. The park's biggest achievement is managing not to look entirely fake, even if this is by design. The landscape architect has been clever enough to let it get a little frayed at the edges, with pockets of wild garlic and pandan, sporadic bursts of dog fennel and bunches of wild grass getting in the way of the stodgy ornamental varieties.

"There are otters here on the river—did you know?"

He does, but he's never felt the urge to see them. He and Jinn spend the next couple of hours looking for them and watching them play.

The otters—a whole family of them lives along the Punggol River—turn out to be a lot more interesting to watch than Sukhin expected. Far more interesting than most people he knows. They hold hands—he never knew that otters held hands. Paws. Whatever.

When he gets home, he changes his sheets, does the laundry and rearranges his books. He goes to his parents' house for tea and dinner, ignoring his mother's questions about how his attempt at bakwan kepiting turned out. "You should do a practice run," she said. After dinner, before he drives home, he takes the boxes that were meant for Jinn's new house and piles them up on his old bed in his old room.

Her old clothes are gone. The woman does not notice at first, but one by one they made their exits, replaced by softer, lovelier spies. When she looks through her things and finally notices that the spies have taken over, it's too late. They have won her over with their softness and loveliness.

The woman is amused but says nothing to the man who sent the spies. He must think she's above being partial to softness and loveliness, so she lets him continue thinking this.

This way, they can both be smug and happy.

XI

THE DOOR TO his office is flung open, the resulting draft sending papers flying from his desk to the floor.

"Sweetie, help."

Sukhin refuses to look up. "What do you want?"

Dennis snatches up the stack of scripts Sukhin is working on and chucks them on the chair on the opposite side. "Look at me. This is important. Something momentous is about to cross our multiverse."

Bloody thickskinnery of the first order. Sukhin weighs his two options: one, throw Dennis out—he needs to finish totalling up and recording the marks for that stack of scripts and this interruption already means he will have to double check that he hasn't missed anything; two, give Dennis the attention he doesn't deserve—it will probably save time in the long run. He stands up and shoots Dennis the coldest stare he can manage, hoping this will scare him off.

No chance. Dennis hops onto Sukhin's desk and stretches out on it, spreading his arms to cover as much surface as possible. "Look at me, look at me. Talk to me, talk to me."

"Get the fuck off my desk."

"Say you'll do whatever I ask." Dennis picks up a random card from

Sukhin's desk, a note from a student with a sketch of a fish. He raises his voice: "Or I'll reveal our love letters to the world."

Mrs Chandra, head of the Economics department, who has the office next door, walks past with a cup of coffee. She gives Sukhin a very strange look. He wants to sink into the floor—Mrs Chandra's husband is one of his father's patients.

Option one it is. Sukhin waves towards the door. "Dennis, go away. I'm trying to work."

"You work too hard, sweets."

This isn't true. For days, Sukhin has done as little as it is possible to do without attracting notice. He's attended a few department meetings, spoken to the Tay about the literature trip he and Natalie are proposing for next year—basically making sure people know he's around and working on something, while spending the rest of the time holed up in his office otherwise occupied. *God, I've become Ken.*

Ken, who has spent the better part of the academic year campaigning for new uniforms for the girls' softball team and nothing much else. "We can't expect our girls to wear polyester," Sukhin heard him say to Tat Meng in the staff pantry just last week. "It's so bad for morale. All the other school teams are wearing Tencel or even merino wool."

"Wool? For a sports uniform? Doesn't sound practical." Tat Meng looked torn between wanting to escape the conversation and needing to question the logic of wool in tropical sportswear.

The glee on Ken's face was apparent even from the other side of the room, where Sukhin sat waiting for a few colleagues to arrive for a meeting. Sukhin turned his head to the wall so that Ken wouldn't see him roll his eyes.

"That's what most people think. People who don't know their technical fabrics." Ken paused, adding, just in case Tat Meng missed his point:

"But I do. I'm always up to date about these things, you know. I make it my business to understand my industry."

Your industry? You're a PE teacher.

"Sukhin, I see you disagree with me."

He forgot to turn his head to the wall that time. Damn. He shrugged and pretended to be busy with his notebook.

"So you want to tell us why merino wool isn't good for activewear? Go ahead."

Sukhin waved him away. Not going to engage.

Ken had other ideas. "I suppose you know all about the moisture-wicking properties of merino wool? And its antimicrobial properties? FYI, this means it doesn't smell. Very important to the girls. It also regulates temperature, so it's perfect for sportswear."

"Yes, absolutely. Merino wool. Great choice." *Go buy it or sell it or start a religion. Or breed the sheep.*

Ken crosses his arms and widens his stance. Sukhin suspects he must have read this in some self-help book about taking charge. "You know? These uniforms are important. Some of us care about the students. We don't walk around like you, wearing blinders."

"Blinkers."

"What?"

"Blinkers. I wear blinkers." Sukhin stood up—time to walk away. "The term 'blinder' is American, but we had the pleasure of being colonised by the British. So I prefer to wear blinkers. Please excuse me—this has been so interesting, but I have a meeting to get to."

Hardly an important meeting, though a convenient means of escape. Sukhin has always detested the formal meetings—the circuitous journeys through the same agendas, the same arguments, the same counter-arguments, the same counter-counter-arguments, year after year, have been tragicomic for as long as Sukhin's been a teacher—but these days he's laughing at himself as much as at the other teachers. Very discomfiting. So he avoids more and more of them and hides in his office and buries his head in science fiction novels and dabbles in cardboard-box architecture—he hasn't been able to stop himself from improving on his designs for Jinn's second cardboard house—and hopes that no one will discover he's really a big fat fraud. Hearing Dennis admonish him for working too hard makes him clench his jaw and gnash his teeth. On one hand, clearly no one suspects he's letting go—Dennis would be the first to hear of this, first through the door to dramatically demand, why, sweet cheeks, why, is everything okay; on the other hand, maybe he's never actually had to work all that hard. But that's ridiculous—there's always so much to do.

"Sweet cheeks, is everything okay?"

"What?" Then he realises he's been standing over Dennis for a few minutes, perfectly silent. Dennis, who is still on his back on Sukhin's desk.

"You need to break free. Which is why I'm here."

"You said you needed help."

"Exactly—so you can break free and help me. Two birds. It's brilliant." He sits up suddenly and now their faces are only centimetres apart. "We're taking your civics class and mine on a combined post-exam outing."

"No."

"Yes—we drew lots and we're together." Dennis wags his eyebrows. "I rigged it. You're welcome. Now neither of us will be stuck with some lame duck."

But we're all lame ducks, Sukhin doesn't say.

"He was lying on his desk!"

"Dennis was lying on his desk? In the Maths department? But why didn't he just go to the lounge?"

"He was lying on Sukhin's desk lah. Mrs Chandra told me."

"What? Aiyah, that woman is such a gossip."

"Yes, I know, but still. Would you lie down on my desk? Are they…?"

"No lah. You're just bitter because it's not you he wants."

"Very funny. Did I tell you he once called my ears lopsided?"

"Twice—but wasn't the problem your hair?"

~

Tomorrow, it will be November—November! It is surprising and unsurprising. The years before this passed just as quickly, just as uneventfully—anchored by the same routine of getting the new batch of first years settled; prepping the second years for their A-Levels; ploughing through the same texts with the same anti-heroes, the same battles, the same deaths; tackling the same kinds of students, all fervent believers in the special-snowflake uniqueness of their cohort, their class, their issues.

He rereads the email he's just written. This should do it—mysterious enough to be attractive, short enough to keep things casual, friendly enough not to rouse suspicion. He clicks send, feeling like he's lobbing a grenade into unknown territory—what if this kills everything? *Well, let's see if I get a reply.*

Anyway, this year—why does he expect this year to be different? He can feel a strange disappointment, now that the flurry of the first-year exams are over, replaced by the gallows atmosphere of the A-Level seatings. A student told him yesterday that she would die if she didn't get an A in her modern literature paper. He was so amused he nearly had a Dennis moment. *Sweetie, no one dies from failing literature. Most of the world can't put a coherent sentence together—you're going to be fine.*

But then he remembered Jinn at A-Levels—pale, anxious and self-flagellating—so he told the girl that she wouldn't fail, that he would eat his copy of *Hamlet* if she did. And now, remembering how relieved she looked, how thrilled to hear him say something so uncharacteristic, he wonders if he should perhaps do this more often with his students. It could be interesting to document the effects of random dramatic affirmations of ability on half his classes, with the other half as the control group.

He stores this in his head to tell Jinn when he sees her—he'll try looking for her again today.

He hasn't seen her in a week.

ʌʌʌ

The email reply comes the next morning—short, polite and to the point.

Yes, come see me the week after next. Anytime after 2pm, Wednesday or Thursday. Please let me know which works better.

He responds immediately. *Wednesday is perfect.*

ʌʌʌ

The joint post-exam outing turns out to be a lot more fun than Sukhin expected. He and Dennis fight for days over the itinerary, then decide to compromise—the Peranakan Museum, so that Dennis can show off his heritage and bore everyone with details about his grandmother's porcelain collection; then a tour of the sculptures in the Central Business District and along the river, where Sukhin will work in a poem-reading or two; then Sentosa for beach volleyball and dinner, for the kids. They hire a bus, buy sunscreen, fight over where to take the students for lunch, compromise again by choosing somewhere they both detest but the students will enjoy, circulate the consent forms, then pat themselves on the back when everything—every last detail, right down to pre-ordering meals for the vegetarian kids, even the difficult little jerk who refuses to eat mushrooms "because that's basically fungi, which is weird"—is done in a week.

Sukhin endures the Peranakan Museum with as much grace as possible, gets through lunch without losing his temper, and then tries his best not to sound too stuffy on his leg of the tour.

He takes the students first to see Salvador Dalí's *Homage to Newton* at UOB Plaza—he assumes they will all have heard of Dalí, so it's an easy start. But Sukhin is irredeemably dull—pointing out key features of the five-metre abstract piece that looks to him like a distorted human skeleton, he goes on about gravity and surrealism until Dennis catches his eye and, grimacing, draws a hand repeatedly across his throat. He stops talking. Off they go to Fernando Botero's *Bird*, just a short walk away. The students like this one better.

"It's so *fat*," one girl says to another.

It is indeed, like all of Botero's creatures—great, fat neck; massive, puffed-out chest; thighs the circumference of its head; bulbous, monstrous toes.

Dennis pronounces judgement: "Far too many carbs."

Even Sukhin laughs.

The animal statues are the best received. The black elephant on a podium in front of the Old Parliament House, a gift from King Chulalongkorn in 1872, is pronounced "stately, like all elephants" by the quietest boy in Dennis' class; they stop for half an hour while everyone but Sukhin takes photos of the Singapura cats playing on Cavenagh Bridge. Sukhin stands apart and refrains from making snarky remarks.

The tour ends with the Merlion at One Fullerton, overlooking Marina Bay. Everyone has seen this one before, of course—it is, after all, the most widely recognised, most culturally appropriated structure in all of Singapore—but up close it is quite a sight. Four storeys of half-lion/half-fish constantly spewing seawater into the bay. Sukhin stares, newly horrified—

well, if they were going for memorable, they nailed it. His class stands around him, also eyeing the Merlion with reluctant awe.

"Incredible," Sukhin says. "In the truest sense of the word."

"I wonder how much the government spends maintaining it." His favourite student, Abi—a quiet, unassuming girl with lovely manners and a knack for asking uncomfortable questions.

Dennis' students are intently watching the Merlion spew seawater while he talks them through their assignment—to calculate the changing speed of the spray. "Everyone take a copy of the diagram, please. Who doesn't have one? Okay, good. Assume there are two pumps—one to get the water from sea level to the base of the Merlion and another to get the water up to its mouth. Best part—assume that the pressure of the seawater entering the pipe changes every time..."

Time for the poem he's prepared for this part of the excursion: "The Merlion" by Alfian Sa'at. Sukhin hands the nearest student a stack of photocopies. "Take one, pass it along."

As his students stare at their sheets, he reads aloud.

> "I wish it had paws," you said,
> "It's quite grotesque the way it is,
> you know, limbless; can you
> imagine it writhing in the water,
> like some post-Chernobyl nightmare?
> I mean, how does it move? Like a
> torpedo? Or does it shoulder itself
> against the currents, gnashing with frustration,
> its furious mane bleached
> the colour of a drowned sun?

But take a second look at it,
how it is poised so terrestrially,
marooned on this rough shore,
as if unsure of its rightful
harbour. Could it be that,
having taken to this unaccustomed limpidity,
it has decided to abandon the seaweed-haunted
depths for land? Perhaps it is even ashamed
(But what a bold front!)
to have been a creature of the sea; look at how
it tries to purge itself of its aquatic ancestry,
in this ceaseless torrent of denial, draining
the body of rivers of histories, lymphatic memories.
What a riddle, this lesser brother of the Sphinx.
What sibling polarity, how its sister's lips are sealed
with self-knowledge and how its own jaws
clamp open in self-doubt, still
surprised after all these years."

"Yet…what brand new sun can dry
the iridescent slime from the scales
and what fresh rain wash the sting of salt
from those chalk-blind eyes?"

A pause.

"And why does it keep spewing that way?
I mean, you know, I mean…"

"I know exactly what you mean," I said,
Eyeing the blond highlights in your black hair
And your blue lenses the shadow of a foreign sky.
"It spews continually if only to ruffle
its own reflection in the water; such reminders
will only scare a creature so eager to reinvent itself."

Another pause.

"Yes," you finally replied, in that acquired accent of yours,
"Well, yes, but I still do wish it had paws."

When he finishes, they are all looking at him. How many of them are thinking about the poem he just read, he wonders, and how many of them are just wondering whether they should bother? How many of them will remember this? Abi—when she's a hotshot lawyer, will she remember that she once had to suffer his reading of "The Merlion" as the afternoon sun beat down on her and twenty-two other students?

Sukhin's stare shifts into the middle distance for a split second. *I must really be getting old—I'm starting to anticipate my exclusion from the next generation's bouts of nostalgia.* "Okay, let's get started. What does the poet have to assume the reader knows about the Merlion, for this poem to work? Any ideas?"

To his relief, there are. The quicker they get through this exercise, the sooner they'll be out of the sun and on their way.

Later, he and Dennis sit under a large umbrella at a café on Siloso Beach, trying to forget they're supposed to be babysitting a bunch of seventeen-year-olds. Dennis is on his phone, scouring online shopping sites for a pair of loafers he thinks he saw on someone who might have been a local fashion designer at either Books Kinokuniya or the lobby of Mandarin Orchard. "I can't remember the guy's name, but he looked really good and those loafers will go with everything I own." Sukhin is reading a book about the evolution of baking and doing his best to ignore Dennis.

Their drinks arrive—lime and soda for Dennis, ice lemon tea for Sukhin. After much discussion, they've reluctantly agreed not to consume any alcohol until the bus takes the children away at nine.

"Why did you become a teacher?"

The delivery is abrupt, but the question has been on Sukhin's mind for hours. While his class broke into groups to discuss the poem, he watched Dennis prance around the Merlion, somehow managing to look ready to hit the beach clubs in a school T-shirt, bermudas and a straw hat. Completely incongruous with the way he taught—shooting questions, clearly and logically positioned, demanding curiosity, demanding proof of knowledge, demanding participation. ("At that height, at h=7.2, is that the minimum speed of the water in order for the Merlion to be spewing? Not dribbling, not dripping—we want it spewing, spouting, gushing, whatever. Is it? Prove it. Peng Siong, how would you begin? What would you define first?") The students looked starstruck; they all wanted to be part of the dialogue without knowing why. Sukhin wanted to be one of them just for five minutes.

Dennis takes a sip of his soda and leans back in his chair. "I couldn't think of any other way to meet you—so I stalked you all the way to NIE and then to our lovely institution, and now here we are." He waves dramatically at the café patio, half-filled with tourists half-heartedly sipping cocktails, half-wishing they had gone to Bali instead. "Sentosa, land of excitement and passionate affairs."

Sukhin sighs. "Dennis."

Dennis stares. "Oh, you're serious. Sorry, sweets." He fiddles with his straw. "You really want to know? I warn you—this isn't a very exciting story."

Sukhin waves him on impatiently. Why do so many people preface their stories like this?

"Okay, so I desperately, desperately wanted to go abroad." Dennis doesn't look at Sukhin. "I know it sounds so awful, sweets, but I wanted to get away from my family so badly. They were driving me nuts."

So when the Ministry of Education offered Dennis a scholarship that would take him out of the four-room flat he shared with his parents and three brothers and deliver him to Cambridge, he jumped at the chance. "I had gone ahead and applied to all the big universities, even though we couldn't afford it. Ballsy, yes? I figured, who cares? If I don't get in, I don't get in." He grins. "So I got in, then I went fishing for scholarships. Took the first one that came through. Everyone was *so* mad at me. My mother went into full Taiwanese-drama mode—went on and on about how I had grown up into this evil, secret-keeping little turd." Dennis rolls his eyes. "*Such* a drama queen. But she came around."

"So, no regrets?"

"Sweetie, please." Dennis waves down the waiter and points at his drink. "Are you seriously asking if there's nothing else I'd rather do than teach F Maths to snooty brats who are constantly waiting for me to mess up?"

"You're so good at it." This comes out sounding like an accusation.

"You sound like a jealous old fishwife talking to a young whore." Dennis puts a hand on Sukhin's shoulder. "Sweets, thirty-five is not that old."

It is. And he'll be thirty-six in two months.

"Anyway, your turn. Why did you want to be a teacher?"

"My father said I couldn't."

The distilled version sounds incredibly silly, so Sukhin ends up having to tell Dennis the much-less-abridged version of the tale. He realises he has never told it to anyone, apart from Jinn. No one has asked him in years why he decided to be a teacher; in the early days, in the first year of teacher's training when everyone wanted to know why everyone else wanted to teach, he had kept his story dim-witted and believable—"It's a stable career and I like working with kids"—and completely false.

And the distilled version isn't completely true. His father hadn't exactly said that he couldn't. But he did say, when Sukhin announced he might go for a degree in English Literature and Linguistics: "But what will you do with it?"

The "but" rankled, that introduction of argument into a topic that Sukhin had not thought of as open to dispute.

"I don't know yet. Something meaningful, I hope." Oh, the naïveté. He understood now why this particular choice of words had confused and frustrated his earnest, practical father, the frame-maker's son who had worked all his life for a place in medical school, who just didn't know how to shoot down his son's loose approximation of ambition without also shooting at his son.

"Meaningful? How?"

Sukhin knew he was on muddy territory—he couldn't answer this for himself. But to his father, he said, "I'd like to make a difference to the way people think, live, operate."

"Med school, Sukhin. Go to med school and be a doctor."

He hadn't expected this total abandonment of subtlety by his father, the articulate Dr Jaswant "Got-the-gift-of-the-gab" Dhillon. The switch of tactic left Sukhin stupefied, unable to continue the free-form development of this idealistic, altruistic train of thought.

"I'd make a horrible doctor," he snapped. "I've been thinking of teaching." He had not, but it was worth the shock on his father's face.

"Teaching? You?"

"Why not?"

His father threw up his hands. "Why?"

They stared at each other across the kitchen table, a fine pair of caricatures—the broad-shouldered, bearded giant and his fine-boned, bird-like son.

"You can do anything you want, Sukhin. Anything." A pause, as his father appeared to search for the right words to move him. "You have an excellent memory; you have a knack for learning; you have always been so logical, so quick, so good with details. Everything you've ever set out to learn, you've learnt. And you have good hands. When we went to to see that school play and I saw the machines you made, all the large and little parts fitting together, moving together, I said to your mother, 'Look at that, he will be a fine surgeon.'"

Sukhin had to force himself not to be carried off by his father's narrative. He felt helpless and angry—why was guilt always his first and strongest emotion when it came to his father?

"Listen to Papa. Don't do this—you've never wanted to teach; you've never shown the slightest interest in teaching anyone anything. All your life, you've only learnt what you want to learn—*being a teacher means learning what other people need to learn*. You won't like that. Listen to me, Sukhin. Do something else. Listen to Papa."

That was the lowest blow, Sukhin felt—the regression to "listen to Papa", the calculated appeal to his boyhood instinct, his unquestioning trust in the one who taught him to walk swim cycle play dead if approached by a bear.

So he refused.

"Oh my god, how Oedipal."

"I don't want to kill him, Dennis."

"You want to discredit him. You've spent—what, ten years, yes?—doing all of this"—big gesture that includes the students in the distance playing some odd fusion of volleyball and football—"to prove him wrong. Sweetie, you are so fucked up."

"I am so fucked up." *I might have been a fine surgeon.* Sukhin brings his forehead down to the table and shuts his eyes.

"Okay, now you're worrying me. I'm going to reel in the children and we're going to get food."

~

Sukhin's head is throbbing. Everything is spinning. Dennis is next to him in bed, snoring, his arms thrown wide. Sukhin realises with distaste that they're both still in yesterday's clothes. He runs a hand through his hair. Sand and something sticky. Ugh.

Stumbling out into the living room, he finds the front door wide open. *What the fuck.*

The clock in the kitchen tells him it's nearly eleven. Good thing it's Saturday. He puts the kettle on, feeling like death. His head is so, so heavy.

A noise from the bedroom. Dennis. Sukhin has almost forgot about him.

"Oh wow, you look like shit."

Sukhin locks himself in the shower for half an hour.

~

"You look terrible."

"Shut up. I brought you cake."

"Rough night?"

Jinn laughs at his recount of the evening before—the chaos of feeding the students and rounding them up when the bus arrived to take them home, the endless rounds of piña coladas (two for twenty dollars), the free shots of rum (the consequence of Dennis buttering up the bartender), the big black gap in his memory between the fourth shot and waking up to find Dennis in his bed.

"He made breakfast and asked if he'd been gentle enough. I should have stabbed him with my teaspoon."

"You'd have missed." She holds up a slice of cake. "This is good. It's been a while since I had lemon cake."

He doesn't tell her that he made it, or that it took him three dry runs to get the texture right.

They chain her bicycle and her backpack to a bench and go for a walk. On the red steel bridge leading to the wetlands reserve, in the fading daylight, they stop to watch dragonflies dart about like manic little biplanes, and he tells her about telling Dennis why he became a teacher.

He repeats that conversation's rather dismal conclusion: "I am so fucked up, Jinn."

"No."

He can't look at her. His heart is suddenly pounding exactly like it did that night so many years ago when he told her about wanting to be a palaeontologist.

She shocks him by taking his shoulders and pulling him closer, then putting her arms around him. He stands quite, quite still. A dragonfly whizzes past and collides with the bridge.

"You're not fucked up, Sukhin," she says, her mouth close to his ear, her face nearly touching his. "You haven't spent ten years trying to prove your father wrong. You've been proving to yourself that you can teach.

And you *are* teaching. You're tired, you want it to be easier, you wish you loved it. But you're not fucked up."

He can't hug her back; he's too busy trying not to weep.

"If you tell me you're fucked up again, I'll beat you. I'll throw you into the river and tell the otters to eat you."

He weeps.

It is a long, low, deep wall in the middle of a garden of long, low, deep walls. It is polished rock, with five rows of rectangular marble tiles, all identical. The tiles on the top row are all inscribed, each one bearing a name, a pair of dates and a small photograph.

Only one tile on the second row is inscribed. The woman reaches out and runs a finger over the name.

"I'm sorry."

She turns. A strange man is standing next to her, carrying a small bunch of flowers. His face is kindly.

"My mother is over there." He points, with the flowers, at another wall close by. Bending a little, he looks closely at the photograph on the only marked tile on the second row. "Sister?"

She nods.

"She looks exactly like you."

The woman and the stranger look at the photograph for a few minutes. He divides his bunch of flowers into two and puts them on the narrow ledge in front of the tile. "Mum won't mind." He walks away.

She raises a hand to her face and finds it wet.

XII

HE RUNS IN the evenings now. One of the PE teachers told him it's time he added some distance to his route.

"Push yourself," she said. "Or your muscles will get lazy."

He doesn't understand how muscles get lazy while they're supposed to be working, but he agrees to push himself. Nisah must know what she's talking about—she's done the Ironman Triathlon twice. Not that he's considering signing up for anything even approaching competitive endurance.

Running, Sukhin has decided, is for the uncoordinated, the stubborn, the posturing. In essence, it's an undemanding sport, requiring no special skill, no more than basic agility, no strategy, no understanding of other players—to be good at this, to want to be good at this, Sukhin thinks as he struggles through the final third of his new six-kilometre route, you'd have to be driven completely by ego or desperation. A woman bounds past him, all lean limbs and designer sportswear, her phone blasting an upbeat, high-pitched song that he doesn't recognise. Sukhin grits his teeth. *Or you're a sociopath, or a maniac.*

Another runner draws abreast. A man of about his age, a bit stockier, tanned and lean and muscular. *Gym monkey.* For a short while, he matches

Sukhin's pace—not hard; Sukhin is slow—and then speeds up, pulling forward. Sukhin quickens his step and lengthens it; the man easily keeps up. *Stupid fuck.*

They don't make eye contact. They don't turn to look at each other. But it's clear that the race is on.

They run, strides matching, past a couple making out on a bench, past a group of in-line skaters on a break, past a family crowded around barbeque pit, kids screaming and pushing each other. Sukhin cringes. *Beasts.* He loses focus and stumbles over a stray paper cup. The man takes the lead. Sukhin draws a deep breath and lunges forward, but it's too late—the paper cup has cost him his momentum and now his feet feel like sandbags.

He ambles along a while, steadily losing speed, the distance between him and the stranger growing with each uninspired step. The race is over, but Sukhin will not go gently into that good night. He silently counts to a thousand, then tries to recall the periodic table to distract himself from the burn in his legs, the rapid constriction of his lungs. But there's no point. Get past the next dustbin, he tells himself, just one more dustbin. *Where are the bloody dustbins?* Finally, he sees one, bright green even in the darkness. He lopes towards it, a mess of limbs, sweat and desperation. Passes it, passes the near-luminous plastic vessel for refuse that's become the anchor of his entire run.

Done. Sukhin comes to a complete stop.

He looks around. He's well past his planned end point, which involved making a loop somewhere way back, and is now in a much quieter section of East Coast Park, well beyond the barbeque pits and the seafood restaurants and the water-ski simulator pond. There doesn't seem to be anyone around and he's never explored this part of the park before, so he walks on, feeling a little like he's breaking into new territory.

But it's just more of the same park—the same trees, the same dustbins, another public shower, another bicycle rental shop, the same pavement guiding the way through polite, coiffed clusters of plants. The only deviant from government-groomed parkness is a group of tents crouching parallel to the shore under a clump of trees, well out of the glare of the street lamps lining the pavement.

As he approaches for a closer look, he sees people outside the tents, some cooking over portable stoves, others talking softly. A small lamp hangs from a branch. A couple of tents are all zipped up, flip-flops arranged in a row outside.

Absolutely baffling. How much fun can it be to camp in a park like this, a hundred metres from a giant parking lot, with McDonald's just a half-hour walk away?

"Hallo! You want water?"

He jumps. The offer comes from a man who appears about his father's age, who's looking at him with concern. Sukhin realises he's still heaving from his run, and he must look a pitiful wreck. He nods, more out of curiosity than thirst, and follows the stranger to one of the tents.

The man hands him a cup of water. "You sit down lah. Rest a bit."

The plastic sheet spread in front of the man's tent looks clean and Sukhin doesn't want to track dirt all over it. But neither does he want to remove his shoes—it just isn't wise to take off your shoes until you are absolutely certain of not being in danger.

"Eh, don't worry lah. Just sit down."

If he refuses, he will probably come off as either a snob or an asshole. So he sits down awkwardly near the edge of the sheet, his feet planted on the grass.

"Just now, I check because somebody say maybe you police," the man says. His tone is friendly, conversational. He watches Sukhin gulp down the water. "Running must bring water, you know."

"I know. Sorry."

"No need sorry. Water free, you just drink." The man smiles. "Funny, right? Last time got house, must pay for water. Now no house, water free. Like that lah, yah?"

Yup. Like that lah.

~

"Police ah?"

"No lah. He say he teacher."

"Then you give him your name and handphone number for what?"

"He say got project, got people cook free dinner, anyone can go. He say he ask if they can bring food here."

"Hah. Don't have lah. Keong, where got people so free one?"

"Aiyah. He say got. If got, got lah. If don't have, same what."

~

Sukhin almost loses his way, but he gets there with five minutes to spare.

The place she has chosen is tucked away from the busier streets, away from the trendy establishments and the ladies who lunch then drink. The façade is an exposed-brick wall with a glass door. A small engraved metal plate hangs above it. Sad Cypress. Odd name for a café.

He goes in. The door is much heavier than it looks; he almost stumbles backwards.

A waiter walks briskly towards him, apologising for the door. Sukhin looks around quickly. Only two tables are occupied and he doesn't see her.

"Mr Dhillon?"

How unnerving. "Yes."

He follows the waiter upstairs, through a short, dark corridor and into a room filled with massive earthen pots of fine-leafed bamboo.

Overhead, small windows puncture the roof, letting in shafts of sunlight. In the centre of the room, at a table for two, she sips tea from a glass teacup. She stands up as he walks towards her. Her dress is plain and grey, falling in a straight line from her shoulders to her ankles.

"Sukhin." Her tone is warmer than he expects.

She hasn't aged much since he last saw her—ten, maybe eleven, years ago. He wonders if she thinks he has.

"Hey Ping, thanks for meeting me."

They sit down. There isn't anything as pedestrian as "just black tea" on the menu, so Sukhin ends up with an indecently priced concoction of pine needles, basil seeds and other un-tea-like things. Ping tells him how nice it is to see him again, after all these years, sounding like she means it. He tells her he's teaching at their old school, wishing he could think of something more interesting to say. They then spend what seems to Sukhin to be an interminably long time talking of random things, both circling the only topic that brings them here.

Sukhin is the first to give up. He had no idea Jinn went missing, he tells Ping.

"You didn't? It was in the papers, all over Facebook. We told everyone."

"I don't read the papers," he admits, feeling stupid. Everyone expects teachers to read the newspapers—why? They're so tiring. "And I'm not on social media."

She doesn't show any surprise. He feels a new respect for lawyers. Anyone else would have at least raised an eyebrow.

"Have you heard from her?" She looks him straight in the eye.

"No."

She takes another sip of tea. "I thought you had. Your email came out of the blue." A pause. "I thought you might have news to share."

No, he tells her, he doesn't. But while trying to hunt Jinn down for a reunion dinner with their old friends from school, he learnt that she was missing. He wasn't sure who to call or ask, but he thought of Ping.

"How did you find me?"

"Oh, I didn't. Someone said you had set up a bakery and Google did the rest."

They sit in silence for a while. Sukhin prods at the pine needles at the bottom of his teapot with his teaspoon. Ping taps a finger soundlessly against the edge of her saucer.

"Congratulations on the bakery—I hear only good things about it."

Ping smiles and looks pleased. "Thank you."

He wonders if she's thinking of her sister—can it be that, like him, Ping can't think of cake without thinking of Jinn? Running a bakery must be a constant reminder of her sister—does she do it on purpose?

"My colleagues got me one of your cakes for my birthday. Very good." Why is he saying all this? He needs to stop talking.

"That's lovely." She sighs, suddenly looking tired. "You know, I was really hoping you had news."

"She wouldn't have looked me up." She didn't.

It's probably why Ping hadn't bothered to try to reach him when Jinn went missing. She would know all about the circumstances of their split—she probably knew more than he did. Jinn always told her everything.

"My sister says it's weird to keep your eyes open while you're kissing someone," Jinn said once, out of nowhere. They were in her room on campus. She was studying for a test; he was fighting the urge to tidy up.

Sukhin was mortified. "You told her *that*?"

"Kiss me—and try doing it with your eyes closed."

"You're nuts."

"Ping says *you* might be. Come on, try closing your eyes."

He felt himself go red. He began to rearrange Jinn's bookshelf. He would never be able to look her sister in the eye again.

And yet here he is, drinking tea in this poncy café, looking her in the eye. Lying to her face. *Our wills and fates do so contrary run.*

~

One of the otter pups has caught a fish. Grabbing it with his two front paws, he takes its head off with his little otter teeth. The crowd goes wild—and every amateur photographer within zooming distance has a go at Fish Caught at Four Thirty-Seven.

The pup looks straight at Sukhin as he gnaws on his victim's guts.

"I don't know where she is," he tells it, leaning a little over the guardrail separating the path from the riverbank. "Sorry."

It's the third day in a row that he hasn't been able to find her. Last week, he only saw her twice. The week before, not at all. He misses the cardboard house, that alley—simpler times. Now that Kim Seng's bicycle has made Jinn a moving target, Sukhin never knows when he'll see her next, or where—last Saturday, he walked four kilometres before he finally found her lurking below a bridge, watching a couple of birds make a nest on an islet in the middle of the river.

"Shhh," she whispered as he approached. "Architects at work."

Half the time, he doesn't find her. She doesn't have a favourite spot in the park, so all he can do is keep walking and hope he encounters her before it's time to turn back—he's set the U-turn time at one hour on weekdays and two hours on weekends.

Maybe she doesn't want to see him. Maybe this is why she insisted on moving here. She always looks pleased to see him, when she sees him.

But he gets the feeling that he isn't ever missed—does he want to be missed?—and that his coming and going doesn't quite matter.

What does? Or rather, what did? Something mattered enough once to set all of this in motion. Some life-event equivalent of a star collapsing into itself, sucking in everything that is or comes close, even light, even time.

"Ping, what happened?" He asked the question before losing the courage to lob it across the table.

She was silent for a few minutes, staring into her teacup. "She never said anything to me. But I'm sure there was something."

"I'm sorry." He was. Ping was lying. Jinn's note was meant for her—so while Sukhin only knew the contents of the note but not the context, she had to know.

Ping waved the apology aside. "It's fine. I'd be curious too." She looked up at him. "I know you loved her."

Was that meant to throw him off balance? It did.

"That was so long ago." He tried to sound casual—but why? They were talking about a missing woman, not a missing pen. "I hope she's all right."

She didn't take the bait. No echo of his sentiments, no indication of her own.

Did he do the right thing, reaching out to Ping? He doesn't even know how much Ping knows. Does she know that the missing Jinn is vagabonding? Is she even looking for her sister? Or does she assume she's dead, rotting somewhere no one will ever look? And what the hell happened? Of course, if Jinn wanted him to know more, he would. But she doesn't. Why? What difference will it make, to her or him? None to him—if she turns out to be a mass murderer, he will still prowl the park for her and bring her cake.

He's past the wetlands now, a long way from where he parked his car. He hasn't been this far out since the day he cycled over to Punggol Park from the east coast, but there's still no sign of her.

Fine—he doesn't need to see her today. He was relieved when he didn't find her yesterday or the day before. He knows she won't ask if he's feeling better or if he wants to talk or anything banal like that, but every now and then he gets a flashback of standing rigid in her arms the last time they met, hungover and weeping, and he wants to throw himself into the river. He blames the rum. He blames Dennis' glib tongue and the bartender's susceptibility to glib tongues. He also blames Jinn—why, she practically coaxed him into tears. What does she think of him now? What will he say to her?

Crying is such a hassle. Especially when the witness to your meltdown—and its palliative—is the girl who once horrified you by crying at everything, everything. The girl whose tendency to cry you treated like an inconvenient, ever-present affliction, like a damaged kidney or malformed lung.

"Sukhin! I can't go in, Sukhin."

He could hear her voice but he couldn't see her. A hand emerged from behind the bushes nearby. It waved. "Over here."

Sukhin hurried over. Crouched behind the bougainvillaea was Jinn, her face a mess of tears, black streaks and smudged red blotches. She was still crying, but no sobbing—thank goodness.

"The service starts in fifteen minutes. We've got to go in. Grace is getting married, Jinn." He stopped. Should he put his arms around her? Would that help? "It's a good thing. Grace wants to get married." He wondered what else would help. "Twenty-four is a bit young, but she knows what she's doing."

A few minutes passed. The crying stopped, but she still looked like a professional mourner.

"Are you going to be okay? Do you want to go home?"

"No, no. I'm okay, I'm okay. I'm super happy for Grace." She took a deep breath and began tearing up again. "It's just such a big thing, you know, one of us getting married."

"Yes, and you're about to miss it." He looked at her in her inglorious snivelling, wiping her face with the backs of her hands, and loved her a little bit less.

In the end, just minutes before the service began, he put his jacket over her head and led her into the church and safely into a pew.

"Sudden attack of photophobia," he told the usher.

There she is suddenly, just over a metre away. He stares at her in sudden wonder. How did she go from that snivelling mess to this mad, marvellous creature who will sleep anywhere and eat discards and still smile like that? *What a marvel you are.*

She's beaming, sweaty—did she run to him? Did he miss that? Yes—the bicycle is way over there, next to that bench. He hopes she locked it.

"Sukhin. You're here."

I am. I am I am I am.

"Brought you a bit of cake." He hesitates, then adds: "Made it myself."

"You clever thing."

Our wills and fates do so contrary run.

~

"Oh, are you taking those boxes away?"

"Pa, we've talked about this, remember? They're for my friend."

"Jaswant!"

"What? Darling, it's been weeks and weeks. I just thought Sukhin changed his mind."

ᨓ

Sukhin's living room is a mess, strewn with cardboard. Sheets and strips and bits and flaps everywhere. In a box, in a haphazard, well-meaning attempt at organisation: craft knives, scalpels, glue and stapler guns, thumb tacks, brushes, wire, pliers, plastic tubing, an assortment of nuts and rivets, a handsaw.

Paper all over the study—old newspapers and magazines taken from the staff lounge, stacks of drawings, both technical and schematic.

The bedroom plays host to all the objects banished for their own good from the living room and the study—document files, favourite books, the hemi-demi-semi-done Guggenheim puzzle.

The kitchen alone is unscathed.

ᨓ

"I tried that route to East Coast Park. Long." They're watching the sunset from one of the bridges in the park.

"Told you."

But it was worth the ride, she tells him. "I took off my shoes and walked in the water for a bit at Changi."

He can easily picture it—she's been doing this at beaches since they were young. Once, she lost her shoes and he had to give up his. The blisters—he can still remember how much they smarted.

"Is Changi one of the fake beaches?"

"No. Well, maybe some parts." Sukhin stretches out his legs. The sun has completely disappeared, but there's a bright orange band across the sky where it was. "But there's a proper bit—the Japanese took a bunch of people there, lined them up along the sea and shot them. There was that guy who found a skull while digging for worms, remember? They say the sea was red, you know, that morning. All day."

"Who's they?"

"My grandmother."

The sky is now a startlingly deep red. Sukhin wishes he hadn't brought up the Changi Beach massacre.

"I remember her. How is she?"

"Stronger than her daughters. Far more stubborn." He tells Jinn about his grandmother telling off his Aunt Lillian for buying less-than-great belacan for the nasi lemak sambal at Sunday lunch, just the day before.

She tells him about helping a group of schoolchildren fish out frog spawn from the river for a project.

"But it's the school holidays."

"Maybe they're supposed to have the frogs ready by the time school starts again."

Sukhin sighs. He hates school holidays, even if it means he's off work as well. Children everywhere. Noise levels at a constant high. Punggol Park isn't immune—the weekend crowds have become thicker with the sound of yelling, energetic children and frustrated, yelling parents desperate to tire them out.

Jinn isn't happy with the heavier traffic either, but "it's still better than Chinatown". She says this matter-of-factly.

Months ago, back when the cardboard castle was still standing, he asked her why Chinatown. Noisy, cramped, full of people—how did she stand it? How did she even end up there?

"I thought I'd like being lost in a crowd. And sometimes I do."

Is oblivion some sort of fantasy of hers? Or just anonymity? The idea of Jinn blending in unnoticed, anywhere, is still somewhat amusing—

he remembers when she was so bloody loud. And not just because she insisted on half-yelling most of the time, protesting when he begged her to keep her voice down, that Loud Enough to Cross a Football Pitch was her natural volume.

Was it a Maths lecture? Yes, it was. He remembers the tap on his shoulder, his classmate Leonard pointing backwards with his thumb. Sukhin looked up and up. The lecture theatre had seats arranged in steep terraced rows circling the projector screen and lecture podium. He was at the bottom, right in front, with his class. Jinn's class was near the back, about twenty rows up.

He couldn't see her but he could see: SUKHIN IM HUNGRY. Each letter in black marker on a piece of foolscap paper, all held up by her classmates, complete with blank spaces between each word.

Mr Chua laughed in the middle of explaining linear regression.

Sukhin wondered if she would be upset if he told her never ever to do this again. He didn't. When the lecture ended, he rushed her straight to the canteen and fed her tea and biscuits.

"There. That should do until five."

"Maybe."

When he offered to get more tea, she said he spoilt her. But she seemed very, very pleased about it. And even more pleased with the tea.

A poke on his shoulder.

"So, Sukhin, when am I getting nasi lemak? I'll help you pound the chilli."

The man walks into the garden of walls. He has never been here. Until recently, he never knew the garden existed.

It takes him half an hour to find her family wall. He looks at her tile, wondering what they put behind it instead of ashes. Some of her old things? Photographs?

From behind him, a voice calls his name.

He wouldn't have come if he knew he wouldn't be alone. The other visitor steps up and links her arm through his. It's as if she expected him, though he knows this is impossible.

"Did you see the obituary? Did you like the photo? I think she would have approved." She speaks lightly, smiling.

He doesn't reply. Frowning, he rereads the inscription on the tile just below the pair of dates: You will be remembered, Jinn Hwa, by the sorrow you caused by your loss.

An epitaph in the second person, addressed to the dead—the man has never known one like this. His heart quickens.

"We saw a grave slab with an inscription like this at the ancient cemetery in Athens when we were there, years ago." Her voice is soft now; he has to lean closer to hear her. "She cried and cried over it." She pauses. "So did I."

XIII

CHRISTMAS DINNER SHOULD be special, they all agree.

Sukhin wants to say something about European paganism, harvest festivals, cultural and religious colonialism and the inappropriateness, therefore, of celebrating Christmas in the Southeast Asian region. But for her sake he keeps quiet.

Jinn spends less time at the kitchen on Rowell Road these days. There are more volunteers now, including a retired chef who used to run a thirty-man kitchen in a big-name Teochew restaurant, and she feels it's time for her to retire into the shadows and let the new people have a go at things. But Kim Seng has insisted on her helping him organise the Christmas dinner—it will be their grandest effort yet, with a fleet of volunteers ferrying people from other parts of the island to the Rowell site.

The families at East Coast Park will be coming too, Jinn told him the week before. She seemed delighted. "Sukhin, how kind," she had said, when he asked Kim Seng and Gopal about the possibility of getting food to the people he'd seen living on the beach. He'd done nothing but take down a name and a number and pass them on, but if Sukhin had a tail, he would have wagged it.

"Healthy food, for Christmas? Hmm. Well, turkey is healthy, right?"

He's agreed to be the meeting scribe, but so far he's written nothing down. Nothing intelligent or actionable—how he hates the word, but it's at least useful—has been said in the last hour and he suspects nothing will be.

"Is turkey too Christian?"

Sukhin blows out his cheeks and sighs loudly. *Too much, too much.*

Every head turns towards him. A long, even stare from Jinn.

He raises his hand in apology. "Sorry, sorry. Please, carry on."

"Turkey is Christian?" Gopal sounds incredulous. "And, um, it's Christmas." Sukhin cheers him on—in his head.

The veggie pirates are meant to be making a list of everything they will need for Christmas dinner—food, lights, candles, more tables, everything—but the discussion hasn't progressed beyond what they should serve.

"Can we have curry?"

"What about turkey curry?"

"Is turkey curry like chicken curry but with turkey?"

"No curry! Curry isn't Christmassy!"

Sukhin wants to strangle them all.

At the head of the table, next to Kim Seng, Jinn lifts a hand and waits for everyone to stop speaking. "We're going to make a list of everything everyone wants. And then we'll vote, and that will decide the menu. Is that okay?"

A murmur, then everyone nods. Relieved, Sukhin organises the Christmas election. When the meeting ends an hour later, there are fourteen items on the dinner menu—turkey is in, and so is fish biryani, roast chicken, mutton rendang, mushroom rice, devil curry, strawberries, kuih dadar, gingerbread, durian pengat, bread pudding, fruit tarts, mince pie and "festive cakes", which no one can define but everyone agrees are necessary.

Kim Seng laughs. "Wah. So rojak." He looks at Jinn. "Okay lah, let's try."

As people start to leave and Gopal accosts Jinn for a tête-à-tête to say something derisive about the new volunteer who brought up the Christianness of turkey, Sukhin goes up to Kim Seng.

"What's the plan?"

"Don't know, honestly." Big, long sigh. "Quite a lot of things to do if we want to get this right. But I don't want to tell them that this is all a little too much, you know? This sort of thing—we have to dare to try lah." He consults his notes. "And food is just part of it, you know—so many other things to take care of."

Sukhin wonders what Kim Seng does when he's not captain of the veggie pirates. Teach? Sell stuff? Manage a gang of criminals? (What's the verb for gangster?) He's articulate, organised, logical and comes across as intelligent without seeming like a know-it-all. People listen to him. Even when he's dressed in tired-looking shorts and a faded football jersey that's too tight for him. What a superpower—and he's using it to organise groups of people who scavenge for vegetables and cook them for other people. Sukhin is unsure whether to think of Kim Seng as a madman or a saint, but he's leaning towards madman—sainthood proper would require being burnt at the stake or crushed by a wheel or something just as gruesome.

"A lot of cake and pastry on the list."

Kim Seng shakes his head. "Yah. That's going to be hard—we've only got that one oven. Time to start looking for sponsors. But Christmas is so busy—it's going to be so hard." He raises a hand to his forehead. "Two hundred people! Last year, I don't think we even had half of that."

Sukhin takes the plunge. "I know someone who may be able to help."

~

"So, can I put you down for cake? For the big dinner."

They're finally leaving Rowell, after an extended discussion about the Christmas set-up and timings with Kim Seng and Gopal. Who knew there could be so many ways to arrange tables and chairs in a back alley?

"Sure. What kind?"

"Surprise me—something special."

"Challenge accepted."

"Kim Seng told me you've offered to help with getting sponsors."

"Nothing's confirmed. But I'll make a few calls."

She puts a hand on his shoulder and sighs. "Thanks, Sukhin. We need all the help we can get."

He starts the car. "School holidays. Might as well keep busy."

The one thing that Sukhin and his father will agree on absolutely is what a wonderful thing it is that Christmas isn't a big deal in the Dhillon household. No parties, no traditions, no gifts, no feasting. If anything, things slow down in December. Sukhin becomes idle and increasingly moody from a combination of being idle and dreading the start of the new school year. Dr Jaswant takes time off from the surgery because all his patients are on vacation, and every year he and Doris say that next year they too will go on vacation.

"Paris. We should go to Paris."

"Paris? Why Paris? Alaska! We could book a cruise. Sukhin, what do you think?"

Sukhin doesn't look up from the laptop he's helping his father reformat. "Sounds brilliant."

"You should come with us."

Doris sets down her coffee mug. "Yes! A family vacation." She turns to Sukhin, whose full attention she's managed to get with her last two words.

"Where would you like to go?"

Home. Time to leave. There is no way he's getting dragged into any discussion of a family vacation, no matter how remote the possibility—if he does, he won't be able to deny knowledge of it later.

But first: "Is it okay if I take a few more boxes?"

His father frowns. "Your friend—she needs more boxes?"

"Yes."

"Hmm."

Doris, sensing an impending impasse, decides to go all in. This is serious, she thinks. There really might be grandchildren in this. This woman's house-moving has taken months, and yet her son, her impatient, antisocial Sukhin, is still helping out. Last week, he asked her for a recipe for Christmas pudding—and wanted to know if there was one that required flambéing. Flambéing! He said he wanted something special. The boxes, all the interest in baking and cooking *and flambéing*—when has he ever been like this before? Not even his old girlfriend had inspired him to cook, and he really, really liked that girl.

"Take all the boxes you need, Sukhin."

"Really?" He expects a little more resistance.

As if on cue, his father chimes in. "Darling, if we need to move..."

The one-track mind, boys and girls, is the secret to a successful medical career.

Sukhin makes a dash for the living room and Doris turns to her husband. "Jas, it's fine. We have plenty to spare."

She will make dried chilli chicken with cashews, his favourite, for dinner. And sugee cookies. He will forgive her.

In the living room, in a Sukhin-sized space between two stacks of boxes, Sukhin is feeling very kindly towards his mother as he carefully searches for the sizes he needs. Perhaps a very short family vacation...

He picks up a promising-looking box and studies it. No. Not sturdy enough.

~

This year, Sukhin hasn't had the time to become idle and moody.

His living room is a scrap heap now; his study is half-full of boxes. Three weeks on, the project has nearly swallowed him whole. He spends every waking hour with it or thinking about it, except when he goes to see Jinn or his parents. Or when he bakes—on his fourth attempt, the Christmas pudding turned out very well. Adding fresh cherries made all the difference, exactly as his mother said it would. He has ordered a kitchen blowtorch—the one he borrowed from Dennis only has three settings for flame intensity and no option for changing flame diameter.

The project, sadly, isn't going as well as the baking. Version Three now, and the sketches alone have taken three days. The first version didn't work at all—his direct translation from memory of wood to cardboard wasn't structurally sound or elegant, and the mechanism was far too clumsy. Straight to the recycling heap—he didn't even need to test it to know it was going to be a waste of time. The second took twice as long to build and looked nothing like the first or the long-dead original. It was modular—good; light—good; but there were too many oddly shaped pieces and he wasn't happy with the structure. But the mechanism worked, earning Two the right to remain in the living room, the lesser but acknowledged elder brother to Three.

He checks the time. 2pm. No time for lunch—he's meeting her in an hour.

As he puts his tools back into their box, Three stares up at him, needy and petulant. *Get your ass back here. These slats won't make themselves.*

Sukhin shakes his head. Internal conversations with inanimate objects now? *Ah, mental decline—I've been expecting you.*

~

Who the hell is that man?

Ten minutes ago, he found Jinn. She's under an origami-esque pavilion halfway through the park. Her backpack is next to her on the long wooden seat; the stranger is on the other side. The man is plainly dressed—outdoor clothes and sensible shoes—and doesn't appear in any way threatening—except that he's speaking to Jinn and leaning towards her in a way that disturbs Sukhin.

Who parks himself under an identical pavilion a short distance away, watching, waiting for the man to leave. Willing him to leave. He wants to go up to Jinn and say something to her and at the stranger, something that will send an unambiguous message to him that he's not wanted here. "*There you are. Is this weirdo bothering you?*"

Is he?

Jinn isn't getting up to leave. She isn't saying much, but that doesn't say much. The man is turned towards her as he speaks, his gestures small but friendly. She is looking ahead, at the river. But she isn't getting up to leave, and she hasn't noticed Sukhin's arrival.

Who the hell is this man?

Half an hour goes by. Finally, the stranger gets up. He smiles at Jinn and does an odd little bow. *Obsequious fuck*. Sukhin stares hard, taking advantage of the unobstructed view of his face. No, he's never seen him before. Then again, maybe he just doesn't remember—there's nothing striking about the stranger. Tallish, medium built, no obvious physical deformities. Handsome? Sukhin doesn't know. Maybe—would Dennis call those good legs?

The stranger passes Sukhin as he leaves. Quick step, good posture, steady gaze. Taller than Sukhin first assumed. Better looking up close—tanned, lean and square-jawed in that annoying wholesome way that all the boys in the swim team had. He doesn't notice Sukhin glowering under the other pavilion.

Jinn doesn't turn to watch the stranger leave, but she looks up at Sukhin as he sits down beside her. He's already decided that he won't ask about the stranger like a loud, loutish lover.

"You smell like cookies."

Uncanny. "You hound."

"Arf."

"Dogs can't eat chocolate."

"Do I look like any old dog? I was bred for chocolate-scoffing." She holds out a hand.

He produces a tin, holding it just out of her reach. "If you keel over and die, I'll leave you here."

"But take the bicycle—key's in my backpack. Now, hand over the cookies."

They share the cookies, which Jinn pronounces too sweet but delicious, and then they go for a walk. She tells him that she cycled to Changi Beach again, and that she saw the otters on her way there.

"Isn't it wonderful how otters just...are? Without thinking about it? No delusions of grandeur or insecurities or anything stupid. Imagine being an otter."

"If I were an otter, I think I could manage delusions of grandeur."

"A snooty otter." She rolls her eyes.

"I'd be adorable."

They discuss, at length, what makes an adorable otter adorable. Jinn decides an otter is adorable by virtue of being an otter, snootiness notwithstanding. She tells him that this means his snootiness, were he an otter, would add no value to the otterdom.

She doesn't tell him about the handsomish stranger.

ᴧᴧ

Three isn't behaving. It's four in the morning and, after hours of tweaks and adjustments, the mechanism still isn't working as it should—the movements are too rigid and regular; the effect is crude.

He will need to find a way to randomise the movements. He must introduce imperfection.

ᴧᴧ

The baking continues to go well. Sukhin is so pleased with the fifth iteration of the Christmas pudding that he drives it over to Dennis' place for an impromptu supper.

"Sweetie, what is that?"

Sukhin realises he's enjoying the horror on Dennis' face. "My new kitchen blowtorch."

He begins to put it together on Dennis' kitchen counter, screwing the torch head with its petrol-pump-like nozzle onto the gas cylinder. The assembled torch looks like a gun attached to a large can of insect spray. He turns it on and a jet of blue flame bursts from the nozzle.

"No. *Mine* is a blowtorch. That is an industrial welding tool."

"It's all-purpose. The reviews are great." In one of the hundreds of reviews he read, someone noted excitedly that "it sears meat like a dragon". That clinched it for Sukhin.

He tells Dennis to switch off the lights. And then, dragon-like, he begins to sear the snowy meringue peaks he's just piled on top of the Christmas pudding. Dennis doesn't say a word, watching mutely as Sukhin pours cherry brandy over the entire pudding and lights it up.

"Behold—the Christmas bomb."

Blue tongues of flame dance over the pudding, luminous in the darkness. The meringue peaks, carefully serrated with a fork just minutes ago, glow like little razor blades. *It's like an alien egg.* Sukhin smiles to himself. He can't wait to see Jinn's face when she sees this.

When the flames die down, he cuts a slice for Dennis and one for himself.

"Not sure about the name, but very fancy—and very good." Dennis takes another mouthful and sighs loudly. "So. This is for *her* somehow, isn't it?"

"It's for—a party." Sukhin shrugs. "It's a pudding, Dennis. Just flour and eggs and sugar and fruit. It's not a big deal."

"You bought a blowtorch. It's a big deal."

Dennis puts the rest of the Christmas bomb into the freezer. He has no idea what he'll do with the massive ball of carbs, but it will keep.

He resumes his seat at the table and leans forward until his face is nearly touching Sukhin's. "Tell me something—are you guys actually dating? Or are you hovering around, silent and hopeful? *One day she'll notice me* and that kind of thing?" He stares at Sukhin, eyes wide. "Oh god, sweetie, that's it, isn't it?"

Sukhin doesn't answer. Why are people so keen on the minutiae of other people's love lives? Why not pester for details on the books they're reading or their sleeping hours? He would love to have someone ask him about his sleeping hours—he's surviving on just over four hours a night these days and is a little surprised to find he's still functioning. It would be nice to discuss this with someone, perhaps get some perspective on whether he should push this further just to see what happens.

"Can we talk about something else?"

"You know, you're a little too old for this to be cute. Can't you just tell her?" Dennis flings up his hands. "Just tell her!"

But there's nothing to tell. The summary of them is too ludicrous to say out loud, to anyone. *My ex-girlfriend now lives in a park. We meet twice a week. It's nice.* There's nothing to tell.

"We're not talking about this."

"God, so stubborn. Sweets, I know you're a lit teacher, but there's really no need to do the suffering unrequited love thing."

"Suffering unrequited love thing—you put it so well."

"And you're hopeless." Dennis eyes the blowtorch, now prostrate on the kitchen table, and raises an eyebrow. "You bring that to her party—she'll definitely pay attention."

"Shut up, Dennis."

~

There he is again.

In the distance, on an elevated portion of the main boardwalk, Jinn and the stranger are walking and talking. He's doing most of the talking, but she appears to be listening. Every now and then, she nods. Her face is calm. The stranger is an eager dog, lively and energetic and silly-looking. He moves around her as he speaks, his gestures dramatic. Today, he is dressed differently—just a shirt and jeans, but very neat. He carries a bright yellow box in one hand.

Is that chocolate? Sukhin grinds his teeth. Furthermore, what is this man doing here in the middle of a Tuesday afternoon? He doesn't look like any sort of wandering vagabond or wandering anything—that shirt looks ironed—so doesn't he have to work?

The stranger and Jinn turn around and start walking in the opposite direction. Sukhin does the same on a lower section of the boardwalk. They all walk in parallel, back and forth along the river, Jinn and the stranger oblivious to Sukhin's presence. Back and forth, back and forth. The man shows no signs of flagging and Sukhin becomes anxious.

Who is he? What is he saying to her?

By the time the stranger leaves, two hours later, Sukhin's mind is a wild and distended thing. He walks off for a bit after deciding not to follow the man, crosses the first bridge he sees, then turns around and walks back in her direction, quickening his pace. By the time he catches up, she's further along the river. He sees her bicycle chained to a bench nearby, the backpack chained to the bicycle.

"Hey." He hopes he doesn't look as frazzled as he feels.

She looks tired. "Hey, Sukhin."

Suddenly, he can't bear it any more. He bursts. "That guy you were talking to. Who is he?"

She doesn't look surprised. This surprises him.

"Just some guy." Placid, not placatory. "No one."

She's holding the bright yellow box.

Two little girls sit unsupervised in a hall with grey walls, watching the adults scurry around in quick mincing steps, some with vases of fresh flowers, some with trays of food. In a corner of the hall, their mother harasses a man in a jacket, the nice one who kindly sat the girls down earlier and gave them a bit of cake from one of the trays.

One of the girls grows bored of watching. She kicks the chair in front of her, making little growling noises. The other girl stops her. She is older; she knows why they are here. She tells the younger girl that she must behave or Grandpa's ghost will take them both away. The younger girl stops kicking the chair.

The older girl invents a quiet game for them to play. They are to guess which flower the other likes best and which flower, least. They look at the flowers in the vases around them. They consider them all.

They have the same favourite—the large, white one that they learn later is called peony. The older girl likes most of the other flowers, but her least favourite is the lily. The younger girl thinks most of the flowers look the same, but hates the one that looks like a spider, but with so many more legs than a regular spider. This, her grandmother tells them later, is the chrysanthemum, much loved by Japanese royalty since ancient times.

"Ugly," says the younger girl. "Spider."

Her sister laughs and takes her hand.

XIV

THREE HAS BEEN chucked—it lies in a corner of the living room next to Two, surrounded by cardboard scraps. Four, he thinks, Four will be it. Sukhin is so sure of this that he's already decided, even at the first phase of construction, to make it larger than its predecessors. The base will occupy six square metres and the entire thing is going to be two metres high, twice the size of Three.

The peacock sofa has been pushed against the bookshelves, forced to defer its place in the living room to Four. The coffee table is a rolling work station, crowded with boxes of tools, bottles of glue, different kinds of wire, string, thread and fishing line, balls of shredded paper—accidents have happened; its surface will no longer be the same again. The television screen is just another surface onto which sketches may be taped.

The study is a cardboard jungle. The desk is invisible, stacked high with magazines and newspapers, overrun by sketches and drawings and prototypes of mechanism parts. Boxes everywhere—piled high on the floor, on the chairs, under the desk. Very little light enters this room now.

The bedroom has put up a better defense. A clear path leads from door to bed to bathroom; a sliver of floor space remains empty in front of the wardrobe. But apart from these last bastions of order, chaos—still more things have been moved here from the study and the living room, boxes that will no longer fit in the study or living room have crept into the corners. In plastic containers that now occupy the bedside table: bits of Three's mechanism that are being saved for transplant into Four and must remain safe from accidental discard.

A single, small box has found its way into the kitchen. Otherwise, the kitchen remains pristine.

Sukhin has given up running, regular meals and scheduled sleep. He no longer fears decrepitude; he eats when he's too hungry to work; he sleeps when he's too tired to handle a blade.

He wakes up on the Sunday before Christmas without caring that it's Sunday or that it's one in the afternoon. He checks his phone—two texts from Dennis, one from his mother, one from Kim Seng, one from an unknown number, offering low-interest loans with immediate approval.

The one from Kim Seng is from two hours ago: "When u coming later? Freezer already clear."

Right. That's today.

Shower, cereal, pudding, car. Sims Avenue, car park, lift.

Kim Seng is outside his flat, arranging objects in a large shelf next to the door. "Eh, hallo. I thought maybe you weren't coming."

Sukhin watches as Kim Seng takes a packet of printer paper, a pair of old sneakers, a phone charger and a can of pickled lettuce out of a very large canvas bag and puts them on the shelf. There's clearly a system—the lettuce joins a few packets of biscuits and a couple of loaves of bread; the phone charger goes on another part of the shelf, next to a small fan.

"Sorry, woke up late." Sukhin picks up a can of tuna from the shelf and puts it back. "What's all this? Need help?"

"No need, no need—I just put everything here, then people come and take what they want. Very easy."

Sukhin takes a toy truck that has fallen onto its side and sets it upright. "But where's all this from?"

"Anywhere," Kim Seng tells him. Everything here is technically rubbish—someone has decided they don't want it and thrown it out. "But we all want different things, right?" Kim Seng regularly makes rounds of his neighbourhood dumpsters and recycling bins, looking for junk that someone else might be able to use. "Recycling isn't simple, you know—a lot of things can't be recycled. And people throw a lot of stuff that can't be recycled into recycling bins. Food also got." Kim Seng sighs and rubs the spot between his eyebrows. "A bit stupid lah, but never mind—if I see anything like that, I take it and put it here. Like this—see? How to recycle? Got metal parts joined to plastic parts and rubber parts here and here. Cannot lah." He shows Sukhin a hair dryer, pointing to its different components. "And this is still working, you know. People are so *wasteful*." He spits out the final word.

Sukhin stares, fascinated—so it's not just veggies, then. The man is some sort of junk heap Robin Hood.

"Got bigger things also. Come in lah, I show you."

Oh my stars.

Two entire bedrooms, piled to the ceiling with all manner of things. Tables, file cabinets, shelves, racks, fans, chairs. A child's toy kitchen. Another child's bicycle. CRT televisions, VCRs, fridges, vacuum cleaners. A massive coat rack. Umbrella stands. Ironing boards. An inflatable pool. Rope. Kim Seng is talking about where he found the inflatable pool—"Someone put it into a recycling bin two blocks away—these idiots don't check the label"—but Sukhin is far away. His heart races a little; he doesn't know why. There is something surreal and hopeful about all this—that, in this nondescript flat, in these two bedrooms where no one sleeps, all of these objects have been rescued by a man who has no reason to, aside from his conviction that "we must not throw good things away", and that they all wait here now for someone to come along and carry them off into the sunset.

"Eh, you okay?"

"Sorry, sorry."

Kim Seng looks at him kindly. "Yah. Scary, right? The things people throw away."

The space in Kim Seng's freezer is only big enough for three puddings. Sukhin has brought eight.

"It's okay," he tells Sukhin. "Let's take these next door—already told my neighbour we might need to borrow space."

All of Kim Seng's neighbours—everyone on this floor—are aiders and abettors of the veggie pirates, as well as regular contributors to and partakers of what he calls the Everyone Shelf. A few of them will be ferrymen on the evening of the party and all of them are donating food, he says happily. Once again, Sukhin marvels at Kim Seng's ability to mobilise people and make them do things—most people he knows can't even name their neighbours. Sukhin can't name his neighbours, not even the guy who's lived next door for two years.

Kim Seng claps him on the back. "Thank you, yah. Your friend called Gopal—she says she'll help. We're all set."

Sukhin nods. Good, good. Crazy, but good. "I'm glad everything worked out."

"Me too—we were all getting super stressed. Without your help, I don't know what we'd do."

Sukhin is embarrassed now. "Please. It's no big deal."

"But it is lah. Lucky for us your friend said yes." Another clap on the back for Sukhin. "And thanks for all the cake."

"Pudding. But no problem."

They've stowed the rest of the pudding in the freezers of three neighbours—Vijendran from next door didn't have enough space—and now they're back outside Kim Seng's flat.

Kim Seng turns to him, arms crossed. "Eh, I ask you—but don't get angry, okay? You and X—how? Got something?"

What the fuck. *You too?*

"Good friends." Sukhin puts his head through the door. "Hey, have you got anything with locking wheels? Ball bearings?"

"She's a good girl, you know. Don't mess around." Kim Seng gives him a stern look. "Wheels? Got. Ball bearings, not sure. Let's have a look."

Slightly dazed, Sukhin follows him into the flat. Threatened by the captain of the veggie pirates—now, now his life is complete.

~

He won't tell Jinn about Kim Seng's menacing *don't mess around*, but he can hear it in his head as he walks up to her. He imagines being made to walk the plank—possibly into the river right here—by the entire Free Kitchen crew while they pelt him with rotten vegetables. "These aren't fit for eating, but at least they won't go to waste now," Kim Seng will patiently explain to onlookers.

"You look tired," he tells her instead.

"I am." She doesn't say why and he doesn't ask.

They read together, under the shade of a large, canopy-like structure in the middle of the river. The words on the pages of his book swim and swim and won't settle. A curious dullness has made a nest in his head, right behind his eyes.

She tells him that it rained the night before for the first time in days. "The frogs sang all night."

He didn't notice that it rained at all last night, or that it hadn't rained this week.

"You're quiet these days, Sukhin."

"I guess I'm tired too." *And you won't tell me who he is.*

He doesn't stay long. But before he goes, he tells her that her Christmas surprise is all sorted. He's decided he will let her light one of the bombs, but he keeps this to himself.

"Going to be a blast."

The intercom buzzes, loud and slightly terrifying. The intercom! Sukhin can't remember the last time anyone used it.

"Sukhin, it's me."

Jinn! He looks at the clock. It's one in the morning. His first thought is that she's been injured or assaulted. He knows it. He's been mad not to have seen this coming, mad not to have insisted that she stay here, mad to have let her roam some stupid park full of crazy people hooligans miscreants fuckers of the first order. He runs to the intercom panel and jabs at the button that unlocks the main gate. A click and the line goes silent.

He grabs his car keys and his phone and runs downstairs—it's faster than taking the lift. He dials the nearest hospital, ready to hit the call button.

Jinn, the backpack and the bicycle wait for him at the lift lobby. None of them appear harmed. Nothing is torn, broken or blood-spattered, but Jinn looks more tired than he's ever seen her—her face strangely wooden, her head and shoulders pitched forward.

"Sorry to wake you."

"I wasn't asleep." He takes the backpack from her. His first instinct is to ask if she's just cycled all the way, three hours, tonight—but he stops himself. Of course she has; what a stupid question. "What happened?"

The expression on her face is the shadow of an old one, grim and stubborn and cold. The look she gives him is slightly, deliberately, out of focus.

She reaches out and presses the Up button. A bright, metallic ding, the lift doors open.

"Let's talk in the morning."

~

"So, tell me what you're making."

She sets down the mugs of tea and sits next to him on the floor. The light coming in from the glass door leading to the balcony is grey and soft. Sukhin has been up for hours and hours, working on Four, begging Four to work with him.

"I don't know if I'll finish it. Harder than I expected." He stares at the tangle of string and cardboard in front of him.

"I'm sorry. I'm in the way, aren't I?" She picks up a piece of cardboard and studies it. "But this was the safest space I could think of."

He watched her sleep last night and the night before, stretched out like a plank under his blanket, her face buried in his pillow, and understood what it meant to be dogged by anxiety—because, suddenly, he wasn't. He's decided he will keep her here by force if necessary and hunt her down and drag her back if she escapes.

"Feeling better?"

"Yes."

"Shall I try to find the fuckface, kill him, dismember him and feed him to crows?"

She smiles. "So dashing, Sukhin."

He takes a sip of tea to hide his scowl. "You should have told me from the start."

"I was going to. Then you stormed up and demanded it."

Smug, wicked wretch. One day, one day, he's going to bite her.

But first, first he will find the fuckface.

A student, she told him. Seminary school. Used to be some sort of marketing consultant, but saw the bright light of god one day when he missed colliding with a truck by less than a hair's breadth after falling asleep at the wheel driving home from work. Decided he would justify the rest of his life by giving it up to the great divinity that saved it, applied to seminary school, et cetera.

"Could have just started taking the bus."

"Sukhin, don't interrupt."

The rest of the story was just as eye-roll-inducing as Sukhin feared. It was as if the guy googled "mid-career change spurred by post-motor-accident revelation paved with predictable obstacles, particularly bouts of self-doubt and paranoia" and decided that he would live the cliché. The thought of Jinn enduring the unabridged version of the story filled him with an uncomfortable mixture of awe, disbelief and envy. The envy is mostly of the man, who managed to find someone to whom he could tell his stupid, dull, uninspiring tale without being stoned or laughed at, but also of Jinn, who managed to look past the ridiculousness and listen to another person go to pieces trying to make sense of some emotional, spiritual turmoil that had zero to do with her.

"But how do you know each other?"

"We don't."

It didn't make sense. He frowned. "And he just showed up one day and started talking?"

Jinn laughed.

No—and yes. She woke up one morning to find him sitting next to her, on the floor where she had laid out her sleeping mat. They were under one of the park pavilions. The sun had just risen. It was drizzling.

"How romantic. Morning light, a drizzle. The stuff of novels."

"He was taking shelter from the rain."

Right. And what kind of weirdo went to parks before sunrise?

Something to do with prayer and running, according to Jinn. Anyway, the man asked if she had spent the night at the park.

"I said yes—no reason to lie."

Stupid, credulous woman. He would have to muzzle her.

The story arc was pretty predictable from that point onwards. Religious fanatic sees woman. Religious fanatic figures out woman is homeless. Religious fanatic decides that woman is part of grand divine test of his faith. Religious fanatic tries to drag woman into safety of church, organised religion and unhomelessness. Religious fanatic persists, in spite of patient resistance by woman. Religious fanatic becomes unwelcome stalker. Woman exits.

Religious fanatic is killed by woman's ex-boyfriend and dismembered and fed to crows.

"He wasn't a fanatic, Sukhin. He really wanted to help."

"And he brought you chocolate."

She gave him a long, narrow look. "Don't be a shit. Those were biblical-verse postcards."

The tipping point, she finally told Sukhin, was when he began showing up in the dead of the night, while she was sleeping, to pray over her. She asked him to stop but he wouldn't. She was meant to be part of his journey, he told her, and he meant to press on until she realised it too. Two nights ago, he broke down, shook her until her head spun and demanded to know why she was making things so hard for him.

"So I came here."

"Should have kicked him in the balls first."

Yes, he will find the fuckface.

For now, though—lunch, laundry, supermarket run. No way he's going to keep feeding her cereal, which is all he's been eating for weeks. That, and all the Christmas pudding that didn't make the cut.

ᵚ

They've all been here since eight in the morning, dicing slicing peeling cutting chopping filleting dipping basting baking broiling. Everyone is sweaty, tired and, ironically, hungry, but spirits are high—Kim Seng, darting in and out of the kitchen in between phone calls and deliveries, manages to keep them all in a state of convivial near-panic. Sukhin is amazed at how much noise twelve adults can generate.

"Eh, where is the bag of onions? I just put it here. Just!"

"Here, here. You left it in the fridge lah. Aiyoh, so much to do...how to finish in time?"

"Can, can—don't stop, don't stop!"

"You all want kopi? I go buy. If I don't have one soon, sure KO."

"Hey guys, does three tablespoons of salt sound like too much? Seems like a lot."

"Just *taruk* lah, okay? If it's too much, we'll add coconut milk. Can't have too much coconut milk, right?"

"When was your last cholesterol check?"

Sukhin is peeling potatoes. He's been peeling potatoes since he arrived three hours ago. Every time he thinks the ordeal is over, a new batch of potatoes arrives. When today is over, he will be done with potatoes forever. *No, I'm afraid I can't make that casserole any more—took a vow on Christmas Eve years ago never to touch another spud.*

Kim Seng sets another bag of potatoes on the kitchen counter in front of Sukhin. The next time his students ask who Sisyphus is, he will bring them here and make them peel potatoes for a big dinner.

"How many sailors are we expecting for dinner?" Sukhin asks, louder than he intended.

Everyone turns to look at him. Choppers, knives, ladles, spoons stop and wait.

This is a little awkward.

"Potatoes prevent scurvy," he explains. No, not good. He tries again: "Sailors used to eat potatoes to prevent scurvy."

Stares, none of comprehension.

"On long journeys at sea."

No one says anything.

"We've got lots of potatoes here." He gestures with the peeler and tries to sound friendly. "So I'm saying, maybe we're expecting many sailors tonight. You know, because of the potatoes."

Stares slowly and carefully shift. Choppers, knives, ladles, spoons tentatively resume motion.

Kim Seng calls out, "Okay, who can take over with the potatoes?" He puts a hand on Sukhin's shoulder. "Go on, take a break."

A hand on his other shoulder. Jinn. "Come. I'll make some tea."

They drink it upstairs, among the rows of micro-greens and edible flowers that finance the Free Kitchen operations. A technician moves from pod to pod, checking the temperature controls and water levels. Another carefully prepares pea tendrils in dainty beds, each the size of a placemat, for delivery.

"Christmas Eve delivery—where the big money is," Raj told them last week.

Sukhin peers at a pod marked "micro carrots". How very, very odd—what would his grandmother think?—that a carrot barely the size of his little finger could be sold for ten times as much as a regular carrot?

Jinn touches his wrist, just for a moment. "Thanks, Sukhin."

"Sorry—I didn't mean to complain about the potatoes."

"No, silly. For everything—Kim Seng says you've been wonderful. You have."

"It's not a big deal."

"You always say that." She's done with her tea. She takes his cup, stacks it onto hers and heads towards the stairwell. "Don't say things you don't mean."

~

"Wah. That's so cool."

"Please. It's an open flame—please, don't try to touch it."

"You sure this is for cooking? Looks like something from my brother's workshop. He's a plumber."

"So just pour the brandy over and light? Just like that?"

"Yes."

~

Everything looks—well, everything looks much better than he expected. Tables and chairs have been set up along the entire back alley, along with candles, cutlery, plates and glasses. Fairy lights dangle from the rooftop edges, criss-crossing over the tables. The pirates and other volunteers have all brought portable lights and lamps from home—most of it is décor from other festivals and some rather random pieces, but no one really minds. Sukhin doesn't; he thinks the large blinking ketupat lamp and the Spider-Man desk light are brilliant Christmas ornaments—who needs stars and angels?

Someone puts on the dinner gong song. As "Perhaps Perhaps Perhaps" begins to play, that silly first line—"You won't admit you love me"—swelling over the street, the crew brings out the food: platters and platters of turkey, potatoes, curry, bread, biryani, rojak—discordant dishes for a mismatched mise-en-scène.

"They're coming, they're coming!"

It's 1909, according to his watch. Nearly on schedule. Sukhin takes the back door, in through the kitchen, past the stark, empty airwell, past Raj's office and out the front entrance of the shophouse. An assortment of cars, minibuses and vans are double-parked along the road; an assortment of people climbs out of them. Some are Free Kitchen regulars; others—staring confused at the dark, quiet row of shophouses, wondering if this has all been some very weird, mean trick—are clearly here for the first time.

This is Group Three, to which Sukhin has been assigned.

"Hello!" He isn't used to raising his voice, especially not while trying to sound cheerful and festive, but he forces himself. "Happy Christmas, everyone. Thanks for coming. Follow me—let's get you comfortable. This way, please."

Group Three begins talking all at once. No one follows Sukhin.

If hell is other people, Christmas is a very special kind of hell.

Sukhin drinks to this, from a bottle of wine stowed in the kitchen fridge among bowls of fruit, after he's finally settled everyone at the long table. The Christmas tok panjang—what an excellent idea, to have groups of ten share a set of dishes, instead of serving everyone individually. A lot less work, and at least people would talk. Well, they can talk to each other—he isn't going back out there. He drinks a bit too much, grateful to whoever brought the wine—probably one of the new volunteers, in a bid to liven things up.

By the time she arrives, he is more than a little tipsy, still hiding in the kitchen, grateful to his Christmas bombs for the excuse of checking on them and planning their grand entrance.

From the outside, a few cheers, then silence.

Gopal rushes into the kitchen. "She's here. Come, you should see this."

Sukhin follows Gopal to the back door. They stand at the doorway, leaning out for a better view. This is instinctive but unnecessary—they're already four steps above the ground, more than enough to appreciate her mastery of the art of spectacle.

A procession, slow and ceremonious, has begun on the farthest end of the alley. Thirty doll-like men and women in white gloves and jackets walk in a straight line along the row of tables, each one bearing a large cake on a platter, every cake lit with as many sparklers as it can tastefully hold. These are cakes whipped up by whimsical hands—frothy, cloud-like, some flecked with gold, some glowing with spun sugar, others topped with ferns and flowers. At the head of the procession, she holds out an architectural marvel with glistening spires, her posture regal, her smile the perfect balance of garden grin and dental advert. Her gold dress marks her out as the key player here, the proper subject of the trio who follow and document the procession—a photographer, his lighting assistant and a girl typing furiously into her phone—and the camera-wielding drone flying overhead, its red lights blinking. Every guest at every table is awestruck, silent. The volunteers have all backed up against the walls, unwilling to mar the scene.

She reaches the last table, all the way at the opposite end of the alley from where she started, and turns around to enjoy the scene she's created. A nod at her posse, and every platter of sparkler-studded dreamlike confectionery is laid onto the tables.

"Merry Christmas, everyone!" Thirty-one birdlike voices in sing-song unison.

Clapping, cheering, excited chatter as the guests contemplate the cakes. Bursting with superlatives, they declare that they have never seen anything quite so wonderful. They stare openly at her, the obvious bearer of these treats, with the same reverence regularly wasted on royalty.

All hail the queen of tarts.

~

"Sukhin."

The anger in Jinn's voice makes him spin around so fast he nearly loses his balance. Gopal takes one look at her and dashes off without a word, leaving them alone in the kitchen.

"Why did you bring her here?"

Her voice is low, but she's pale and shaking, her arms stiff at her sides. He doesn't move from the doorway. Outside, a few voices pipe up in a decent rendition of "Feliz Navidad". He steps into the kitchen and closes the door.

"I thought—you might—she's your sister."

"I know that." If looks could kill… "What were you thinking?"

Sukhin didn't know—it hadn't been an elaborate plan. Desserts were required; he knew a baker—and he wanted to see what would happen if she saw her sister again. Not that he had any clue what would actually happen. How could he? *And that's the whole point of an experiment, isn't it? No, dumbfuck, it is not; an experiment should, ideally, test a hypothesis.*

To his horror, she begins to cry. "Why did you do this?"

"I just wanted to help—" But it isn't true. He just wanted to know.

"Has she seen me? Does she know I'm here? What have you told her? Why, why did you do this?" Her voice cracks. She scratches at her cheeks, her neck, her wrists.

"I haven't told her anything. Jinn—"

"Oh Sukhin, what is wrong with you."

She takes a few steps back, away from him and the bright kitchen lights. Her weeping is animal-like, mewling and gasping and guttural.

She clenches and unclenches her hands over and over, then wraps them tightly around her neck, palms pressed tight against her throat.

He doesn't move. He didn't expect this—but what did he expect? Inviting Ping into Jinn's new territory—nothing short of chaos could have ensued, and he knew that.

"I'm sorry." He is.

She turns around and walks out the way she came, through the dark shophouse and out the front entrance.

There's a knock on the back door as he's about to follow her—the timing is so perfect that he almost laughs. It swings open and Gopal steps in. "Your turn, Sukhin. Let's light up."

Just as well—he knows he won't find her.

~

"Okay, did we get everything?"

"Let's see. Miss Teo… Photos with homeless peeps—done and done and done. Photos with organiser chief dude—done. Photos with kitchen help—done. Photos with cake, whole—done. Photos with cake, sliced—done. Yes, we've got everything."

"What about the servers?"

"Done. We've got them entering the alley, standing in a row, close-ups of the better-looking ones. We have them setting down the cakes, mingling with people. And we have that cute shot of all of them surrounding Miss Teo."

"Did you check the drone footage? All good?"

"All good. Candlelight showed up better than we'd hoped."

"Okay, great. Get all the pics and vids uploaded, send the link to the usual people. They've all received the press release, right?"

"Of course—three days ago."

"Good job. Is Eling done with the social media bits?"

~

Ping accosts him afterwards, when the guests have left and clean-up is about to begin. He stares, surprised to see her.

"I thought you'd gone."

"About to leave—just thought I'd say hi. And bye." She laughs.

"Thanks for doing this."

"Oh no—thank you for asking." She leans over, gives him a half-hug. "Merry Christmas, Sukhin. That really was lovely—and such great PR. Cakes on me, anytime."

"Thanks."

"And this." She gestures at the tables, the décor, the remnants of dinner. "How good of you to help with—this. I think—I think she would have approved."

He doesn't respond. All he can think is that she's using the past tense.

The man has not asked the woman if she is happy. He doesn't dare.

The woman has not given any thought to happiness. She doesn't care.

It has been months and months since she died. It occurred to her, at some point, that she might experience some sort of void, a diminishing sense of being anything. But there isn't a void. Quite the opposite—her heart and her days are full.

She knows that he watches her, and that he is sometimes afraid of her going away. She knows he will feel better if she promises him that she won't ever leave, but she doesn't like to make promises.

Instead, she makes him copious amounts of tea and holds his hand while they take walks together in the neighbourhood after dark. In return, he drinks the copious amounts of tea and holds her hand while they take walks together in the neighbourhood after dark.

It is, for both of them, a lot.

XV

AN ORANGE CHIFFON cake rises in the oven as he contemplates the nearly finished Four. It's his third orange chiffon—the first was an utter disaster, limp and damp; the second was fluffy but not nearly orange enough.

Four is a beauty. Another trip to Kim Seng's for a couple of parts, a few final adjustments to the mechanism—and Four will be complete.

And then what?

Sukhin isn't sure what he will do with Four once he's finished. He can't think of anyone who could use it—what use could it possibly be to anyone? He might keep it himself—why not? He designed it to be entirely collapsible, after all, so it will fit into a box and he can keep it in the study, always knowing that it's there if he wants it. Lonesome. Waiting. Hopeful.

The smell of butter reaching browning point fills the apartment, elevating it from being the place that keeps him to being the place that keeps him and *this*. This, this is why all those damned supermarkets put their bakeries near the entrance—to cast a spell on all who enter, to chemically compel everyone to buy the overpriced organic stuff and the pointless health food no one really wants to eat. *Oh, I smell brown butter; better balance it out by buying some of that vile gluten-free pasta.*

The cake looks promising through the oven door. Golden-brown, plump in its rounded mold, steadily swelling at 180 degrees Celsius—who decides that it can't be 182 instead? Candied strips of orange peel glisten on top—wait, was it a mistake to have added them before perfecting the texture? Will they alter the chemical reactions in any way? He snarls at the cake in the oven. If this turns out well, he can never make it without the candied orange—unless he makes another one without the candied orange. Tomorrow. He'll do that tomorrow.

He's looked everywhere he can think of.

This morning, he went back to Chinatown. He parked the car in the same multi-storey horror he always parked in whenever he went to see her, took the same route to the alley, hoped to see the pile of boxes somehow reincarnated. But the alley was completely empty. Not a shred of evidence anywhere that she once lived there, in a house of boxes that he once brought crashing down with a bag of tacky decorations.

Of course he will keep Four—what man gives up the light of his life? He stares in wonder at the two-metre-high cardboard structure that has taken him weeks to build, that has demanded—and received—hefty sacrifices of time, sleep and thought. Did he really build this? How? Is this what it means to be visited by a muse? Working on and on in oblivion, not caring for anything outside the orbit of the task, knowing that it is the centre of everything that gives life meaning—he hasn't felt this way in years. And now there's so little left to do. Standing on a stool, Sukhin lifts Four's roof and looks at the system of string, slats and grooves inside. Maybe he will add more ball bearings to the sliding bits.

Last night, he roamed the park in Punggol for hours. Up and down along the river, checking every bridge and every pavilion, every bench, everywhere he could think of. No sign of her. He even asked the otters.

He cuts himself a slice of cake. Good colour, inside and out. Good texture, even distribution of tiny air bubbles with no obvious pockets. He takes a bite. Ah, seven out of ten. It's light enough to justify the term "chiffon" and flavourful without being too orangey, which he hates in any cake or pudding. A bit on the sweet side for Sukhin—but a cake is a cake, and the orange peel bits help with that. When she comes back, she will be pleased—she's always liked orange chiffon.

She'll be back—all her things are here, in his apartment. It's only been two days. All he has to do is wait.

~

X's weird boyfriend-not-boyfriend has dropped by to ask if he has any more ball bearings to spare. Didn't even call first—just appeared out of nowhere. Kim Seng scans the piles of rescued furniture, trying to think of what could possibly have ball bearings here that he can extract for the guy—he's become quite fond of him; the fellow did his best to help over Christmas and X seems to like him.

"More ball bearings? What are you making?"

"Nothing."

Kim Seng pauses in mid-crawl. He's under a table, making his way towards a box of random odds and ends he's salvaged over the years. "Nothing?" Seriously? He's a little irritated. How can it be nothing? Why do people say things like that?

Sukhin sighs. "It's a project."

"Everything is a project." Kim Seng emerges from under the table with the box.

They dig through the contents of the box together. Everything is either a bit broken off something else or the remnant of something broken—antennae, brackets, hooks, handles, wheels, lids, doors and parts of toys and random machines. Sukhin helps himself to a couple of wheels and a doorknob. No ball bearings, though.

"Sorry—but if I find something, I'll call you, okay?"

Sukhin wonders if he should ask Kim Seng if he's heard from Jinn—on one hand, he'll have to endure a strange look or three, perhaps an awkward question; on the other, Kim Seng might know something.

"Thanks." Sukhin pauses. Should he ask? "Have you heard from her since Christmas Eve?"

"No." The strange look, on cue. "You two quarrelled ah?" And the awkward question.

"Yes." Sukhin looks away. No point lying about that one—Kim Seng is clearly just fishing. By now, Gopal would have said something to him—to everyone. Sukhin can imagine the lot of them discussing him, indignant on the behalf of their X.

And of course they'd be right. He deserves nothing less than righteous indignation—he ruined the evening for her, unboxed who knows what demons, drove her away from her safe places, showed himself to be a thoughtless fiend. If only someone would just punch him in the eye in exchange for her safe return, he would wash their feet with his tears and dry them with his very best towels.

"You young people—too much energy."

Kim Seng begins to lecture him on the virtues of balance—"All arguments start because people don't think about the other side in the first place, and all arguments continue because people don't listen to the other side"—but Sukhin isn't listening. Next to a shelf stuffed with old records, half hidden by a filing cabinet—is that what he thinks it could be?

He waves to interrupt Kim Seng, then points at his quarry. "May I have that?"

They spend a good half-hour moving things out of the way so they can fish it out and take a closer look. It's a hand-cranked sewing machine—

a relic from his mother's girlhood. His grandmother had kept hers for years—and Sukhin was allowed to try it once—before Aunt Lillian gave it away to the karung guni man. Ah Mah refused to speak to her for weeks.

"It doesn't work lah. And there's a whole chunk missing. What are you going to do with it?"

Sukhin kneels next to it and cranks the handle. He watches the wheels turn, lost in speculation.

"Aiyoh, you. Take lah, take lah."

~

The doorbell rings and he jumps—but it's not her.

"Let me in. I come bearing gifts."

"Go away, Dennis. Christmas is over."

"Twelve days, sweetie. So it's day four."

There's no point hoping Dennis will go away—there's a higher chance of global nuclear disarmament before the new year. Sukhin opens the door. "I don't do Christmas. This is a pagan household."

"So Happy Winter Solstice then." Dennis kisses him on the cheek. "I have wine—we'll drink to the rain deities and beg them to spare Orchard Road from floods this year." Brandishing a bottle, he shoves a large box wrapped in silver paper into Sukhin's arms and bounces into the living room.

And stops.

"Sweetie?" He hugs the bottle of wine close to his chest. "We've been teleported onto another planet, where everything's made of cardboard and no one has heard of housekeeping."

"Don't be dramatic."

Dennis' eyes widen. "Dramatic?" He raises his voice. "Dramatic? *What is this?*" He gestures at the living room, at the piles of boxes and cardboard scraps, at Four in the middle of it all. "What are you doing?"

"Nothing."

Dennis walks up to Four and circles it—once, twice. He reaches out and gingerly strokes the outer shell. "Did you make this?" He traces the edges of a few interlocking pieces of cardboard with a fingertip. "How—? Are these all individual pieces?"

"Yes."

"But there are so many!" Dennis circles Four again, frowning, incredulous. "You cut all of these by hand? All of them? There must be thousands!"

Three thousand, eight hundred and seventy-six.

"But what is it? Some sort of shrine?" He slides the door open. "A walk-in wardrobe?"

"Please, Dennis. Don't touch it." Sukhin wants to drag him away, but what if he struggles and damages Four? "Please don't touch it."

"Calm down—I'm just looking." He pokes his head inside and looks up at the network of strings, wires and pulleys. He inspects the newly installed hand crank on one of the side panels. "God, honestly, what have you got here? A torture chamber?" He shakes his head, stepping away from Four, taking Sukhin firmly by the elbow. "Tell me what's going on, sweet cheeks. What's all this for?"

Sukhin can't answer. He still doesn't know.

"Oh my god—is that our sofa?"

~

Chinatown again. Duxton Plain Park in the middle of the afternoon, around the time that they used to take their walks here. Everything is the same—the trees, the quiet, the odd loiterers.

He didn't expect to find her and he hasn't. He's walked up and down the path three times and now he's at her favourite bench. He's even brought a book. He imagined finding her here, reading, looking up when he arrived, saying, "Oh, there you are—good, you've brought a book." He'd shrug and say, "You're observant today."

Not that he expected to find her here. She isn't here. He isn't disappointed—he never expected to find her.

He opens the book but doesn't read. He studies the few people who pass.

An hour later, he leaves. Back in his apartment, he spends the next twelve hours ripping pages out of old magazines and tearing these down into strips, then rolling them into paper balls not greater than two centimetres in diameter. He falls asleep with aching shoulders.

ʍʌ

After much careful deliberation and dedicated product research, Sukhin goes to the supermarket for a dozen canisters of portable-stove fuel refills, two different kinds of instant coffee (one with sugar, one without), biscuits (plain, with fruit, with nuts, without nuts), shampoo (no sulphates) and shower gel (no sulphates), and adds these to the bags in the boot before driving down to East Coast Park. This forces him to make two trips from the car park instead of one, but Keong goes with him the second time.

"Eh, sorry, I haven't said thank you. The dinner that day—very good."

"Glad you enjoyed it."

Sukhin struggles not to pant with the effort of carrying the large sack that he and Kim Seng filled yesterday at a fruit wholesaler's. Take them all, the pirates had been told. Crates and crates of apples, all part of a two-week-late shipment that the supermarkets had rejected—the guy in charge explained that there was now no room for these because a new shipment was arriving in a few days, and no point in sending them back to the supplier in Australia because they had been written off as damages. Sukhin was aghast—marginalised fruit? Had it really come to this? *What a piece of work is man!*

When they finally reach the cluster of tents that make up the park's homeless village and stop outside Keong's, Sukhin is hot, sweaty and angry that he didn't think to bring a trolley. He scans the area, looking for her. It's unlikely that she would come here and live among strangers, but he feels better now that he's looked. No, no tall skinny short-haired very possibly scowling woman in the vicinity.

"You okay ah?"

"Yes."

"The dinner—you all work very hard, yah?" Keong gestures at the other tents. "Everyone said everything very nice. My wife very happy—got somewhere to go, can sit and eat nicely." Keong offers him a cup of water. "And my children like the cakes."

"What sort of cake do they like, exactly?"

∿

What a good idea it was to put in lights.

Sukhin sits in the belly of Four, congratulating himself. The lights are tiny, dim and battery-operated, slotted at random throughout the inner layer of the shell—not at all sophisticated, but the effect is unexpectedly pleasing. He feels like he's in a candlelit cave, much like the one he saw in that documentary on modern English Satanists—who probably use the same kind of lights, everything being made in China and all.

He's inspected the mechanism and made sure that the baskets on the topmost layer are loaded. The wires and strings are all in the correct grooves and slots, every layer connected in a loop through a system of wheels—one taken from a broken pram, two from a trolley suitcase, two from a disused handcart, the largest borrowed from his mother's old bicycle—and a series of simple pulleys made of thread spools and toilet-paper cores. Everything is anchored to a wooden bedpost, which rotates by the grace of a hand-cranked system inspired by the sewing machine he pilfered from Kim Seng's scavenged heap. As testament to this, that machine's handle is now this one's.

And now, for the moment he's lived for for the last few weeks. Holding his breath, his chest a big ball of anxiety, Sukhin reaches for the handle and turns it.

Moments later, he is smiling.

The world is a good and beautiful place.

Four works like a dream.

He takes it all apart.

He puts it back together again.

Five orange chiffon cakes sit in the fridge, each one whole except for the slice cut out of it at tasting point.

Four stands in the living room, surveying its kingdom.

The cardboard scraps, the bits and pieces, the dismembered boxes, the gutted toys and things—all gone. The tools are all accounted for, safely returned to their boxes. The refugees from the living room and study have returned to their proper places; the bedroom is itself again.

This morning, Sukhin drove to his parents' to return a few unused boxes. His father was thrilled. His mother bit her tongue.

The study, too, is back to normal—files and reference tomes back in their shelves, books back where they belong, the desk finally clear from all clutter. Sukhin sits at his desk and looks around. It's been so long since he's last sat here and actually worked that it feels like someone else's desk. Sighing, he turns on the computer.

He hasn't done a scrap of work in the last month and school starts again in three days. More than two hundred unread emails wait in his inbox. He hasn't reviewed, let alone approved, his entire team's lesson plans for the next six months. This should scare him, but it doesn't. He knows what he'll get: a humdrum pile of recycled lesson plans, with book titles, characters and authors changed and perhaps an additional word or two thrown in, everything vague and obfuscated—and, too often, unintelligible.

He downloads one lesson plan. Lynnette's. Might as well start at the bottom of the barrel.

"This lesson will cover a key passage in *Wuthering Heights*, in which the characters Hamlet and Catherine are forced by circumstances to confront each other, and themselves. Students will be asked to analyse the following passage, paying attention to how Shakespeare builds tension in the scene."

Sukhin chokes on his tea.

He shuts down the computer and makes himself a gin and tonic. It's four in the afternoon.

~

The intercom, at nearly two in the morning. Sukhin doesn't wait for anyone to speak—he knows who it is. He unlocks the gate, then goes to the door.

He opens it and waits for her. She walks up to the open doorway and stands there, facing him. He forces himself to meet her gaze instead of looking down at his feet.

"You all right?"

"Yes."

"Can we talk in the morning?"

"Yes."

Sukhin steps aside so she can enter, then closes the door behind her. He wonders where she's been, but he's not going to ask. Right now, it's enough that she's back. And that she looks calm, even if a little haggard—and grim. This is a bigger relief for him than her return, he realises.

He can handle haggard, and grim is nothing compared to the look on her face he remembers from the other night.

Like Dennis, she stops at the sight of fully-assembled Four, the elephant in his living room.

"Sukhin, it's beautiful."

Nothing could have moved him more. He takes her hand. "Come on."

They approach Four like a couple of supplicants, silent, heads bowed. He slides the door open slowly and enters, thinking how bizarre it is that his life so far has managed to lead up to this moment. She follows him into Four, shutting the door, and they sit down in total darkness. He waits a short while before turning on the lights, wanting this to last a little longer than he knows it will. In the dim, scattered light, he watches her look around, her eyes growing wide as she takes in the layers and layers of scale-like cardboard pieces surrounding them, interlocking and undulating, stretching up and up to form a vault.

"Oh, it's like an alien egg." She's grinning suddenly, and so is he.

He holds a finger to his lips, then reaches for the handle and turns it.

A whirr as the wheels turn in response and, overhead, a complex dance of strings and wires begins, setting in motion three layers of slats that now start to slide and shift from side to side, each layer built to turn and twist at a different rhythm. At the very top, invisible but ever so important, rows and rows of wire baskets tilt and tremble, shaking out their contents bit by bit into the moving layers below. Released, tumbling in all directions, these little balls of paper acquire a different cadence in every layer, falling, finally, randomly, through the last of the slats and through the air and onto

Jinn, who whispers, "A rain machine", and

Sukhin, who allows himself to kiss her hand.

"Yes."

Years ago, when they parted, she felt lost and afraid.

She took long, meandering walks and wondered why she couldn't bring herself to call him. She cannot remember now exactly what prevented her—was it just foolish pride? Inertia? It was something stupid that only the young can afford.

In a curious, roundabout way that was part cowardice and part romance, she gathered things she felt might make him think of her. A nice round stone she found on one of her walks. An old copy of Gone With the Wind. *A book of illustrated cake recipes. She put these things into a box and wrote his name in capitals on the side in black marker, exactly the way she had written his name on all his school books.*

She went to his house and left it just inside the gate, which was never locked. Then she went home and waited.

XVI

IN THE MORNING, when he wakes up, he's alone in bed and she's gone. At first, he panics. And then he sniffs—in the air: a combination of shampoo and soap and Earl Grey. Stepping out into the living room, squinting against the daylight, he finds her curled up on the peacock sofa, which remains backed against the bookshelves on one side of the room. She's drinking tea, looking thoughtfully at the rain machine. Her hair is wet, all slicked back against her head.

"You look like a sixties gangster."

"You *snored*."

Sukhin goes into the kitchen and makes himself a cup of tea, then cuts a few slices of orange chiffon number three and takes them to her on a plate. "Cake as reparations."

"Cunning man."

"I even bake." He sits down on the other end of the sofa.

"I still can't believe you made this."

He frowns. "Well, it took five tries to get the texture exactly right, but it's really not that hard. The one you're having now—it's got candied orange peel on top. I quite like it—"

"I mean the rain machine."

"Right."

In the daytime, now that all the surrounding debris has been removed, Four looks less and less like a warrior-worthy space pod and more and more like a giant curled-up pangolin—rotund, scaly, somewhat cute. This is rather unsettling for Sukhin—hours and hours of research, of poring over drawings of futuristic furniture, ancient war machines and cruel-looking medieval automata, and he ends up with a pangolin.

"It's wonderful, Sukhin." She takes a sip of tea. "Do you remember ours?"

Of course he does—what a stupid question.

They spent weeks working on it together, shut up in the drama room after school. There was a whole team working on the sets, but the rain machine fell to Sukhin and he'd already finished a made-to-scale prototype by the time she had volunteered to help with the production.

They built the frames first, out of wood, one set for each side of the stage, then the delicate bamboo beams across them. And then came the strings and things. The paper rain, Sukhin explained to the girl with the loud but oddly attractive laugh, would fall from perforated tubes strung up along the beams and anchored by the frames, rather like a complex clothesline, with four sets of strings controlling four sets of tubes, controlled in turn by two people standing on opposite sides of the framework, just off stage. Terribly simple, yes? No. While she was more than adept at the woodwork, she was hopeless at the strings. She broke them, she got entangled in them, she didn't understand how taut or not a string had to be tied and to what effect. It drove him mad.

What drove him madder was how she'd howl and fuss and sigh every time anything went wrong—such a waste of time and energy. But he stayed calm, repaired every string she broke and looked forward to 8.30 every night, when they would lock up the drama room and go to the McDonald's nearby and talk for a couple of hours over greasy fries, burgers and sundaes.

"My mother never lets me eat at McDonald's," he told her.

"I never listen to my mother," she told him.

Once the strings were done, Sukhin spent all his breaks alone in the drama room, learning how to twitch and flick and tug at the strings until he could control the rain tubes like a master puppeteer. He knew it was a silly, perfectly useless skill, but still it thrilled him to play storm god with little paper balls.

She watched him demonstrate how to make it drizzle and pour, and how to make it rain steadily, going from light to heavy by changing his grip on the strings. She was ecstatic. "That looks amazing—and we're done!"

"No, we're not," he told her. "You're part of the machine too."

It took him two weeks to teach her how to make it rain. She fumbled at the strings, knotted them up and broke most of them, and he had to fix them while she sank onto the floor and went on about how hopeless she was, how this was never going to work, how he'd better find someone else. He came very close, very often, to telling her to just shut up and keep practising.

But it finally happened one night—tugging lightly at her sets of strings, she managed to pull off an even drizzle. She looked at him, grinning madly. A little later, with a bit of a struggle, she set off and maintained a steady, insistent shower.

"Sukhin, I've got it! Do I get to say 'eureka' now? I've always wanted to say that."

He laughed, then went over to the opposite side of the set-up and started working his own strings. The entire machine came to life—strings flying, tubes rocking, a boy and a girl applying the laws of motion, paper precipitation everywhere. With Sukhin shouting instructions across the room, they joined forces to unleash a great downpour, going on and on until the tubes ran out of rain.

She ran up and threw her arms around him, and he let her. They danced around the room, laughing, triumphant. Sukhin had never danced around a room before, but that night it felt absolutely right to be absolutely foolish.

When they had danced themselves breathless, they filled up the rain tubes and made it rain again.

"Yes, I do remember it." He reaches out to take the last slice of cake from her plate.

"You were such a slave driver."

"You were a terrible slave."

"Spoken like a true slave driver."

Smiling to herself, she goes to the kitchen and opens the fridge. "I see you've been busy." She takes out another one of the chiffon cakes and begins to rummage in a drawer for a knife.

She's back, she's calm and she's eating. Watching her from across the apartment, he's struck by an immense sense of relief. The grim shadow that was on her face last night is gone, and all she wants to do right now, it seems, is have her cake and eat it while staring at the pangolin. He sips his tea and leans back against the sofa. This, this is the idyll, isn't it: cake and tea served with a side of banter, with her. And yet, now that the drama and tension he's expected and already made space for—the uncomfortable conversation, the profuse apologies and, perhaps, more of her weeping—have been wiped out, Sukhin feels strangely bereft. And cheated—yes, cheated—out of a well-deserved, crazy, cathartic showdown.

God, I'm messed up.

She's filling up the kettle. "Shall I make you another cup of tea too?"

He says yes; he thanks her. He sounds chirpy, even to himself.

Why does he want to be raged at? Because that's what he wants now, really. To have her shout at him, demand an explanation for hurling Ping into the kingdom she's acquired all by herself, the weird kitchen realm in which she's this sainted sage-pirate-chef instead of a refugee from whatever it is she's run away from. Has she really managed to shrug off that entire evening?

She hands him a mug. "Here you go."

He remembers the anguish on her face, the way she clawed at herself.

"I found some lapsang souchong in the cupboard. Smells amazing." She scans the bookshelves, then picks up the book she was reading the week before. *The Name of the Rose*. One of his favourites.

He thinks of the weeping, the horrible little sounds she made. *Sukhin, what is wrong with you.*

He stands. "I need to get some work done, okay? I'll be in my study."

She doesn't answer, already lost in her book.

"Go ahead."

Her face lights up. She stares at the handle, as if willing it to cooperate, then takes it and turns it. Seconds later, the heavens open. He watches her through the handmade rain, still trying to decide if he's more pleased or frustrated that she's returned. What is she doing here? Why did she bother coming back? And he will have to go shopping soon. *My girl, your sleeve is hanging by the grace of some divinity.*

When the brief shower ends, she turns to him, paper balls stuck in her hair.

"Let's do that again."

"Okay."

She tiptoes to refill the baskets. He decides he will get her pyjamas as well.

〰

In the dark, just an arm's length away, all she is is a soft shape. He decides it has to be now—when the sun rises and she's a woman again, he won't have the courage.

"Are you awake?"

The soft shape replies with a low, non-committal growl.

"Can we talk? About Christmas Eve." He sighs.

The blanket shifts. The soft shape turns around and edges closer. It stops just centimetres from him. It has a nose now. He turns onto his side, facing it. If he stretches his neck, he can touch that nose with his. But he won't.

"And I'd like you to tell me—why." There, he's said it.

It has eyes now. "Why?"

It's very close. He can feel its breath on his face.

"Would you be happier if I told you?"

"Yes." He doesn't know, but it could be true.

"Okay then. Tomorrow."

〰

It's 7.30 and they're sitting on the balcony, drinking iced tea and watching the sky change over the neighbourhood. Bringing out the kitchen stools and the tea and just idling here is Jinn's idea—Sukhin reads here every now and then, but mostly he just comes out to hang the laundry. In fact, he's thought of closing up the balcony and turning it into space for more bookshelves, but he's never got around to it.

It's surprisingly pleasant on the balcony. There's a nice bit of breeze, and while he can hear the neighbourhood children, the noise is far off enough that it's easy to ignore. *Maybe I'll keep the balcony.*

He turns to ask her what she thinks about roast pumpkin and leeks for dinner.

"So basically I lost my mind," she says, squeezing lemon into her glass.

Sukhin stares, wide-eyed. All thoughts of roast vegetables dissipate.

"I'm not sure how much you want to know, Sukhin." She stirs her drink with a finger. The ice cubes clink against the glass. "Or how much I should tell you. But stop me when you've heard enough." She pauses. "If I'm still going on."

The losing of a mind, she tells him, is a messy and terrifying thing. It just wanders off and can't, or won't, find its way back. "At first, I didn't realise that I'd lost it. And when I did, I couldn't lure it back."

She's nuts. The truly mad, he thinks as she talks about trying to entice her mind to return with holidays and yoga, must be able to talk about going mad like this—casually, almost flippantly. *You went to the cinema over the weekend? I went mad.*

The first time her mind wandered off was after a death.

"Yes, I know—very cliché. And actually, there were two."

The first was Isaac's. He sat next to her at work and handled the more conventional over-the-top glitzy parties, while she had ended up specialising in the bizarre end of the socialite-party spectrum.

She raises a hand. "Sshhhh, Sukhin. Yes, the socialite-party spectrum. We had a chart on the wall with numbers and everything—I made it."

"Where would Kubla Khan's pleasure-dome be?"

"Sunny with caves of ice? Pah. Level Three—closer to glitz."

The sky is dark now. The children are gone. The balcony has a light, but Sukhin doesn't turn it on.

So, Isaac. Jinn didn't know him very well, but they sometimes went for lunch together when neither of them had better plans. And then one day she went to work and he wasn't there. No one knew where he was, or if he was down with something; no one socialised with Isaac outside of the office. No one thought much about it, though everyone complained that it was terribly inconvenient, with one of the biggest parties of the year happening that weekend. After two days, their boss called the emergency contact on his personnel file—Isaac had put down his mother's number—and found out that he'd had a heart attack and died.

"A heart attack, Sukhin. At thirty-two. The man played tennis twice a week and ate salads for lunch every day. The year before, he climbed Mount Kerinci."

Sukhin makes a face. *Mountaineers.* And immediately regrets it. The man is dead, he tells himself. *Try not to be a shit.*

She went to the wake, then to the funeral. She cleared his desk and ferried everything to his sister's house. And then she took over all the events he'd been assigned. When the last of Isaac's parties was done and every bottle of Champagne signed for, she quit. She didn't know exactly why, but it definitely had something to do with not wanting to drop dead and leave behind a to-do list that started with "Check if elephants are allowed on hotel garden path".

"Wow—which hotel?"

"The Capella."

"And are they?"

"No."

She didn't go back to work. She didn't want to think. She had a thought, once, about what the world would be like if it had been her heart and not Isaac's that had given up, but she shut it down. She didn't want to think. For two months, she spent her days reading, watching television, sleeping and going to the grocery store several times a day to buy crisps and ice-cream bars.

"And then my mind started going off by itself."

"Where did it go?"

"Oh, all sorts of places, I suppose."

She would lose hours, sometimes days. She'd start reading a book in the morning and then realise it was dark outside, with no idea what had happened in between. It was usually like this, but sometimes she would come around and find that she'd done things that she couldn't remember doing. She might feel a little tired or a little hungry, or sometimes an urge to listen to a particular song, and there would be a stretch of nothing, and then she'd find herself in the kitchen surrounded by plates and plates of marmalade sandwiches, or lying in her bedroom with Bowie's "Starman" playing at maximum volume on loop. Once, she came to on one of those tourist boats with wheels, the kind that drive around the city and then into the water.

"That was somewhat fun, but I got worried—what if I found myself running across a highway, or jumping from a plane?"

"God."

"So I went to see a doctor."

At the swanky hospital that her mother insisted on, they ran a series of tests. She was made to lie still in machines, run on a treadmill, bleed and spit into a number of tubes, breathe into some sort of accordion-like contraption and then wear a helmet-like thing with wires attached to a machine.

"Very sci-fi horror flick." He tries to sound light-hearted, but it comes out leaden.

"Very. But they found nothing."

"Nothing?"

"Nothing."

The doctors said it might be stress- and anxiety-related. That's when she tried yoga. Didn't help at all. She took some website's advice and went on a cruise, on which she hid herself in her room and refused to leave—she didn't know why. And then to Bali, where she had a panic attack at a traditional kecak performance, certain that one of the players was not who he was.

"Not who he was?"

"I don't even know who I thought he was supposed to be, or who he was pretending to be. It was all very weird."

The psychiatrist said it might help if she went back to work or at least found a way to add some sort of routine back into her life.

"I looked, but none of the jobs I could do were any better than the one I'd left. Everything just seemed so lame."

She didn't go back to the hospital. She didn't get a job. She watched a lot more television than she ever thought possible.

And then her grandmother died.

She stands up. "Shall I make dinner?"

"Is that the end of your story?"

"That's all for tonight."

~

Sukhin barely survives the first day of school. The hordes. The noise. The hours.

By 12.30, when he goes to the canteen to get his tea and sandwiches, he is a raging mess. Watching him leave, muttering to himself, Mrs Chan decides she will say a prayer for him to the Goddess of Mercy when she's at the temple tonight. *Poor Mr Dhillon, why so old still never get married? His parents must be so worried.*

He eats his sandwiches and drinks his tea under his desk, with the lights turned off and his desk lamp rerouted so that he can read. *King Solomon's*

Mines again, his old favourite, worn out and dog-eared from being read over and over and over since he was about ten. Even now, its power over him hasn't diminished. Hunched over the yellowed pages under his desk, Sukhin lopes after Quartermain and gang in spirit, shielding his eyes from the desert sun, clambering up a mountain slope in his polished Oxfords. A knock on the door nearly causes Sukhin to yelp in fright. *Fuckity fuck.* His breath quickens but he stays quiet, sinking slowly into the floor. Another knock and someone tries the handle, but Sukhin has locked the door—thank goodness.

Later, two voices:

"Have you seen Mr Dhillon?" Hussein, the office receptionist. "I tried calling, but the line is engaged." He peers through the small glass panel in the door. "But there's no one here."

Sukhin remembers lifting the telephone receiver and burying it under a stack of administrative forms in November, in a fit of post-exam passive resistance.

"Not today, but I was in class all morning. Just going for lunch now." Mrs Chandra, from next door.

"There's a package for him downstairs."

"I'll let him know when I see him."

"Thanks!"

Curious—who would send something here?

~

The apartment smells of ginger, lime and a few things else. Jinn is bent over at the stove, peering through the glass lid of his largest pot. Next to her, on the kitchen counter: every bowl and plate he owns, and both chopping boards. The table is strewn with vegetable peel, seeds, ginger shavings and—guts.

"I'm making fish soup. You owe Mr Loh twelve dollars for the fish."

"Who's Mr Loh?"

"The security guard. I asked him for money and directions to the wet market."

Sukhin squeezes his eyes shut. He owes the security guard money. Will the madness stop, please?

She straightens and turns around. "It'll be ready in a couple of hours. Tea?"

She puts the kettle on. He starts washing up, beginning with the bowls.

"Granny dying—that was difficult." She opens the cupboard above the sink and takes out a box of teabags. "She wasn't ill at all. She just collapsed while gardening, and that was it."

"Were you close?" He doesn't remember her ever talking about her grandmother.

"Yes, but she wasn't one of those lovely old ladies, you know? Very old school, rather strict. Made sure we learnt to cook."

"I never knew you could cook."

"I didn't always like it. And my mum didn't want us anywhere near the kitchen—I think she always meant for her girls to be tai tais." Jinn rolls her eyes as she hands Sukhin a mug of steaming tea. "But Granny made us go over every Sunday to help cook dinner. And she taught us how to bake, so we could pitch in at the bakery if she needed to play mahjong on Sunday afternoons."

This delightful woman created the kind of posthumous chaos only soap-opera scriptwriters could calmly imagine when it was discovered, at the will reading, that she had left the bakery to Ping and Jinn, and everything else—her house on Duchess Road, the house Jinn's uncle lived in, the apartment Jinn lived in, her properties in Jakarta and Kuala Lumpur, her Hong Kong stocks, every last cent she had—to Jinn alone.

Sukhin almost gasps. "That's a lot."

"I didn't even know half of that existed."

Her uncle—and her parents—contested the will.

"They said I wasn't of sound mind. My uncle told everyone that I must have tricked Granny somehow." She doesn't sound the slightest bit bothered.

"What did Ping do?"

"Nothing." She shrugs. "Ping said she didn't want to take sides." She refills her mug with hot water, then reaches for Sukhin's.

And that was when her mind just pottered off.

She checks on the soup. "Almost done—would you like rice with this, or shall we keep things light?"

"So what happened?" He frowns.

"Tomorrow. And let's not bother with the rice."

"Why not today? I'm not planning to have you killed at dawn." He hands her a paper bag. "See? I bought you pyjamas."

"Of course—she should have just asked the king of Samarkand for PJs."

He's reading in bed when she comes out of the bathroom, frowning.

"Where's my toothbrush?"

"It's the yellow one."

"No, mine's blue."

"I threw that out this morning. Yours is the yellow one." He continues reading.

"You got me pyjamas yesterday. Sukhin, stop buying me things."

"Fine. Whatever." He holds out a hand, not looking at her. "Give me the toothbrush."

"No."

"Well, you're welcome, then."

He lies in bed after he turns off the lights and wonders if it will always be like this—a general cosiness of a level approaching domestic bliss, but never quite there, punctuated every so often by some protest over toiletries or clothes or whatever.

The soft shape rolls over and comes towards him in a sort of lengthwise shuffle. "Thank you for the toothbrush," it says. "And the pyjamas."

He smiles, knowing it can't see him.

It's stopped moving. "I can't quite describe it. Things just got weirder and weirder."

The lawyers kept calling. Her mother kept asking whether she thought she deserved everything. And she found she couldn't leave her apartment any more.

"I'd open the door and the corridor would grow longer and longer, and I just couldn't."

At first, she kept trying. It was always the same—she would open the door, and the corridor outside her apartment would stretch and stretch and stretch, not even stopping when it got hard for her to see the start of the stairwell. But when the delivery men arrived, the corridor would behave. After a while, she gave up.

"And I tried talking to Ping, many times—I'd call her at the office, and she sometimes came to see me and she'd say I mustn't be difficult, when I was so lucky." A pause. "She kept calling me lucky."

He tries to imagine what it must have been like for her, to lose her grandmother and then everyone's empathy. He can't.

"I didn't understand anything. Nothing made sense. And I kept waking up and getting the days wrong."

The soft shape comes a little closer. He turns to face it. That nose again.

"I just knew I couldn't any more. I couldn't. So I stopped, and I left."

A long silence. He wonders if it's gone to sleep.

It hasn't. "And when you brought her, when I saw her—"

It stays very still. He whispers, even though it's hopelessly silly and he can't remember if she likes Dylan Thomas and he feels like a fool, because it's dark and because he wants to:

> Never and never, my girl riding far and near
> In the land of the hearthstone tales, and spelled asleep,
> Fear or believe that the wolf in a sheepwhite hood
> Loping and bleating roughly and blithely shall leap,
> My dear, my dear,
> Out of a lair in the flocked leaves in the dew dipped year
> To eat your heart in the house in the rosy wood.

He puts his arms around it. It lets him.

They are at a café. They met here once before, and she has chosen the same table. He notes the sentimentality.

Sipping from a glass teacup, she is full of false cheer. Everything is good; everyone is well. What about him? Is everything good? Is everyone well? She watches him carefully as she tells him how very perfect life is. She waits for him to ask her questions; she wants to tell him more.

The man doesn't say much. He listens. He doesn't ask her questions.

They talk, circling each other for a little over an hour. They finish their tea. The man leaves. She watches him, wishing she dared to follow.

XVII

"ONE MORE THING, Mr Dhillon."

He's already risen from his seat and taken a step towards the door, but he turns around and sits back down. "Of course, Mrs Tay."

The principal is a fan of sustained eye contact. Sukhin isn't. And so every conversation they've ever had has involved his persistent efforts to break her visual equivalent of a chokehold, usually in vain.

"I wanted to say how pleased I am with your contributions to the school. I've been told many, many times how lucky we are to have you."

He struggles to keep from grimacing. Is the Tay being sarcastic?

"You've been here…" She breaks off the staring match to look down at a piece of paper on her desk. Sukhin takes a deep breath and blinks rapidly. "Ten years." And the match resumes.

"Yes."

"Our youngest Head of Department." She treats him to a cheerless smile. "Mr Narayan was very—passionate—in his support of you."

Sukhin nods, returning the smile with a grim one of his own. "Yes. Mr Narayan was very kind." Where is this all going?

"I've been thinking, and Mr Leong agrees with me…" She pauses and sits up straighter, then clears her throat. *God, the drama—if you weren't a principal, you'd be a third-rate soap actress.* "…that you're ready to take on a bigger role here."

What? "What?"

"We need a Director of Academic Studies."

"Mr Zahidi is Director of Academic Studies."

"Mr Zahidi is retiring in July." She holds up a hand to pre-empt an interruption. "I know that's seven months off, but I like to be prepared."

Sukhin, meanwhile, is so unprepared for this that he does something he never, ever, does with the Tay—he invites her to elaborate. "So you want *me* to be director of academic studies?"

"Yes. Mr Leong and I feel you'll be a good fit with the rest of the senior management committee." Another creepy smile. "So between now and July, you'll work with Mr Zahidi, learn the ropes…get a firm handle on curriculum planning. And we'll be sending you for advanced leadership training, of course."

By the time he recovers enough from the shock to clamber after her, she's moved on.

"…so I'd also like you to lead the GoTech committee we're setting up soon."

Mrs Tay launches into a lengthy explanation of the need to emphasise technology adoption at a higher level at pre-university "because we live in such a fast-paced world". Her eyes continue their relentless gaze—"It's like she's trying for spontaneous telekinesis," Dennis once remarked—and Sukhin's head begins to pound. Did she actually say "fast-paced world"? And what is this GoTech crap? He hears her say something about tablets, and then something else that ends with "…interactive videos for English literature lessons."

He rocks in his chair to destabilise it, then pitches himself and the chair forward.

~

Where are the bloody scissors?

Sukhin puts his cup of tea on his chair for a moment while he reaches up and rummages in his top drawer. He wonders if the packet of biscuits is worth all this ridiculous blind fumbling. Yes, it is—he's starving. Wait. So is it worth even more, then? Is it, perhaps, worth the risk of standing up, looking into the drawer, locating the scissors, grabbing it and then sinking back to the floor? Just five seconds should do it—but what if someone sees him and comes in?

He should live on the wild side, like Alice, head of the Maths department, who's put up a calendar over the window in her office door.

"Wah, Alice, can do like that ah?" In the pantry earlier, over curry puffs left over from someone's birthday party, Tat Meng came right out and said exactly what Sukhin had been thinking when he first noticed the white card blocking her window.

"Who says cannot?"

Tat Meng and Sukhin looked at each other, nodding. Okay, fair. Technically, there were no rules governing the transparency levels of door inserts.

"But if we're allowed to do that, everyone would do it."

"So if everybody do, you do. Nobody do, you don't do." Alice sighs. "You two ah. Are you sheep, or are you men?"

He's worried he might be a sheep. Meek, indecisive, useless without a guy with a stick. Here he is, damned with eating biscuits under his desk because he doesn't have the gall to break an unwritten rule on school office doors. Here he is, hiding, instead of openly telling people he'd rather not speak with them. And later, he will go home and spend the rest of the evening—like he's done every single evening for a week—trying to decide if he shouldn't just drag Jinn to a doctor.

"Have you had any…episodes since you left?" he finally asked her last night, after deciding, after much deliberation, that the word "episode" wasn't too much of a euphemism.

No, she hadn't lost a single day since that morning when she put a bag over her head and left her flat.

"You put a bag over your head?"

"So the corridor wouldn't recognise me. How else could I have escaped?"

Straight-faced, she speared a slice of carrot with her fork and popped it into her mouth. No doctor would assume she was joking—and Sukhin can only hope. He turns on his desk-lamp-turned-under-desk-lamp and begins going through the notes for his next lesson. Surely everyone's a little mad? How mad does one have to be in order to be properly mad? He's talked about this in class so many times, but in a strictly *Hamlet* universe—and now when he looks at Jinn and thinks about everything she's told him, all the verse, all the arguments, just fly from him.

So basically, I lost my mind.

But has she regained it? Is the madness quite firmly a thing of the past, or is it an evolving part of her? She has said nothing about recovering—but that could be because she's recovered. Is that even the right word? Do people recover from madness? He's heard stories of people recovering from trauma, from conditions like post-traumatic stress disorder, but is that the same thing as recovering from mental illness?

Are people mad if they say they're mad? Or even *because* they say they're mad? *To define true madness, what is't but to be nothing else but mad?*

His leg has fallen asleep.

I'm the teacher who spends all my breaks under my desk, hiding from my students and my colleagues.

And I've been asked to be Director of Academic Studies.

It's a mad, mad world.

~

She isn't home. Not stretched out on the floor or on the sofa, reading. Not world-watching on the balcony. Not messing up the kitchen or making tea or drinking it. Not in the bedroom or the study or the bathroom. Not hiding in the rain machine—he checks it twice.

Okay, she's gone out.

He puts on a Lou Reed record, surprised to find himself so calm. He takes a deep breath to check—yes, perfectly calm. People can become accustomed to anything, he realises—in his case, to the impulses of a self-declared madwoman and the capriciousness of life lived with her. Any moment now, she might come through the door and tell him that she's found a—a boat that will take her to Bangladesh, to a commune where she'll spend the remainder of her days meditating and planting rice. Or that she's going to help set up the local chapter of a guerilla eco-terrorist group. Or that she's going to go to live under the pedestrian bridge near the Esplanade.

And it will be all right—he'll poke his nose into things as far as she will allow, then he'll hang out at the margins, just in case.

Easy.

Not so easy: figuring what he's going to do with this appointment that the Tay has decided to favour him with. Unperturbed by his collapse in her office yesterday, which he blamed on a dizzy spell before pretending to stumble about and out of the room as quickly as a nausea-ridden man can be expected to, she sent him an email afterwards and accosted him today right after the morning assembly.

"Mr Dhillon, I'm surprised you even have to consider."

"It's a great responsibility." He put on his gravest expression.

She pinned him down for a few seconds with a thumbtack stare but looked less irate as she reminded him of the deadline she had set out in her email. "Tomorrow, Mr Dhillon. Let me know at the end of tomorrow."

Sukhin doesn't understand why him. Especially as he's the only one who would turn the promotion down—not that the Tay knows this. She probably assumes, like everyone else will, that he's immensely flattered by this and is now busy counting the years until he takes over as Principal. He shudders—if that's where he's headed, he will throw himself off the balcony.

It's raining. He looks out the front window and hopes she'll be back soon. Did she bring an umbrella?

Wretched woman. Where is she?

ᴍ

The day guard jumps. On his phone screen, the host of a Japanese variety show urges two juggling contestants to *come on, try another pumpkin.*

Another sharp rap on the door of the security post. The guard looks out the glass window. It's raining too hard to see clearly, but there's someone right outside. He opens the door.

It's the sour-faced man. Mr Dhillon. #04-03. He's under a large black umbrella, his glasses completely fogged up.

"Hello."

"Ah, hello."

"Sorry, but have you seen my friend?"

"Your friend?"

"Woman. Short hair. About this tall." Mr Dhillon holds up a hand, knife-like, to his cheekbone. "I think you told her where the wet market is, sometime last week."

Ah, yes, that nice lady. "She went out around three."

"Did she say where she was going?"

The guard gives Mr Dhillon an incredulous look. Who ever tells the guards where they're going? "No."

They both turn to look at the clock on the wall. 8.15. 8.16.

"Raining lah, maybe she stopped somewhere."

"Thanks, Mr Loh." Mr Dhillon reaches into his pocket and hands the guard an envelope. "And here's the money I owe you. Thanks."

The guard stares, first at the envelope and then at the retreating rain-blurred figure. It's the first time Mr Dhillon of #04-03 has called him by name.

Just before nine, the door opens and she walks in, cheeks flushed, swinging an empty bag. He looks up from his book, frowning. She's wet through and dripping all over the floor. He growls, but only in his head, *It's late, where have you been?*

"Go shower and put on some dry clothes."

She sniffs appreciatively. "That smells lovely."

"Chicken and leeks."

"Sounds delicious."

"You're not getting any until you've showered and changed. Look at you." He does, and she's glowing, radiant with some secret, metaphysical joy. Would he ever return home at the end of the day, after a day of classes and meetings and lesson plans, looking like this? "You're mopping all of this up later, you know."

She pushes the wet hair from her forehead and grins. "It's just rain, Sukhin. Just water." Her tone is indulgent.

He mops up while she showers, wondering if madness is the secret to all his problems. If he were mad, he wouldn't have to avoid anyone—

they'd avoid him. And mad people aren't good candidates for Director of Academic Studies, so that would be out of the question. Or, if he were mad, he'd accept—and not think about how bizarre it is that the man who cannot quite teach will be responsible for the entire curriculum.

"I've been thinking that perhaps I should stop," he tells Jinn over dinner. "I'm not much of a teacher."

"Would not being a teacher make you a better human?"

"I don't know. I don't know what else I would do." He doesn't, and he doesn't.

She steals a forkful of leek from his plate. "Well, would not being a teacher make you want to be a better human?"

"I don't know."

She puts down her fork and puts her hand on his. "You must think carefully about this."

He stares at her hand. "Okay."

"People aren't like otters." She speaks slowly, measuring out every word. "An otter doesn't have to try to be a better otter. It can just be, and it will be the best otter that it can be. But if we don't try to be better humans, we start becoming worse humans." She gestures with her fork. "A gift and a curse."

"I wish I were an otter."

She nods sagely. "Yes, and you'd be an adorable snooty thing. We've talked about this before, Sukhin."

The neighbourhood dogs have struck up an impromptu concert. From the big house at the corner, from the unit upstairs, from other houses and apartment blocks on other streets cutting across Sukhin's, the members of this canine choir know their parts—each individual bark is pitched for maximum effect;

every bark combines with the others to create the most jarring cacophony possible; every new volley of barks begins just as the one before it ends.

Sukhin and Jinn lean over the balcony railing. A dog walking a man struts down the road, its nose in the air, pointedly ignoring the performance.

"Definitely not a sheep," Sukhin mumbles.

The dog goes up to a gate and wags its tail at the two larger dogs behind it.

"Look at it, trying to make friends." She gestures with her mug.

"It's taunting them. Look—obviously, it's saying, 'You may bark yourselves hoarse you're inside I'm outside my tail's nicer.'"

"You'd be a snooty dog. How surprising." She rolls her eyes. "Anyway, you'll ask around?"

Before the canine concert began, she asked if he would mind asking his colleagues for old textbooks. She and Kim Seng are collecting them to give to some of the Free Kitchen regulars and the families at the beach.

"Isn't there a government assistance scheme that gives out free textbooks?"

"Not to junior college kids."

"Oh." He felt guilty for not knowing this and was relieved when the barking began, disrupting his thoughts.

"Sure, I'll ask tomorrow." He'll put a collection box in the pantry, maybe send an email around.

"Thanks, Sukhin."

He thinks about the veggie pirates, the soup kitchen, her latest collection efforts at the wet market two streets away. And now this textbook drive.

"Did you have a plan, when you left? Did you know what you wanted to do?"

"No."

"No clue at all?"

"No."

She takes his mug and goes inside. He follows her. "And the note?"

"I needed Ping to know I was leaving because I wanted to." She opens a tin on the kitchen counter and helps herself to a slice of the cake he made yesterday. Pineapple upside-down—his Aunt Lillian's recipe.

"Did it matter?" He hands her a plate.

She looks thoughtful—but it isn't clear if she's thinking about the cake or the note. "Delicious—you've added something different to this one." A cake-filled pause. "Yes. Everyone was calling me insane—I wanted her to know that I understood what I was doing."

I love you. I've tried to cross the space between us, but I don't want to any more. So I will turn it into a chasm. I'm leaving. I take nothing with me, and I leave nothing behind. I can't talk to anyone because I will only say terrible things. I must go. I'm not coming back—count on that. Forgive me for what I do.

"But at this point you were losing your mind? I added some thyme."

"Well, yes." She laughs—he doesn't expect this. "Sukhin, if you're trying to make sense of all of this, don't. I just didn't want to be labelled mad. Not by her."

He remembers something else she said, that day when she told him about the note. "And you wanted them to think you could be dead?"

"Yes." She's started on another slice.

"But why?"

"Lovely flavour." A big bite. "All proper tragedies end in death. It's the final-final thing."

"But you're not dead."

"But I'm not alive." She pauses. "Either way, it can't be proven. As long as they don't find me, I'm like Schrödinger's cat."

"So you're neither dead nor alive, and also equally dead and alive." *And you're neither a cat nor a wave particle,* he wants to add but doesn't. "So what now?"

"I'm waiting." She doesn't elaborate. She starts to talk about whether the textbook drive should include novels as well, even the dreadful vampire-romance variety, because "we shouldn't ignore books teenagers actually want to read, right?"

Utterly baffled but unable to ask her to please, please tell him what she's waiting for, Sukhin goes for a run.

ᨓ

"You can't not take it."

"But what's the point?" Sukhin unlocks his office and stares at the stack of printed lesson plans on his desk. They're three weeks overdue, but he hasn't had the strength to start. "Dennis, go away. I've got work to do."

He sits down, tired and irritated. How does Dennis even know about the Tay offering him the role? So much for her going on and on in her email about how this was all meant to be strictly confidential. He's written to ask her for another week to think about it, citing Head of Department responsibilities that can't be put off. Not a lie—he gives the lesson plans a long look—but he wishes he had just gone up to her office and turned down the position.

Why doesn't he? What is he waiting for? Alice is right. What a sheep he is.

He never wanted to be Head of the English Department—but here he is, three years on, trying not to fuck up too badly. What difference would it really make to accept the role the Tay is practically forcing on him, take the extra money and spend another few years trying not to fuck up too badly? If he has to choose between mundane and mundane with more money, the choice is obvious. But maybe he should dream beyond mundane and mundane with more money? But wouldn't everyone think it awfully weak and unambitious of him if he turned it down? This bothers him much, much more than he ever thought it would. He disappoints himself—why does the respect of people he doesn't actually like even matter? But it does. Oh, to be an otter.

"Sukhin, are you okay?"

"Yes. Sorry."

Dennis drapes himself over the chair across from Sukhin's, his legs over one of the arm rests and his head thrown over the other. "Sweetie, you have to take the job. Or someone lame will pounce on it." He turns to face Sukhin. "Just think—you'll be on the *inside*."

"The inside of what?" He wishes the lesson plans were on the inside of a furnace.

"Who cares? You'll know everything."

"I don't want to know everything. And it's Director of Academic Studies, Dennis, not Chief Spy—you have that one sewn up."

Dennis waves this off. "One day, you could stage a coup. Bring down the Tay. Bring down our enemies. Bring down—Ken."

Sukhin raises his eyebrows at the mention of Ken. "I see you have this all planned. So how will I do all of these really fun things?"

"Stop asking me questions. Use your imagination, sweets."

"Fine. I'll be in the inner circle. I'll orchestrate a scandal, then stage a coup. I'll turn this school into a mob co-op."

"You take care of the senior management team. I'll work with the peasantry."

Sukhin laughs, then sighs. Must every conversation degenerate into a farce? "Dennis, seriously. I really don't know about this role."

"Why? We have nothing to lose but our chains!"

~

It is nearly five. Most of the other teachers will have gone home by now, and the ones who haven't are likely to be trapped in class. Staring at his empty glass, Sukhin decides that he will venture into the pantry for a refill—and he should hurry, before the last period ends.

As he's about to enter, he stops. Someone has just said his name.

"But why Sukhin?"

He is just out of sight, just beyond the door frame. Should he stay or should he go?

"Probably the safest choice. I mean, look at him."

Who is this fuckface? Okay, he should go. Turn around quietly and go back to his office.

"Safest? Heh. You mean he's bulliable."

"Totally—Mrs Tay and Mr Leong get an extra vote for their agenda every time the committee has to vote on anything. Of course they want him!"

"He's not so bad lah. He'll stand up to them." This sounds like Renchun.

"Hah. You think because he's this angry weird dude, he'll stand up to them? Please lah. He'll just sit back and enjoy the easy life." This is Ken.

"Yah. And then later on, he'll be safest choice for VP."

"Huh. I can't imagine Sukhin as Vice-Principal."

"No need to imagine. It's always the quiet, pathetic, zero-backbone type that gets all these promotions. Everyone just feels safer around them." *Just who is this venomous fuckface?*

"I can be like that! Why didn't anyone tell me earlier?"

Laughter. Sukhin backs away from the door, his face flushed with shame and anger. Shouldn't have eavesdropped, didn't need to hear any of that. He touches his forehead. It's cold and clammy, and his head hurts. He goes back to his office and locks his door, then sits in the dark, under his desk.

By the time he leaves, it is dark outside. No one else is around. He cycles home thinking of the scene that greeted him last night—Jinn milling about the kitchen, cooking with unruffled, no, unruffleable calm.

He opens his door to find her milling about the kitchen, cooking with unruffleable calm.

"Come, Sukhin, taste this." She holds up a spoon. "We made tomato soup at Rowell today. Imagine—hand-pureed tomatoes, basil, coriander."

He goes to her.

This isn't madness. If it is, it's a far, far better thing to be.

A year after her death, the man makes the woman a kite.

It's an onion. Virulent green layers puff out in the wind, causing it to dip and rise and dip and rise. It is unstable, unwieldy and ugly. Children point and ask their parents what it is. So far, no one has said "onion".

The man and the woman spend hours flying it on the same field where they once flew kites as bright-eyed twentysomethings. The field has shrunk to make way for some concrete monster, but it is still green as green can be. Their onion looks like a runaway tuft of grass.

This makes the woman giggle like an idiot.

The man says nothing. But his heart is as light as their onion.

XVIII

THIRTY-EIGHT MINUTES and thirteen seconds today, from the time he enters the bathroom after his run to getting his bicycle to the back of the gardening shed. What the fuck—weeks of running every bloody morning and cycling every bloody evening and not even a thirty-second improvement? Fine. He'll take seventeen seconds for now, but this—he glares at his bicycle—is not over.

The canteen is crowded, as always, with loitering students, but the regulars at the drinks stall know better than to get in the way of Mr Dhillon and his first teh si gao kosong. The infrequent customers, the more casual partakers of caffeine, are quickly shooed aside by Mrs Chan, as much for their well-being as for Mr Dhillon's convenience.

Sukhin's cup of tea is already waiting for him on the counter. As he takes it and turns to go, Mrs Chan says for the nth time, "Your cake very good, Mr Dhillon."

Unknown to Sukhin, the pineapple upside-down cake he presented to Mrs Chan three days ago has become for her A Very Big Deal. It dominates every single one of her conversations; it has been described in eye-watering detail to every one of the other stall-keepers; it has been declared the best cake she's ever had. Sukhin himself has been elevated in status, from That Handsome Teacher Who Isn't Married Yet, Poor Thing, to That Handsome Teacher Who Is So Kind But Isn't Married Yet, Why Are Women So Picky, He Can Bake Like An Angel.

"I'm glad you like it, Mrs Chan." Also for the nth time, before he runs off, but after he decides he will bring her a different cake next week.

Also unknown to Sukhin, it is the second cup of tea that Mrs Chan has prepared for him that he carries lovingly to his office—the first, which had a spot too much milk in it, was quickly dispensed to someone else. And so it is this second cup that Sukhin relishes in the silence of his office as he rereads the notes for his first lesson of the day, that he knocks over, just missing the pile of unread, unreviewed lesson plans.

"Oh, fuck. Fuck fuck fuck fuck fuck."

He jumps up and back in time to save himself the ignominy of walking around for the rest of the day in tea-spattered trousers, but that is all—tea is everywhere. A large pool forms in the middle of the desk, from which a stream begins to flow towards Sukhin, who now makes frantic grabs at random things within reach. A dam. He must make a dam. A stapler, a ring binder, a few admin forms, an old issue of *Time*, and then the entire stack of lesson plans. Thankfully, the dam is a success—it cuts off the stream and contains the tea, lake-like, within it. He steps back to survey the damage. Appalling. How does half a cup of anything cover so much ground? Everything on his desk now has tea on it.

No. Next to the dam, in front of him, there is a thin, rectangular package—this is clean and dry. And addressed to him. And utterly alien. Sukhin doesn't recognise it, but staring at it in bewilderment does not make it disappear. It only stares back. Sukhin doesn't move, feeling like a character in a very bad horror movie. Or a third-rate student composition: "Suddenly, a package appeared before him. His name was on it. He knew it had to hold the clue to the mystery. A voice boomed, 'OPEN IT.'"

The bell rings for assembly.

Sukhin jumps. With some effort, he gathers his tea-besmirched lesson notes and leaves his office. He checks, twice, that the door is locked, then rushes to the school courtyard. His form class is surprised to see him late—he's normally there before they are—but they know him well enough not to comment. At the best of times, their Mr Dhillon is patient but exacting, kind but difficult to please. Right now, he looks like a caricature of himself at his worst—brow deeply furrowed, lips pressed tightly together, jaw clenched, eyes firmly fixed on the middle distance. Sukhin doesn't bother taking attendance; he doesn't hear their muttered good mornings; he drifts absently to his first lesson in the classroom block farthest away from the courtyard, for the first time barely registering the hectic post-assembly clamour of students rushing in every direction, chattering loudly, filling the air with the unabashed inanity of youth.

It strikes him only as he's about to enter the classroom that the explanation for the package isn't at all mysterious, but disappointingly banal. On his way out of the Tay's office two weeks ago, after he managed to bring his chair down, someone had passed him something saying something—this must be that something passed; for the life of him he cannot remember the something said. He must have put this on his desk, then printed out those lesson plans and put them over the package without even noticing it. Unsurprising—he mostly worked under his desk last week, after all, while he struggled with the worst case of start-of-term blues he'd ever had.

He's still struggling with the worst case of start-of-term blues he's ever had, but it's getting better. He's survived a few staff meetings, a consultation with a group of students and a short but intense discussion with the Tay on the requirements of being Director of Academic Studies, in which he managed to stall for more time while appearing to be keen on the role, though it mystified him, even while he was talking to her, that he couldn't just thank her, decline and walk away. But he couldn't, and he can't, because it keeps springing back on him, clawing at him, the thought that *Of course I must take it. Only fools turn down promotions.*

If he could only leave out the "of course", it would be decided.

"Mr Dhillon?" A student pokes her head out the door, a quizzical smile on her face. "Are you okay?"

He's been standing outside the door, in full view of the entire classroom, for fuck knows how long. He must look utterly mad—ah well, by the time the lesson is done, who knows what else they will think? He isn't sure he cares. "Yes, Anne. Thanks. Sorry. Coming in now."

Sukhin nods at the class as he enters, mumbles good morning, then steps up to the projector. He looks at the students, at their young, open faces, and is filled with envy. *You have no idea yet what you'll do, what you'll want to do, and that's okay—and you expect everything and nothing, and that's...perfect.*

He dives into the introduction he's prepared, before his mind has a chance to wander off. "Last year, we did quite a bit of poetry—mostly classics, the big names, lines of poetry that will jump out at you over and over again all your lives, in novels and plays and films and songs and even adverts."

He places the piece he's chosen for today's lesson on the projector but doesn't turn it on.

"This year, let's listen to other voices. It's too easy to forget these when you're doing your A-Levels, but trust me—you will be better readers if you allow yourselves to venture a little further than the syllabus, the required readings, the canon." There is much more he'd like to say, but he won't. They're young, and he will sound far too old. All he allows himself is:

"The older I am, the more I regret the distances untravelled. And the boundaries I let people convince me were there."

A stillness settles over the room as Sukhin studies the students, disconcerted by what he's just said because it's so funny and cliché and stupid and true. The students study Sukhin, their faces comically serious. They aren't used to personal revelations of any sort by Mr Dhillon, but they can tell this is a Big One. Sukhin smiles at their gravity—it's like being in a parody of one of those awful inspiring-teacher movies, though right now, for the life of him, he can't remember a single one. Whatever.

"I thought we'd start with something local, so I've chosen this untitled poem by Cyril Wong." Sukhin turns on the projector, then adjusts the focus to sharpen the text. He's copied this one out by hand and it feels a little odd to see his own handwriting looming large on the wall, but he ignores this and starts to read out loud.

> We are in the same car, two men
> making out in a deserted alleyway.
> As we grope and cling, the car
> rolls, we fail to care, half-suspecting
> it is our kiss propelling the vehicle
> out into the street. Behind you,
> I see my parents on the sidewalk
> fainting comically to the ground
> at the sight of us, a wrist to the brow.
> I want to laugh but I cannot do so
> with my tongue in your mouth.
> The car seems to know exactly
> where to go. More people seem to drop

as we drive by: Father Arro
who told me God existed by virtue
of trees and the sun's rise and fall,
every teacher who favoured us
for busting our asses to please them,
the rest of your family who have
yet to learn about us. They collapse
in spite of themselves. Buildings
are starting to sway too as we pass.
Soon the Parliament House is
caving unto itself. I watch
the Merlion wobble and topple
into the river with an unimpressive
splash. Churches, flats and malls
shudder to rubble in our wake.
Somehow we are still kissing,
you with your eyes closed, mine
wide open, as our ride takes us
to a shore and straight into the sea.
We are unable to stop kissing,
as waves gorge on our car,
darting fishes or an occasional
squid bouncing off the windshield.
We stop when we reach a world
where no person or building may
fall at the spectacle of our embrace.
I think we are almost there. Already,
the car is filling with water, warm

as saliva in a lover's mouth. We
soar across a galaxy of plankton
undistracted by our kiss, water
rising intimately around our necks,
our destination so close we can
taste the ocean on our lips.

When he's done reading, the silence is heavy. Sukhin feels it against his chest and in his belly. The students are busy figuring out how they're expected to react. Some stare alternately at him and the projector screen, unable to conceal their shock. Most of the class are rereading the poem, frowning, scrutinising every line. Is this really a poem about two men kissing? Is there a joke somewhere they're missing? A complex, satirical metaphor for cronyism? A few students lean back in their chairs, carefully arranging their faces into imitations of the most blasé expressions they've seen on television.

Sukhin tackles the elephant in the room by his massive tusks. "So. Why would anyone find this poem shocking?" He pauses to make sure he has their attention. "What shocks *you*? Why?"

ᵥᵥ

His desk is tea-free again. A mountain of paper towels lies sodden in the bin. The stack of lesson plans is in there somewhere too, wiped out by the flood.

There is a divinity that shapes our ends, rough-hew them how we will.

Sorry, he imagines saying to his team at the next department meeting, *I'm not reviewing any lesson plans this term. Tea or water, a flood is a flood. I'm not particularly religious, but I'm not going against any divinity, just to be on the safe side*. Sukhin smiles. Could he get away with it? They all think he's weird enough; this probably won't change things much.

Well, if he gets away with making a class of seventeen-year-olds read and discuss a poem about two men kissing in Singapore, wrapped in the same breath and rhythm as the Parliament House and the precious Merlion, he can get away with anything. And if he doesn't, then the lesson plans—and the Tay's poncy-sounding new job—won't matter anyway.

Sukhin picks up the mystery package formerly thought of as the parcel from hell or proof that he's being observed by a network of spies. The envelope is heavy white card, too heavy for figuring out the contents just by feeling it, the kind of envelope wedding invitations used to come in back in the eighties, when they were all delivered by hand. He recalls his parents' friends arriving at the house, presenting the stiff envelope over tea and cake, adding some glamorous titbit about the wedding—the groom insisting on Raffles Hotel, or the wedding dress costing "as much as our first house, haha"—and his parents gushing appropriately at intervals. But this isn't an invite—it's far too large and there's too much bulk to it. *What the hell is this?* Sukhin rolls his eyes. Is he so desperate for drama? He tears it open.

A book. Weary, dog-eared, JINN on its cover in black marker. Her notebook from junior college, filled with random lesson notes, funny quotes, nonsense doodles and badly drawn caricatures of their teachers and friends. He flips through it, frowning and smiling, suddenly seventeen again.

And a letter. From Ping—of course, he should have known. The letter is both warm and cold, friend-ish but not friendly, an unstructured tumble of thoughts and information in a delicate, looping script. They are finally packing up her things, Ping writes, never naming "her", and she thought he might appreciate a memento. There's an obituary coming out soon, she adds, to close things off properly. She wants to be the one to tell him. "You loved her too"—this, buried somewhere between a brief mention of a memorial service to which he is not invited and something trite about how it's time everyone moved on, is the sum of their bond, and he's suddenly moved by this strange, second-hand connection that has compelled her to reach out like this. And just as suddenly, he is struck by some nameless emotion, wedged between remorse and pity, because he can't write back and tell her that Jinn is alive and safe.

The last paragraph is odd.

"This is the end, I suppose—I wish she knew there won't be any chrysanthemums. Little one, I'm doing the flowers myself."

He folds up the letter and puts it in his pocket, where it remains for the rest of the school day. Patient and still, it sits there as Sukhin reads the poem about two men kissing in a car to another class, and then another. It snuggles against his thigh as he talks about the poem, after the first class, with two students keen to find out what other voices Sukhin will share with them this year. It listens as a boy comes up to Sukhin after the second class and whispers a hasty thank-you and then cries; it waits out the awkward silence that follows. It rests, safe in his pocket, as Sukhin drinks another cup of tea at three-thirty, this time carefully setting the paper cup down on his desk before turning his attention back to the letter. It allows itself to be unfolded, so he can read it again.

He doesn't quite understand. An obituary? A memorial service? Is this one of those faddish closure rites dreamt up for people who want to cut ties with family members? *We didn't want an alcoholic in the family, you know, so we sent him off and had a memorial service. The agency we hired to close things off even did up an "obituary" for us, to put in the papers. You know, we want everyone to know this man isn't family any more, that kind of thing. All very tasteful and organised.*

When he shows her the letter, Jinn isn't surprised or confused. She reads and rereads it, nodding to herself, smiling. "She knew exactly what to do."

She tears the letter up, scrunches up the pieces into little balls and adds them to the rain machine's hoard.

"In two weeks, Sukhin, I'll be dead. Finally." She laughs. "I hope she'll use a nice photo for the obituary."

ɯ

Later, over dinner, she explains, very briefly: "It's been seven years, so now I can be declared legally dead. And that's what they're doing."

"And before?"

"Just missing."

"Legally dead? You mean in all public records and all that? Can people do that?"

"Yes."

"And what's next?"

"I die." She ladles gravy onto her plate. "You're the lit teacher, Sukhin. All tragedies end with death and maybe a funeral. And, in my case, the rightful division of property." She smiles. "Tell me, what comes after death?"

He has no idea. He looks at the smiling woman across the table, heaping mash onto her fork, talking about dying the week after as if she's talking of cake or dinner—no, far more casually than she would talk of cake—and he wonders how this has become his life. He wants to tell her that nothing matters, really, but her being here. That when she dies, he would like this—his life, his home, everything that surrounds them now—to be her grave. He imagines her saying, *God, Sukhin, how morbid.*

So instead he folds his arms and smiles ruefully. "Are we going to talk about the afterlife over Guinness stew? Really."

"No." She laughs. "Though it's really very good—you must teach me how."

He finds himself starting to talk about browning meat, then about caramelising onions, and in his head he is thinking,

This is enough. For me, it is enough.

He hopes it is enough for her. He asked her, weeks ago, if she was ever frightened, being alone, living on the streets. She was slicing apples for pies to take to the East Coast Park families; he was helping her prepare the dough.

"Yes. At the beginning. But it didn't last—after a while, I realised I needed very little. A bit to eat, somewhere to clean myself, something to sleep on, space to think, a couple of books. I was okay."

"You weren't afraid of being robbed, or attacked?"

"No. I didn't have anything to steal, really." She ate a slice of apple and reached out to feed him one. "And I stayed out of everyone's way. No one notices us, Sukhin—people pretend that we don't exist. No one's supposed to be homeless here." She didn't sound enraged or upset.

Sukhin felt ashamed and uncomfortable. He supposed he was "people" in this case, not "us". He helped whenever he could, at Rowell and at East Coast Park, ferrying food and Jinn and running errands, but he couldn't pretend he was doing it for any reason but her. He wasn't eyebrow-deep in things, the way Jinn and Kim Seng and Gopal were—they were talking lately of buying a second-hand van and starting a mobile soup kitchen. They sat at his kitchen table and did sums and argued and laughed and drank crazy amounts of tea, and he watched them from the sofa, pretending to be lost in his books.

"You guys are incredible," he said, shaking his head.

They understood what he was really saying. They laughed. "What to do, Sukhin? We have too much free time." Kim Seng winked, and they all laughed again.

By the end of that evening, battling a severe case of reverse schadenfreude, Sukhin had agreed to help hunt for the van and drive it once a week. It was so ridiculous, so haphazardly planned—and so unlikely to succeed, so why not? And he couldn't help but be caught up in their whirlwind, even if they seemed so happy to leave so much un—that was it, though, just un. Undone, unplanned, unaccounted for. He didn't know if he envied them more for their devil-may-care glamour or their joy in it.

She seemed to read his thoughts. Later, after Kim Seng and Gopal left, she told him, "You'll see. It will all work out—we'll try, and we'll adapt. Like animals."

"Like otters?"

"Like all animals, Sukhin. God, you've become so fixated on otters for some reason."

He helped her bake six pies, and by the time they were done, it was past two in the morning and they both had shadows under their eyes. The entire apartment smelled glorious. He wondered if all of these lovely buttery things really made a difference to anyone, if it mattered to anyone that they were eating apple pie crumbed and sliced and stewed and baked by these four hands in this small kitchen instead of some frozen-thawed job made by machine in some factory who knew where. It probably didn't, but who knew?

"You know what your problem is, Sukhin?"

"You're about to tell me."

She patted his cheek, sighing dramatically. "You're too much of a thinker. Relax. Your thinking face isn't quite so handsome."

He must have his thinking face on again, now. What was he saying? Something about Guinness stew, but what? She's looking at him across the table, snickering. Staring down at his plate, he realises she's stolen about a third of his dinner.

"Here. Out of the goodness of my dying heart." She reaches across to feed him a chunk of carrot. He rolls his eyes and opens his mouth.

This is enough.

~

"Aren't you worried at all?" he asks the soft shape in his bed.

"About what?"

"I don't know. Everything? The future? I mean, you're about to be officially dead."

"Next week. Yes."

"Not worried? Not a drop?" He moves closer, closer to the soft shape.

It turns towards him. He can feel its hair on his face as he takes it in his arms and buries his face in its neck.

"No, Sukhin. Not a drop."

~

Dennis is waiting for him at the bottom of the back stairs.

"I heard about the poem."

"Oh."

"I think it's very sweet. And very brave."

Sukhin stares at his shoes. They stare back at him. Dennis leans across and kisses him on the cheek, then walks away.

At assembly, the students tell each other that Mr Dhillon is looking—distant? dreamy?

"Shocked?" Yes, maybe shocked.

Back at his desk, the first email he sees is from the Tay. She wants to know, by the end of today, whether he'll accept the role of Director of Academic Studies. She wants him to carefully consider his career not just at this school, but holistically—in education. She wants him to know what a great opportunity this is, how much they are all looking forward to helping him develop his leadership potential. She wants him to know that she will of course be disappointed should he decide not to accept, but—

Sukhin pushes his chair away from the desk, stands up and looks around his office. It's only a box—how has he never seen this? He thinks about all the boxes he hacked apart and sliced into bits and put together again to make the rain machine, and he feels the urge to take up an axe a saw a chisel and do the same to this one. Turn it into a rain machine, turn everything in it into rain, add bits of carpet for texture, throw in a couple of chairs for comfortable viewing. He will tell the Tay: *Thanks for giving me and my career so much thought, but I've decided to go in for installation art instead.*

As he straightens his shirt and adjusts his collar, he thinks about that old Japanese tale about the fisherman led by the turtle into deep blue depths, coaxed to linger there awhile by the princess of the underwater realm, while a hundred years goes by on the surface in what seems like only three days underwater. The same chain of thoughts encircles him, the one that always—and quickly—finds him every time he recalls this story. How horrible, to go home and find it missing. How horrible, all that lost time. That turtle—what an asshole. And that princess—what a nasty piece of marine biology.

He opens the door and steps out of his box.

"Sukhin, is that you? Have you got a minute? Something's wrong with my computer. Can you take a look?" Mrs Chandra, from inside hers.

"Sorry—later? I've got to see Mrs Tay about something urgent."

He turns off the lights and closes the door behind him. He doesn't lock it. The walk to the principal's office takes less than five minutes, but it feels like forever. He can hear her inside, talking on the phone—

or harassing some poor sod with a soliloquy. Sukhin knocks on the door anyway. It will only take a minute, after all, to tell her.

He will say no to the princess.

He will not stay at the bottom of the sea.

ACKNOWLEDGEMENTS

THANK YOU, THANK YOU, AND THANK YOU AGAIN:

Kevin Seah, who supplied me with relentless cheer, who was first to read every chapter, who fell in love with Jinn.

My mother, Alison Loh, for allowing me to be a perfect monster, and Dhruv Doshi and Ryn Suthipradit, for keeping me on the path of least crazy, while I wrote and raged.

James Wynn-Higgins, Abirama Thanikasalam, Jeremy Ee, Joanna Lim and Corrine Chia, for believing.

Nishta Geetha Thevaraja, for listening, always.

M, for that one earnest, unexpected remark in Seville, without which I would never have dared to dare to do this.

Cyril Wong, for gracing the universe with the untitled poem in the final chapter.

Edmund Wee and the incredible team at Epigram Books—especially Jason Erik Lundberg, Qin Yi, Chris Toh and Nicholas Chua—for the unending support, guidance and patience, in spite of my resting bitch face and my inability to refrain from argument.